OUT OF THE SHALLOWS

by Ben Osborne

'A champion is someone who gets up when they can't'

– Jack Dempsey

Chapter 1

ENGLAND HAD VANISHED.

Much of the Severn Bridge towers had gone the same way, along with the swirling grey-brown waters of the Bristol Channel below.

Not two hours ago, when Danny Rawlings first set foot on track, the sea fret was merely a forecast. Now it hung there, like a bad smell.

He could hear the muffled crackle of the grandstand somewhere nearby.

Sounded like the crowd was down on last year, he thought, perhaps saving Christmas money for a nicer day.

The cool watery air made the silks cling to his race-trim body, as if it were a muggy summer's day. He could feel the machine-gun patter of his pulse tickle against his padded body protector.

It felt like he was treading grapes as he led stable star Salamanca by hand in squelchy circles among twelve rivals, though the trade papers had this down as a two-horse race – the big showdown: Salamanca *v* Artemis.

By far the best two staying chasers around they rightly topped the weights in this Grade Three handicap and, while each stood at over seventeen hands and were giants in both stature and ability, both had wisely been dismounted to ease the hefty burden during this delay.

Since the Pardubicka fifteen months ago, Danny's star chaser had thrived as much as his relationship with Meg. When last seen out, Salamanca had put on a show of jumping and staying power to complete a four-timer in the Scottish National at Ayr in April.

3

Danny hoped for a repeat performance but knew there'd be questions to answer on this belated seasonal return. Back on home soil, he longed to add the Welsh version to Salamanca's glowing CV.

Meanwhile nothing could come close to lowering the yellow and blue vertically striped colours of Artemis in six outings last winter and he currently raced off a mark of 170, carrying top weight of twelve stone, giving four pounds away to the 166-rated Salamanca on eleven stone ten pounds.

They were now rated so far clear the official assessor would soon need to frame a separate handicap for these two in relation to the rest, like they did with Arkle and Flying Bolt in the Sixties.

Awaiting them were twenty-two fences over an extended three miles and five furlongs, almost two foggy circuits of heavy ground.

Perhaps not seeing what lay ahead was a blessing.

Danny suspected Salamanca would relish the prospect more than him.

Secretly he hoped the legend of Sabrina – goddess of the River Severn – would whisk them away on her chariot. After drowning there, her ghostly figure was said to roam the banks in the rolling mists, warding off travellers from suffering the same fate, so Danny's history teacher Mr Thomas reckoned years back. It was about the only thing that stayed with him from school – that and the bullying.

Artemis' trainer and jockey Bert Mills looked as nervous as Danny felt. For the first time this fortysomething looked old. Danny couldn't recall ever seeing his neighbour in such a bad way. It was even rarer Bert would let any weakness or vulnerability show up on the racetrack. Danny was even tempted once to ask for the name of his sports psychologist though he reckoned that in itself would show a sign of weakness.

'Good job Salamanca's got big shoulders, seeing as he's carrying the rest of the yard's nags,' Danny overheard Bert saying once.

A bit bloody rich, Danny thought at the time, as Artemis was essentially bankrolling both Bert's farm and stables.

All Danny's plans, workouts and race tactics had long since been safely locked in; this race had been earmarked months ago. For him it was more about stemming anxiety enough to properly execute. That's why he had let his mind get lost in a maze of memories as they'd paraded and then hacked down to the start.

He remounted and then drew alongside Bert. 'Relax, I'll take it easy on you.' Bert looked sad. 'Don't take all my quotes in the papers to heart. It's just words.'

Bert finally turned to face Danny but looked right through him. 'Sometimes it's best to know when you're beaten, you'll know that soon enough.'

Those words were more like the Bert he knew, though there was no conviction behind the voice. Danny sensed this was more a private admission of defeat than a battle cry.

'I'll still win,' Danny said, hoping for something better back.

'In your dreams boy,' Bert croaked, 'bit parched that's all.'

'Keep your mouth open on the way round,' Danny said and smiled, surprised by the disarming honesty of his chief threat. 'That'll quench your thirst.'

Wordlessly Bert urged Artemis to walk on, clearly in no mood for the usual banter.

Danny sensed a brightening lift in the fog, and could now see the Advanced Flag Operator in his white lab coat, standing before the first turn, fluorescent yellow flag at the ready if there was a false start.

And then the steward and starter, both in green padded coats, tweed peaked caps and wellies, returned sharing a smile and a joke after checking they could see the second-last from the final fence. That would be enough for the race to go ahead.

The steward ducked the rail and left for his box up in the stands while the starter repeatedly checked his watch as he paced to his rostrum on the inner.

5

Danny tried to ignore the latest betting from the speakers but the reformed gambler found it hard to bloke it out: 'Artemis is your even money favourite, Salamanca, seven-to-four and it's sixteens bar the pair.'

Danny wiped the back of his shiny gloves on his white breeches, and snapped the outer goggles in place.

The starter was now in position. 'Walk in jockeys! Walk in! Ready!'

The orange tape snapped and they were off.

Initially Danny sat off the early pace, allowing a couple of confirmed frontrunners their moment, this wasn't a sprint. He glanced across at Bert, also seemingly in no hurry.

It was left hand down as they piloted into the back straight and a line of four stiffish fences. Veils of patchy cloud felt like the cool of a wet face-balm. It was if the mists had washed away all the colours, even the lush green turf had faded to grey.

Up ahead the leaders spread a flock of seagulls pecking the prints left in the turf by novices in an earlier chase on the race-card.

All he heard was the dull rhythmic thud of hooves, snorts of blowing steam and then came the jockeys' growls as they asked for a big one at the first plain fence.

Danny sat quietly and let his charge pop over safely, no heroics. A race couldn't be won at the first, but could easily be lost there.

Salamanca put in a low, efficient jump, nudging the birch, but no harm done.

He then quickly found his trademark rhythm but as they reached the final fence before the second bend, Danny sensed the pace wasn't searching enough for his out-and-out stayer and moved up within a length of the rag Old Lag's Iron hugging the rail.

When Danny attacked the line of stiff birch, Salamanca stood back on his hocks, making a perfect shape over the fence. They left the ground in second and came out the other side in first. A shake of the reins helped push home that advantage to a few lengths.

Negotiating the bend, Salamanca sluiced through the deep ground like a clipper riding the wind. Danny was where he needed to be, safety out in front, no risk of being brought down or hampered, in charge of his own destiny.

The nerves had turned to excitement. That was until, from the milky swirls of mist, a ghostly black shape appeared. Initially he feared it was a faller galloping loose the wrong way. Danny found it particularly hard to ignore as it was heading *his* way.

He anxiously glanced over to see a person dressed in black from a balaclava down to flapping tails of a full-length covert coat. Danny could make out the broad shoulders, legs like tree trunks and branches for arms. This was no Sabrina come to take them away.

More likely some sad mindless prick looking to steal my headlines, Danny fumed.

At that moment Danny lost all focus. He had no contingency plan for something like this.

Why would a protestor pick the one day when no one could see the stunt, Danny thought, what a loser.

Confusion turned to anger as he snapped the misted goggles away from his face, make sure this Emily Davison-wannabe could see his eyes.

'Out the fucking way, idiot!'

Salamanca's ears pricked up, though the haunting shape appeared less interested in Danny's protestations. It just kept coming, silently, almost as if floating over the soggy ground.

Danny gathered the reins in his right hand and waved his left arm to ward off the invader. Yet it did no good. The figure came closer and closer. And so was the next fence. Danny's left hand recaptured the reins; he'd need both on the steering wheel to negotiate both these obstacles now almost upon them.

Then he yanked sharply on the left rein but the now worldly Salamanca was in no mood to play games, seemingly intent on getting home by the shortest route possible. At that moment 'the Tank' was steering like one.

Caught up in the heat of battle, a small vengeful part of Danny wanted to steamroller the trespasser but he staved off the urge, yanking again at the reins, enough to leave his mount no option but to trust his master and bank to the inner rail, deftly sidestepping a head-on collision.

They now found themselves racing on a narrow strip of muddy ground, chewed up by the two previous steeplechases at the meeting. He glanced over his shoulder and opened his mouth to vent his fury, but he saw nothing there, not even pursuing rivals to warn them. What the hell?

Holding a big lead in such a prestigious race, he'd never have believed he could feel this angry or confused. He only hoped the remainder of the field had also swerved in time. Last thing he wanted was to win by default, a hollow victory.

There was no time to reorganise for the next fence, so he switched on autopilot and let Salamanca take over. Never one to play safe by taking an extra stride the bold nine-year-old stood off a good four yards from the orange take-off board.

Knees bent and feet tucked, Salamanca flew through the heavy air. But inexplicably his landing gear came out early and his forelegs parted the birch. Danny was shunted to the buckle end of the reins and desperately pushed back in the stirrups just to stay on. He then gathered the reins and his composure.

Salamanca showed only a dent in pride not confidence when he then took the open ditch with a surgeon's accuracy and landed with the surefootedness of an Olympic gymnast, the outstretched forelegs comfortably impacting the spongy turf.

Between the final two fences of the first lap Danny felt a peculiar dream-like sense of isolation. He was more spooked by the pitch-invader than his horse.

Here we go, Danny thought. Three-two-one. Salamanca answered the call and from somewhere found another exhibition leap.

They splashed through the ground in front of the stands for the first time.

Ride as if no one was watching, he thought. Mind, it didn't sound like anyone was, the silence was deafening. Danny's shoulders dropped slightly. He was on the clear second favourite

8

and there wasn't even a ripple of applause to feed off. It's as if there'd been a fire alarm.

Sod them, Danny thought, as they galloped past a sea of advertising hoardings on the track's inner and then banked left to go out into the country on the second and final lap.

He kind of felt flat too. Things were happening too easily. Had he missed the yellow flag that voided the race?

Danny wasn't hung up on superstitions but he knew Salamanca rarely won without a scary moment. He would be the first to admit he was a flawed champion, reliant more on bossing the opposition with brute strength and stamina, rather than agility and prowess.

As the sense of anticipation grew so did his confidence. Instead of treating each fence as a barrier to success, he saw them as a means to gain yet another length on the pack.

Down the far side, they continued to find a metronomic rhythm. There's was a partnership of understanding and trust, like an old married couple.

Salamanca's trim belly tickled the birch of the final fence before banking left on the run for home. He was making some of the stiffest regulation fences in Britain seem like the baby ones in the schooling ring back home.

On the bend, Danny afforded a glance over his shoulder, just to make sure one hadn't found a second wind. Despite the visibility improving by the stride, Danny couldn't see anything of the pursuers, not even the safety car or ambulance on the inside of the track.

Here came the final fence, all that was in the way of success and a place in the history books. Danny asked for a positive jump to keep his charge focused. Salamanca appeared to read the signals transmitted down the reins and met it on the perfect stride. His strong hind legs pushed the soggy turf, catapulting his muscular frame skyward.

They landed running but needn't have. Danny wished he could bottle a leap like that for when it really mattered. This race was already over and he eased to a hack canter before allowing the new Welsh Grand National winner the luxury of walking across the finish line.

By the time he'd turned Salamanca round, he glanced down the run-in only then to see the movement of the second lumbering over the final fence. He couldn't make out the colours of the silks but he felt sure it wasn't Artemis. There was no way any horse could beat the reigning champion by a fence, not even Salamanca. Something must have gone wrong with the hot favourite, either pulling up lame or crashing out with an uncharacteristic fall due to the fog. That seemed unthinkable for a chaser with the jumping prowess up there with legends past and present like Arkle and Sprinter Sacre. It was more likely Bert had been brought down by that glory-hunter roaming the track.

Salamanca wasn't even blowing hard. Danny was relieved as he'd expected a tough race for his comeback and this would set him up for what promised to be a long and fruitful winter campaign.

Danny kept his celebrations muted until he saw all the rivals home safely. When five more emerge from the gloom, he couldn't hold on any longer for Artemis as there were reporters, sponsors and racegoers waiting in and around the winners' circle.

He left the track and set off down the asphalt path to a smattering of applause. Had most of the punters backed Artemis, or could they sense something greater was wrong? Danny wasted no time relieving Salamanca of his weight. Instead of being allowed to bask in the glory in front of the press pack, Danny was ushered directly to the weighing room, carrying a saddle laden with lead.

He was still buzzing with a tingle of electricity as he stepped off the electronic steel plate.

Off to his right he was sobered by the sight of two of the racecourse security team rush by in a blur of their black FBI-style jackets and caps, closely followed by a crowd safety employee, in his fluorescent yellow bib. Now he suspected that he felt the same way as the crowd.

When a strong hand gripped his shoulder, Danny jumped.

It was the seasoned racing hack Cameron Lightfoot. He combed his yellowy smoker's fingers through a thick brush of matching hair. Whatever the weather he was never seen in public without a polo neck sweater, or a silk scarf or cravat, all patterned by tiny coloured silks of the leading owners of the modern thoroughbred. Danny had heard it was to hide a birthmark but he didn't want to offend by asking directly. It certainly wasn't to cover a second chin; there wasn't an ounce on Cameron; he was a rare breed in the press room. Perhaps the forty-a-day habit helped there. This canny Scotsman was a useful contact.

Danny looked at him and then over to the course security rushing about with serious faces. The clerk of the course was climbing into a Range Rover parked up on the inside of the track near the lollypop stick of the finish line.

Cam shoved a voice recorder in Danny's face and asked, 'What happened out there Danny?'

'I won.' Danny shook his head perplexedly. 'Don't think Paxman's got anything to worry about.'

'Not the result, I'm after the juicy details,' Cam said. 'This'll get my copy on the front page.'

Danny shook his head again.

'Come on Danny, don't go shy on me,' Cam said. 'I'll make it worth our while, but be quick, they'll all be after this one.'

'One what?' Danny asked. There were more police rushing by the window.

'Biding your time to get the best offer, I get you,' Cam said and grabbed Danny's arm, 'but mine's on the table for an hour, I want an exclusive. You've got my number, left a dozen missed messages on your phone this past week, asking about Salamanca's build-up.'

'Sorry,' Danny said distantly. 'It was a busy week.'

'Well, you could make up for it by giving me the scoop,' Cam said. 'If you suddenly *remember* or hear something, anything, be sure to call me.'

'Hear anything?' Danny asked. 'Seems you know more than me.'

11

'Don't say no one's told you.'

Chapter 2

THERE WERE MORE BLACK SHAPES, something like he'd just glimpsed out on track.

They were beyond frosted glass embossed with *Mr C. Dent – Director of Racing and Clerk of Chepstow Racecourse.*

When Clive Dent's knuckles rattled the glass, the shapes moved.

For Chepstow's chief to feel the need to knock on his own door, Danny suspected those inside were important.

Danny glanced back at the ten seated jockeys colouring the corridor. It was like being called up to see the Head all over again. Their muddy silks and breeches clung to their bodies. Some were slouched, others were hunched, all looked as anxious as Danny felt, as if they *had* been told.

Danny broke the icy silence, 'I'm guessing this is no Stewards' Enquiry.'

'A more serious enquiry I'm afraid,' Dent replied flatly. 'You'll then be briefed before facing the Press.'

'Police in there?' Danny asked. As Clive nodded, Danny's mouth went dry again. 'Give me something to work with, Clive.'

Clive just pushed the door open.

Inside there were two men. One sat at Clive's desk and a uniform stood nearby.

The seated man looked the wrong side of fifty with receding grey hair brushed forward and there were shadows beneath his brown eyes. He'd already unbuttoned his black tailored suit and loosened his tie. Danny glanced up at the wall clock.

'Please take a seat, this shouldn't take long,' the suit said in a cockney brogue. 'I'm DCI Keyes heading this enquiry and this is PC Mavers, part of the on-course police presence.'

Danny smelt beer. 'And you were part of the hospitality.'

Mavers had clearly dispensed of his fluorescent jacket. He was about half Keyes' age and probably the same weight, though his bulk was more muscle than fat. He stood there like a Queen's Guard, ramrod back, wide shoulders square, chin and nose up.

This lightweight was trying to look all intimidating, Danny bet, a proper jobsworth.

He found it hard to stem his hatred of authority, clashes with them as a teen still fresh as manure. Mavers was taking notes, or least pretending to.

'Sit,' Keyes ordered.

Danny didn't hesitate taking the weight off his aching feet, itchy with sweat. 'What is this?'

'One of the runners didn't come back from the big race,' Keyes said as he leant in.

'I'm sorry,' Danny said and then shrugged, still waiting for an answer. 'But that doesn't explain why you lot are here.'

'Neither did the jockey,' Keyes added.

'Wha-' Danny heard himself swallow. 'Dead?' He swallowed again. 'Who?'

'We're investigating the suspected disappearance of jockey Bert Mills and his horse Artemis,' Keyes replied, glancing down at a race-card marked by ink. 'Tell me what you saw out there?'

'Disappearance?' Danny asked and then smiled nervously, as if this must be some sick practical joke. 'Bert wouldn't get lost round Chepstow. He knows every blade of grass out there, so does his horse!' Danny ran a hand through his thick hair he'd let grow a few inches. 'He must've fallen or unseated, then Bert couldn't stop Artemis from bolting, have you *investigated* that?'

'This was no accident,' Keyes replied.

'I'm struggling here,' Danny said, wiping mud from his cheek. 'You say Bert and Artemis didn't complete – okay, I can get my head round that, but they don't just vanish from the face of the planet. Unless Sabrina-'

'Sabrina?'

'Nothing.'

'This isn't a joke, Daniel,' Keyes said. 'Now what did you see?'

'I'd be guessing as much as you,' Danny said. 'It was like a smokers' den out there and any case, my eyes were fixed on winning.'

14

'At all costs?' Mavers piped up. 'Bet you were glad your chief threat was taken out of the race.'

When Danny looked up, he saw a uniform not a person. He suddenly found his voice. 'Perhaps if I had no morals, but that didn't enter my head, as it did yours. I wanted to beat Artemis on merit, prove to the Press and public my boy was the champ. Why this finger pointing? Jesus, this is supposed to be a career highlight, not being given the third degree by a pair of-'

'Enough!' Keyes snapped.

'Well!' Danny said and sighed loudly as he sat back, as if deflating. He was struggling to come down from the heightened racing state. It felt like he'd downed a vat of coffee. He feared he'd say something he'd regret. 'Look, it's not spotless but this is a cleaner sport than most, we play fair and by the rules, best horse wins.'

'I've read racing thrillers,' Keyes said. 'It's not as straight as you're saying.'

'That's fiction! I can tell you now,' Danny said, palm pressed against his chest, as if taking a solemn oath. 'I didn't, nor did *any* of the other jockeys out there, have anything to do with all this.'

'Your loyalty is commendable, as it is predictable,' Mavers said.

Danny looked up and replied, 'You're making it hard for me to like you.'

'We're not here to make friends,' Mavers said.

'We'll take witness statements from them all,' Keyes added and then glanced over at the frosted glass of the door.

'All this for a missing person, that's probably not missing,' Danny said.

'We believe Bert and Artemis were kidnapped,' Keyes said.

'Kidnapped,' Danny repeated, as if to make it seem any more real.

'And the first forty-eight hours in these cases is our golden period. It offers the best chance of finding them alive. Now before

15

any more of those hours are lost, let's start again, what did you see out there?'

'There was something, a man. Didn't see him do anything myself but I didn't need to, he had no bloody right being there.'

'Go on,' Keyes said and clicked the button of a voice recorder on the desk.

'First off I thought it was just a dog walker that got lost in the fog or something, but there was no dog. He should've been on a leash, mind. Nearly broadsided Salamanca, he was that big. Might've been some animal protestor, or tree hugger out to get himself some headlines. Do more harm than good them lot. Either way I only just missed the idiot turning into the home-straight first time. He came right at me, or so I thought. As quick as he'd appeared, he was gone.'

'What was he wearing?'

'Head to foot in black he was,' Danny said. 'The face was covered, possibly a mask, or a scarf, balaclava, I dunno.'

'But you're certain it was a man.'

'Couldn't be a hundred per cent as I was turning the screw right then, going over thirty,' Danny said, 'but I've never seen a woman that shape, had broader shoulders than Salamanca.'

Danny's eyes then sought the uncluttered surface of the mahogany desk as he still tried to get his head around the news. 'Who the hell would kidnap Bert? I mean, he was hard to like but just as hard to dislike, mostly kept himself to himself.'

'We have reason to believe Mr Mills had recently been subjected to threats,' Keyes said. 'Not long ago he came to us expressing such concerns.'

'Is that why you're at the races today?' Danny asked.

'I'll do the questioning,' Keyes snapped, patience seemingly now thin as his hair. Danny noticed a sponsor's guest badge tied to his lapel.

'I just don't understand why you're grilling me,' Danny said.

'And not the others?' Keyes interjected.

'And not out there searching for Bert.'

16

'Racecourse security and crowd control are searching the track right now.'

'So there's a chance he isn't missing then,' Danny said and raised his hands.

Keyes' smartphone then buzzed into life. He swiped a finger across the screen and after a few more touches he turned it to show Danny. 'This was posted to Bert last week.'

'What is it?'

'Look.'

Danny squinted at the white screen. It showed a photo of a creased A4 piece of paper. Stuck to it were newspaper lettering, different sizes and caps: **14 DayS**.

'Call this a threat?' Danny said, 'You should hear what's said in the changing room.'

There was a whirring. It was only then Danny noticed a fax machine on a desk next to a PC in the corner. Mavers went over to check what it was spewing out. He ripped off a sheet and showed it to his senior. Keyes studied it closely but didn't share this. That stoked Danny's curiosity. 'A new lead come in?'

Keyes' sharp eyes looked over the sheet at Danny and he then put it face down on the desk.

'Bert witnessed someone posting that letter by hand on the thirteenth,' Keyes said.

'Unlucky for some,' Danny muttered nervously.

'My colleague here took a statement,' Keyes added, 'Bert said that someone fitted your description.'

'No!' Danny said. 'Bert's lying.'

'We understand you have a history,' Mavers asked. 'Bet he was a nightmare neighbour.'

'We might be neighbours but his yard would be four streets away if we were in Cardiff. I'm not close to Bert in any sense of the word.'

'That's funny because we were led to believe you knew him well,' Mavers asked.

'Everyone knew him … knows him,' Danny replied. 'He'd been around with the likes of Peter Scudamore and Brendan

17

Powell, part of the furniture in the weighing room.' His fingers combed through his thick hair again. 'Can't believe this is happening, I knew things were going too well.'

'What else do you know?' Keyes asked.

'He was acting odd down at the start.'

'In what way.'

'Quiet,' Danny said. 'As if he wasn't up for the fight.'

'And that's out of character?'

'He's no quitter, I'll give him that,' Danny said, 'and he gives as good as he gets, bell on every tooth before the big races. Even renamed his yard up-valley Sunnyside Farm, just to make very sure I knew who had the south facing slope.'

'Bet that wound you up,' Mavers said.

'Laughed it off, as my dad used to tell me, "empty vessels make the most noise",' Danny replied. 'Any road, whenever the sun makes an appearance up there it's like a solar event, locals drop to their knees praying.'

Keyes said, 'Were you enemies?'

'On the track, maybe, bit of healthy competition never hurt anyone, but there was never anything personal. I don't do mind games myself, let my riding do the talking. He hated getting beat.'

'Are you a sore loser, Daniel?'

'Show me a good loser,' Danny replied, 'and I'll show you a loser.'

'Has he ever disappeared before?'

Danny shook his head. 'Only when he holidays at some small cottage down in Lyme Regis, same week every year. Other than that, his job was his life and his horses were his family. He'd never desert them like you're suggesting.'

'Does he own this cottage?'

'If not he should've done, went there enough.' Danny shrugged. 'He told me it's where his parents took him as a kid, so probably holds special memories he likes to revisit. He's not married, guess his two jobs keep him busy and stressed enough, but he's got a son, Leo, but you'd know that by now. Occasionally see him harvesting crops or herding the cattle in the

18

nearby fields. Not so much these days. The slump in milk prices meant Bert had to diversify and try his hand at training racehorses. It helped there were twenty or so boxes in a stable block going begging on his land.'

'And as far as you could see, he was happy with where both sides of his business were going?' Keyes asked.

Danny shrugged. 'I'm not his shrink or accountant.'

'We're just trying to ascertain his state of mind in recent weeks,' Keyes replied.

'I heard he was never quite the same after his wife walked out on him,' Danny replied, 'leaving him to bring up Leo alone. That break up apparently broke him up, too, soon became a bit of a recluse. Mind, it's not hard to be, up there. Perhaps pressure of it finally got to him. This is only rumours going around the jockeys' room. Only time I'd see him was in his silks or in the tractor mostly from nodding not speaking distance.'

Mavers now leant forward and pinched the corner of the sheet, 'Sir?'

Keyes nodded.

Danny felt like shaking his head again.

Mavers flipped over the sheet. Keyes told Danny, 'Read it.'

Danny didn't move.

'OK, I'll read it for you,' Mavers said. 'This is what you told the trade press and some of the nationals yesterday. I quote: 'This is revenge, I'll take Artemis down, it's Salamanca's time. Bert Mills won't know what's hit him, the king is dead, long live the king.'

'That's just harmless banter,' Danny pleaded. 'The sponsor's wanted a sound bite, they were billing this as the big showdown see. They wanted fighting talk, you know, like at weigh-ins before the big boxing bouts, but it was just fun and games, helps get our sport on the back pages for once, nothing meant by it. I know it doesn't sound good now, but do you really think I'd choose those words if I had all this planned.'

Danny's leg started to go, like a dog lost in a dream.

19

Mavers said, 'With the new "king" Salamanca in the yard, you won't be short of a bob or two.'

'Yeah, but he's our cash cow, just about bankrolls the whole of Silver Belle Stables.'

'We know Bert had turned down a string of escalating offers for his estate in recent months,' Keyes said.

'Well, if you think all this is revenge for him saying no,' Danny said, 'ask them!'

'We're about to,' Keyes said and leant in. 'Well?'

'Me?!' Danny shouted. 'No! Why the hell would I want his farm. Look, I'm like Bert – a one hit wonder. Last thing I want to do is expand the business. What's his yard got that mine hasn't?'

'It's south facing for starters,' Mavers said.

Danny looked up and said to Keyes, 'He's definitely not helping.'

'We have to eliminate you from our enquiries you understand,' Keyes said.

'Believe me, there's very little I understand right now,' Danny said. 'Other than Bert has been telling lies behind my back, when I see him I'll fucking k-' He stopped himself.

'What will you do Danny?' Keyes asked.

Danny leant forward. 'I'll kiss him. Welcome a good friend back to the valleys.'

Keyes sighed. 'Back to the race. You say the man appeared, what then?'

'He was like a man on a mission,' Danny said, 'but then so was I. And once I'd dodged that bullet, I set my eyes on the next fence. Got enough to contend with in a National let alone some loon acting up.'

'Were the other runners as lucky?'

'I was leading, remember,' Danny said, 'they don't supply us with wing mirrors.'

'But you've got a neck,' Keyes said. 'Surely you were looking.'

'I'm not one of these rubberneckers that slow up out of some morbid curiosity. I had a race to win.'

'But you must check where your main rival was,' Mavers said.

'My boy's an out-and-out stayer you see and I wasn't happy with the pace they'd gone on the first lap. By then I was forcing the gallop, make it a proper stamina test. From that point on, I was hoping never to see another rival again.'

'Seems like you got your wish,' Mavers said. 'At least with Artemis.'

'I've had enough of this,' Danny growled and stood.

'Where are you going?' Keyes demanded.

'Go look for Bert,' Danny said, 'instead of wasting time here.'

'You'll only be wasting time out there,' Mavers said, staring Danny down to size. 'The course has already been searched and been given the all-clear.'

'Are we done then,' Danny and stood. 'I've got a man to see about a horse. Wouldn't want to eat into any more of your "golden period".'

'You haven't got a ride in the next,' Keyes said, thumbing his race-card.

'Toby Gleeson's selling a filly down near Taunton,' Danny said. 'Might just buy it with some of these winnings.'

Keyes closed the race-card. 'We're done.'

Danny didn't expect that. Having wanted to get away, he suddenly felt there was unfinished business here. He needed to be sure his name was clear. He certainly couldn't find any comfort in the fact he might not have to face nemesis Artemis when Salamanca lined up on a six-timer in the inaugural Cardiff Open at Ely Park in five weeks' time.

'Go on, send the next in,' Keyes added, 'unless you've got something else to tell us.'

Danny asked, 'Have you taken Bert's kitbag?'

Keyes looked to Mavers, who said, 'Already checked, sir. It's clear to go, nothing of interest. As yet there's no crime, so I've left it in the weighing room.'

'If you like I'll drop it round to his son Leo when I get back,' Danny said.

Keyes nodded at Danny and then over to the door.

Danny suspected no one in that room had got the answers they were after.

Moments ago Danny was desperate to leave but strangely now he was free to go, he felt unsettled, as if he was leaving the room with business left undone.

Mavers showed him out. In the corridor, the PC called to the jockey of the third, Kelvin McDonald. Before he returned to Clive's office, Mavers handed Danny a card, 'If you hear or see anything suspicious, we're giving everyone connected to the case this number, call us to save you being passed from one department to another. Don't hold anything back however irrelevant it may seem, Bert's safety is at stake.'

Danny took the card and returned to the weighing room. The lines of metal wall pegs were lost behind nests of suits and silks.

He peeled off his colours and breeches, soiled by sweat and mud. A quick spray of deodorant under the arms and he was ready enough to go.

As he left, there was Bert's bag already zipped up. Danny went over and after glancing over both shoulders, he felt compelled to check if anything might be missing. There was a pair of tights to wear under the breeches, spare goggles, socks, pants, all neatly packed. The police couldn't have been that thorough in their search. There was also a half-full Evian bottle. He couldn't resist a quick swig before setting off on the drive to Devon. As Danny's chapped lips touched the mouth of the plastic bottle, he recoiled more from surprise than disgust. He liked neat Vodka.

Jesus, Bert! Danny sighed. So that's your secret, he guessed, no wonder he looked like nothing in the world could hurt him down at the start of each race.

So it wasn't fire in his belly out on the track, but a numbing measure of magic water. It seemed like Bert had found his sports psychologist in a bottle. But the Dutch courage didn't seem enough this time as he recalled Bert's face circling in the mists in front of the stands. Except there was enough here to floor a man of Bert's size, unless he'd become immune to its effects over time. It certainly explained Bert's thirstiness in the minutes before he vanished.

Danny replaced the cap and thought about reporting the find but if the police had already seen the bottle, it clearly wasn't significant to their enquiries and even if they hadn't, Danny couldn't bear being the grass that got Bert a lengthy ban if he finally showed up.

He zipped up and slipped soundlessly from a fire exit. Last thing he wanted was to sign a race-card, or face any more unanswerable questions from Cameron and co.

He'd often allowed himself to dream of landing a Welsh National but he'd only feel this flat once he'd woken up.

He then wondered what on earth Bert must be feeling right then, if he was lucky enough to feel anything. He quickly banished that morbid imagining but back it came, as if his thoughts had Tourette's.

Chapter 3

DANNY FELT THE TINGLE OF ANTICIPATION.

He glanced at the clock in the van's dashboard. *Best leave it another five.*

This was the best bit. No chance yet of any dreams being crushed, or bubbles being deflated.

You must be an optimist or insane to be in this game his dad always reckoned. As far as Danny was concerned, he was about to meet the next Salamanca.

That wasn't why he was early. It was an excuse to get away from the chaos on track and besides, he didn't want to let down old friend Toby Gleeson though that was more out of self-preservation. Like Danny, he'd done time – two charges of GBH effectively ended his riding career in the late Eighties, particularly as the victim was an owner daring to question his tactics on a ride. He later revealed to Danny he'd studied the art of training racehorses while inside, whereas Danny had learnt how to pick locks.

Stony reckoned Toby's mood could turn like an angry drunk. Short man syndrome, he'd put it down as, probably in the hope that fear would make others, metaphorically at least, look up to him. Danny had hoped that Napoleon complex had gone with age as he hated conflict and there was hopefully some bargaining to be done.

Something about the thumbnail of the filly Powder Keg, emailed to him a few days before, drew him here. Once he'd checked the bloodlines of her pedigree and her French form he knew she was worth a visit at the very least.

He looked up at the darkening skies. He glanced again at the time and then returned to the racing app open on his tablet – a combined Christmas present from his girlfriend Meg and four-year-old son Jack, who now saw her as his real mum. He still couldn't believe she'd blown her savings on him. When Meg thought he was giving her the silent treatment, he didn't put her straight. Anything to hide the fact he'd got a bit choked up when he saw the present.

Instead he offered to take it back but she was having none of it. He then resolved to make her soon-to-be twenty-first birthday present that little bit extra special.

He began to stare, but not see the small screen as he allowed his mind's eye to drift back to those fleeting moments on track. Despite only a few hours passing since the Chepstow happenings, Danny had replayed countlessly the moment that black figure came at them. If he had successfully taken out Artemis in behind, surely the police would've come across the carnage on the turn for home.

He focused again on the tablet's screen in his hands. He kept checking the live news feed but updates on the fallout from the Welsh National were proving as elusive as Bert and Artemis themselves.

His finger touched the classified section. With Rhys no longer on the payroll, he desperately needed to retain a stable jockey as he was being stretched enough by training and travelling duties. He'd had enough dealings with jockeys' agents and the freelancers on their books. Despite being made out to be the next Lester Piggott or Steve Cauthen, many were going through the motions and Danny felt lucky if they even listened to riding orders.

The only adverts were for shares in a juvenile colt already broken in and ready to race on the Flat in the spring, alongside an invitation to declare entries for the upcoming regional trials of the Shetland Grand National to qualify for the final at Olympia and an advert to pre-book the final remaining tickets for the grand opening of Ely Park racetrack.

He slipped the tablet in the glove box and walked up the arcing driveway to an impressive stone barn conversion. The business was out the back.

Danny knocked. Toby Gleeson emerged from behind the heavy oak door. The ex-jumper had a Flat jockey's build, except for the muffin top over his denims' belt.

'Looking well, boss,' Danny said.

Toby ran his hands over his belly like an expectant mother, seemingly proud of what he'd produced. 'After years of

25

living without, it's good to eat more like a horse than a jockey these days. Feel like I'm making up for lost time.'

'Can't wait for that day,' Danny said. 'But got too many irons in the fire to hang up the saddle just yet.'

'And I just might have another for you.' Danny offered his hand. 'Wait till you see the little madam, then you'll really want to shake on it. This way son.'

Danny filled the silence with, 'You going to the grand opening day for Ely Park?'

'Ah yes, Ely Park, rebirth of Cardiff's very own racetrack eighty years after its death. Recall my grandpa saying he rode there a few times back in its heyday,' Toby replied. 'Seems to me they're trying to recapture the glamour of those glory days, good luck with that project.'

'It'll be Wales' answer to Chelters,' Danny argued.

'If you like,' Toby said dismissively. 'The world is a very different place these days, don't reckon there's room for two Cheltenhams. It'll be the poor relation if you ask me.'

I wasn't, Danny wanted to say, but didn't want the sale to be off before it was ever on. 'I designed the track if you don't mind,' he said defensively, like a proud parent.

'Really?' Toby questioned. 'Paper said it was a joint effort.'

Danny nodded. 'Well, on the race-card I'll share that honour with Ralph Samuel. He insisted.'

'I'd tell that Ralph where to go,' Toby said.

'I would,' Danny said, 'if he wasn't the owner as well.'

'Wealthy businessman?' Toby asked. 'Power mad, them lot.'

'No,' Danny said. 'He inherited it.'

'Won't have anything good enough to send there anyhow,' Toby said.

'What about this one?' Danny asked. 'I've made the track horse-friendly, flat with easy turns, ideal for a youngster like this.'

'You're selling the filly better than I could,' Toby said. 'Come on, this way.'

As they turned into a courtyard, Danny felt his heart thump at the possibility of an exciting new recruit to Silver Belle Stables.

But when he saw the goods, his pulse soon settled.

'Is that it?' Danny asked with a sigh.

'Cover her ears,' Toby called over to the lad taking a tight grip of her reins. '*It* is a filly, and she has a name you know, Powder Keg.'

Toby was a Devonian as long as Danny could recall, but was a Londoner born and bred. Danny could sense he was hankering for a return to the suburbs of the capital but he guessed that would mean giving up the game he loved as land round there was in a different league to rural West Country.

'Looks more like a pinto,' Danny said.

'Funny little thing for sure but she's a half-sister to seven Flat winners.'

'That's not why I'm here.'

'Why then? Surely her family tree needs strong roots.'

'If she hadn't been out of the smart hurdler Boil Over I wouldn't have come.' And standing there looking at her lightly-made offspring, Danny sorely wished he hadn't. 'Not exactly Black Beauty is she.' Toby frowned, making Danny add, 'All I'm saying, she's no model.'

'Have you seen a model try to run?' Toby said. 'Since when is she entering a beauty contest any road?'

'Tell that to the players round a sales ring, I'm just thinking of her resale value if she doesn't deliver on track in Britain.'

'She did in France, no reason why she can't here,' Toby said as he ran a hand down her hind leg covered in white splatters, like a painter's radio. She kicked out.

Danny gave Toby a knowing look.

'Alright, she's a character, made no secret of that,' Toby said, holding his hands up.

In racing Danny read that to mean she was a temperamental sod. 'Great.'

27

'Don't think I don't know what you're doing,' Toby said. 'Looking for problems that aren't there so you can keep knocking lumps of her price. I won the Triumph Hurdle when you were filling nappies.'

Danny scanned the filly closely as if she were a barcode. Like buying a second-hand car on sight, he checked the goods: her teeth, skin, eyes, feet and back were good. He couldn't help but be taken by her gleaming black coat, like freshly valeted riding boots. She appeared sound, with good limbs, a well put together and proportioned filly, if a little on the small side. Her tail flashed as his hand ran over the white blaze on her forehead.

She's a grower, he thought.

He then watched her walk in circles. Everything appeared in good order. She'd passed the MOT. 'She hasn't got much up front,' he said, running a hand through her mane. 'Short neck, small head and ears.'

'They said the same about Arkle, never stopped him,' Toby said. 'And she's only three, plenty of time to fill out, might even make a chaser one day.'

'You seem to have forgotten all racehorses celebrate their birthday on New Year's Day – that's next week when she'll be four.'

'Don't play me for a fool, Danny,' Toby added. 'I won't go a penny below the asking.'

Silently they stood there in a battle of wills. Danny's hand skated over the white brushstrokes down her withers. 'Next you'll be saying those are go-faster stripes.'

Briefly Toby's frown melted to a smile. 'Fifty grand is the very best I can do.' Danny pursed his lips. 'If I put her through the Cheltenham breeze-ups in April, there'll be plenty of big fish ready to bite.' Danny waited for more. Toby added, 'You wouldn't want my nippers to go wanting next Christmas.'

'Now you're sounding desperate, Toby.'

'Couldn't be more wrong,' Toby replied, pointedly holding his gaze.

Before turning his back on the filly, Danny said, 'I want to see her in action.'

'You can send her over a few round the schooling ring nothing more.'

There was no room for the heart ruling the head in this game. Danny knew the smaller the yard, the smaller the margins. And he was always only a few sympathetic purchases away from going into the red.

Danny climbed on and just as he'd bunched up the reins, Powder Keg bucked, kicking out her hind legs and catching Danny by surprise and tossing him forward. He jumped off before he was thrown off. He still landed with a smack of hands and knees on the tarmac.

'Bloody hell,' Danny said, shaken. 'She's an effing fruitcake.'

'It's not her, it's you,' Toby said defensively. 'You need to convince her who's boss in her eyes, you're the herd leader now.'

'Don't reckon I want to be her bloody boss.'

'You will,' Toby said. 'She hasn't had her morning hack, so no wonder she's as fresh as paint, soon settle down out there. Nothing a morning half-hour in your field won't sort.'

Danny dragged her to the schooling ring. Apparently she was as reluctant as he was.

He popped her over a few poles and she made a good shape once into stride but when he eased off, she pulled herself up at the first opportunity. He was no more convinced. She was giving him every excuse to walk away.

However, she left Danny always coming back to the positives. There was definitely something about her. A presence. He'd rather have a prodigious talent with a few quirks than a reliable slowcoach. Danny's instinct was to take a punt.

'Thing is, I like you Toby and I like her, but there's something I don't like,' Danny said.

'The price,' Toby said and rolled his eyes.

'As Meat Loaf once shouted, two out of three ain't bad,' Danny replied.

'This is coming from a Welsh National winner. Saw it on the telly, you've got the money.'

29

'Forty-five.' Danny offered his hand.

'Fifty,' Toby replied, holding firm. 'Take her or leave her.'

They shook on it. Danny said, 'Still can't help but think I'm being royally shafted here.'

'I'm never one to short change,' Toby replied. 'And to prove it, she comes with her very own pal Zola over there.'

Out came a stable lass leading a Shetland pony.

Danny looked over and shook his head. 'No, no, no, wait a minute, that wasn't part of the bargain.'

'Funny, I'm sure I mentioned him,' Toby said.

'I'll stick with Powder Keg, ta. Got enough mouths to feed as it is,' Danny said. 'What you trying to do, make me go bust? It's this girl I'm taking, otherwise the sale's off.'

'Very well,' Toby said. 'But Powder Keg won't do a tap without this little fella in the yard.'

'I'll take the risk.'

Toby raised his eyebrows. 'Don't say I didn't warn you.'

As if on cue, Powder Keg looked down for the Shetland, who nearly yanked the girl's arms off. The filly bowed her head and her bristly mouth touched Zola's thick mane.

Danny offered to take the reins off the stable lass. 'What's his name again?'

'Zola,' Toby said.

'Still support the Blues then,' Danny said.

'And I'll never change, though don't get to see them no more,' Toby said. 'Only cos I can't get down there much, what with all my commitments here. I'm no fair-weather fan mind. Stamford Bridge is where my ashes will be scattered.'

'When you started sounding like a salesman on some crappy shopping channel my bullshit radar picked up,' Danny said sharply. 'No wonder you haven't shifted her if she comes with baggage. Wish you'd let on before we'd shaken.'

'Think of it as a bonus prize,' Toby said, raising his hands. 'Bet you want Jack to take up riding, could get him started on this chap.'

'I've already got a pony, Ronny. He's more than enough.'

30

'But they're inseparable these two, best buddies,' Toby said. 'And he's quick, could nearly use this little fella as a lead horse to some of mine,' Toby added.

Danny then had an idea. Zola might in fact turn out to be a bonus. 'I will, if you tell me why you're really selling Powder Keg? I mean, an unbeaten French import, that's not good business.'

Toby bit his lip. 'My bank and creditors are getting as twitchy as me. They'll want the lot. What's the point of having a decent horse without a stable to keep it?'

Danny felt like repeating, 'Wish you'd let on before we'd shaken.' Instead he said, 'Sorry, mate. She's going to a good home. I'll make sure she's ridden right, I'll only put the best on her.'

Toby moved in close and gripped Danny's arm tight enough for it to hurt. Was the little man in him coming out? 'Make sure you do, cos if anything happens I'll come after you.'

'You're hurting me,' Danny replied, trying not to lose his cool. Toby was too close for Danny to be comfortable facing him. He could feel a brush of warm air over his ear. He fought off a shiver.

'This is hurting me more,' Toby growled. 'It's like selling one of my daughters, I had big plans for her, she was my last hope to save the yard and all I've worked for since being released. She might be yours, but I still see her as one of my own, worth a hundred humans. So, if I hear she's not being treated well, you'll be seeing me sooner than you think.'

Danny felt his heart working again. He was left wondering which one of them was actually about to hand over fifty grand.

'As long as you understand,' Toby added as he backed off and then smiled. 'You look as if you need a drink, come inside while I get the paperwork sorted.'

*   *   *   *

Up by the ridge the weak winter sun set the treetops ablaze as Danny unloaded the new addition to Silver Belle Stables.

31

He led Powder Keg into the loosebox alongside Salamanca's left vacant from when one of the yard's lesser lights Big Time Charlie didn't return having been sold after winning a claimer over Taunton hurdles last week. He was hoping the yard's stable star would set a good example as a neighbour and be a calming influence on this young flighty French thing.

When Danny led her Shetland pal Zola away, he looked back at Powder Keg, whose black head appeared and then looked about over the metal V in the half-open stable door. He rushed back.

As he feared she immediately exhibited signs of stress. As he unbolted the door, she shuffled back and then kicked out at the wall. Danny hurriedly tied up Zola and rushed to settle Powder Keg.

'There girl, I know, it's all a bit strange and new here. Calm yourself, shush, I'm not taking him away for good.'

Danny ran a hand down her coal-black face. She'd now settled enough for him to check her legs and breathed out when he saw they were in better condition than the paintwork of the wall.

'We'll have to get you out and about first light, see the sights, show you it's not such a bad place up here, eh girl.' He looked into her eyes and then blew gently on her lips. From his jacket, he removed an emergency pack of mints. Powder Keg soon devoured the sweetener from his palm. He hoped within days she'd learn to trust this strange man before her. He couldn't help but smile when she began licking his arm.

'Seems Toby was right, you are a lively one, that's for sure.' As he slowly backed out of the stable and then bolted the door, Danny left with, 'Back in a tick.'

He then led her Shetland sidekick Zola down to the lower field.

Since Silver Belle was no longer around, Danny could see Ronny had cut a lonely figure. His flaxen coat, ruby eyes and boundless energy had all dimmed since the grey mare he used to look up to in more ways than one had died. Perhaps Powder Keg wouldn't miss Zola for a few hours a week when she was out doing work on the gallops, or schooling.

Ronny had his head over the bottom rung of the fence separating the lower field off. That was until he'd spotted Danny and Zola. He came bounding over to the gate. Danny lifted the latch and squeezed Zola through. He ran a hand through Ronny's shaggy mane. Danny was as pensive as Zola appeared to be about how the two Shetlands would bond, if at all.

When Danny was happy to let Zola off her leash, Ronny began to run away, hopping and bucking. Zola chased after but had no hope in catching up, clearly not blessed with the speed or athleticism of his footballing namesake. It was only then Danny realised the relative speed Ronny could reach. He recalled Toby saying Zola was quick. What did that make Ronny? It gave him an idea.

Now for the tricky bit, he thought, as he trudged back to Silver Belle House.

Chapter 4

'HOW MUCH?' MEG ASKED.

'Come have a look at her first?'

'How much, Danny?'

'She won both her starts in France and her full sister won the Grade Two Kingwell Hurdle at Wincanton and that one fetched fifty-five thousand going through the ring last year. I only paid a fraction of that.'

'What fraction Danny?'

Danny felt like he was burning calories doing the maths. 'Ten-elevenths.'

She paused. 'Fifty thousand! You spent fifty on a jumper, we'll never get it back.'

'Keep it down, Jack's asleep. I knew you'd be like this.'

'Can you blame me,' Meg said. 'Could've bought my mam's council house for that.'

'But your mam's house is unlikely to win the Triumph Hurdle at Cheltenham in March.'

'And Powder Keg is?'

'All I'm saying is, at least there's a chance,' Danny said 'Speculate to accumulate, stand still and you're a sitting duck, that's the game we're in, you'll get used to it.'

'But blowing the bank on one new recruit, you'll never retire.'

'Who says I wanna retire? Racing gets into your blood, reckon I'll drop dead doing this, it's what I know, it's all I'm good at,' Danny explained. 'Anyway what's with the sudden money worries when, for once, we have money. And we're not even married yet.' Meg gave him a look. 'I said *yet*,' Danny added. 'We've been through this, I don't want to rush in like I did with Sara.'

'It's not that I'm worried about,' Meg said.

'Then what?'

'There's a gambler in you and there always will be, waiting to come out and play,' Meg said.

'Like I said, you've got to take risks in this game. Stand still and others will overtake.'

'When I first came here,' she said, 'I saw you when the yard was in a financial mess and then I see you now. I know which I prefer. I just don't want us to go back there, that's all.'

'And we never will, not with the likes of Powder Keg on board. We need new blood in the yard, Salamanca won't go on forever. I get gyp all the time from the lads in the jockeys' room that I run a one-horse yard. I brush it off with the jealousy line, but it does hurt, cos I know it's true. I've put a Salamanca nameplate on the *outside* of the trophy cabinet in my office. Anyway, even if she doesn't deliver on track, she can certainly deliver as our very own foundation mare once her racing career is over.' Meg's face softened slightly. Danny hoped her attitude would too. 'She can help replace Silver Belle.'

'She'll never replace Silver Belle,' Meg said. 'Nothing can replace her.'

'I know,' Danny conceded. 'But there's something about her Meg, soon as I set eyes on her. Bit like when I first saw you.'

'That won't work on me,' she said and frowned. 'I'll never fall for it.'

'But perhaps you'll fall for this,' he said and marshalled her by the hand. They turned into the stables and there she was. The ink-black filly stood proud, like a statue, calmly surveying the stable courtyard from her new home.

Meg gathered pace as she went over and then silently ran a hand down Powder Keg's glossy neck and shoulders. She then looked deep into her intelligent brown eyes. 'Hey, girl.'

Danny stepped back from this intimate moment. He hoped the filly's temperamental side wouldn't rear its ugly head and spoil it before they'd bonded, but she remained placid as the yard's seasoned hack.

Meg beamed a smile. Her eyes were as blue and sparkly as the Med. It reminded him of the first time they'd met when he'd interviewed her for the post as a stable lass here.

'Welcome to Silver Belle Stables,' she whispered. 'I'll be looking after you.' She turned to Danny . 'Won't I?' Danny

35

suspected that was a rhetorical question. Danny opened his mouth but she got in first. 'No buts, Danny!'

'It's too late, you've told her now,' Danny said. 'Wouldn't dare disappoint the new women in my life.'

* * * *

The late morning sunlight streaming through the window turned the TV screen white. After working the horses since six, they both sat silently, too tired to care. Probably a good thing, Danny thought, only crap on at this hour.

Danny flicked it off. There were three dance competition dresses in pink, peacock blue and lime green draped neatly over the coffee table, their sequins dazzled like diamonds. Apparently she had to choose one for the Glamorgan trial that evening. He was banking on this competitive spirit as he had another trial in mind for her. He came over and moved one of the dresses, so he could sit and look her in the eye.

'What have I done now?' she asked.

'You know you were asking about getting a ride on one of our runners, making the use of the licence you'd taken out.'

'Yeah.'

'Come with me,' Danny said. 'I want to show you something.'

'Not another one, Danny.'

Silently he led her to the schooling ring where he'd set up three makeshift jumps, each jacked up on two tyres either side. These knee-high practice fences would give Danny an idea of Ronny's jumping technique. Tied to the rails, Ronny stood chewing grass.

Danny wished he'd a camera to capture Meg's face as he gave her a riding hat and then the reins.

'It's not exactly what I had in mind,' Megan said. 'We're short enough of work riders for our proper string let alone the Shetlands. Cute as they are, they don't pay the bills.'

'Don't be so sure,' Danny said, adjusting the final pole in place.

36

'I don't understand.'

'You will,' Danny said. 'Think of this as a means to an end.'

'Stop talking riddles, Danny.'

'Just get on and I'll explain after,' Danny replied and glanced at Ronny.

Meg shook her head. 'No.'

'Why?

'Isn't it a bit of a come down,' Meg said. 'I'm used to riding the real thing now.'

Danny didn't want to reveal the grander plan just yet. He feared she'd have one eye on him inspecting her every move in the saddle. This was about her and the pony. Instead he told her, 'It'll help break Ronny in for when Jack's ready and tall enough to ride out.'

When Danny was too old to ride and too tired to train, he secretly wanted his racing life to live on vicariously through Jack. He'd never let on, not wanting to be seen as one of those pushy parents.

'So I'm the guinea pig,' Meg said. 'You said yourself he's a livewire.'

'All Shetlands are,' Danny said, letting go of Ronny's tack, 'This fella was growing old before his time with no Silver Belle down there, you'll be giving him some variety, reckon it'll spice his life up a bit. Anyway you're lighter *and* have a lighter touch than me.'

Danny checked his watch.

'I'm not keeping you,' Meg said and scowled.

'I'm timing you,' Danny said.

'I'm schooling a Shetland, this isn't the Epsom Derby,' Meg said. 'Give the poor lad a break, he's a virgin over these poles, let him have some fun.'

For once Danny was glad she wasn't taking his side. Perhaps she had connected with the pony.

She kicked Ronny in the belly but the pony smelt the ground as if searching for more grass. 'Nothing but woodchip in there, Ronny. Come on boy, show Meg what I saw in the field. Take it easy on him.'

'Me take it easy on him!' she shouted back. Her voice acted like a starter's pistol and Ronny bolted. Danny saw her struggle to stop her being fired out the back door, but she had the horsemanship to grip the reins and regain her equilibrium just in time to meet the first pole on a perfect stride.

Pick 'em up, Danny pleaded, as Ronny raised his front legs, clearing the pole like an equestrian high jumper at Olympia. The Rocket had already set his sights on the second pole. He'd got a taste for the game already. His stunted legs scurried along at full racing speed despite Meg pulling back desperately on the reins for her life.

Suddenly Danny felt the ground shift.

His smile had gone.

Questions fired through his head. Is this what it felt like having a stroke? He grabbed the fence post but his arms suddenly felt weak. He grabbed the wooden fence of the schooling ring. Was it a panic attack? If it was epilepsy, he could kiss goodbye to riding.

Recently he could hardly ignore the RAF jets traversing the valleys on their low-fly sortie. He looked to the skies for an answer but there was nothing, just bruised cloud.

He quickly regained his equilibrium enough to let go of the wooden fencepost.

'Boy that was good,' Meg said, pulling up alongside.

'Did you feel the earth move then?' Danny said.

'Steady, Danny, I said it was good but-'

'No, the earth actually shook,' Danny said.

She laughed. 'Perhaps you should cut down on the morning coffees.'

'It's not a caffeine buzz, I tell you. I know it's crazy,' Danny said.

She stepped off Ronny.

'It's important, Meg, did you feel anything?' Danny snapped.

38

'Alright, Danny! No need to go all weird on me,' she replied. 'Think I'll leave it there.'

'But Ronny needs more of this.'

'I don't,' she replied.

'So that's it.'

'Didn't say that, we'll go again after we've all had a night's sleep.'

From his fleece Danny produced the classified ad sections he'd printed off from the internet. Danny showed her the notice to all entries in the regional trials for the Shetland Pony Grand National. The Glamorgan qualifiers were taking place this Sunday.

As Meg studied the clipping, Danny said, 'I've seen enough, we go for the trials.'

'Danny, it's all a bit *My Little Pony*, I'm past all that,' Meg said. 'How old do you think I am?'

'Old enough to realise all the Irish boys were broken in on the pony circuit there – never did A.P. or Ruby any harm. Best way is to cut your teeth on this little fella. If you can control him in a competitive race, handling a seasoned thoroughbred will be a doddle. It'll give you both valuable race-riding experience.'

'But I'm nearly twenty-one. That's for kids.'

'Says here they've opened up a division for late starters, twenty-one years and under, and you fall in their height and weight restrictions.'

Meg's frown had gone. 'But we haven't even registered.'

'No?' Danny said and produced another sheet from his fleece. 'I took a punt.'

'But you didn't know I'd come up to scratch,' Meg said.

'Seems I've got more faith in you,' Danny said. 'Ronny was my only worry and he seems up for this, look at him.'

Danny left the schooling ring with a cocktail of emotions. He was chuffed with Meg and Ronny but now felt less sure about himself.

This wasn't the time for a health scare, Danny thought grimly, life was going well, possibly too well.

That afternoon he sat at his desk nursing a medicinal whisky with the *Racing Post* open at the Chepstow report dominated by Bert's vanishing act. Salamanca's win managed just a column inch.

In came Meg and said, 'These came for you.'

She held back a clutch of white and pink envelopes to her chest. Danny suspected they were early birthday cards but didn't ask, not to let on he'd remembered. Instead he shuffled his post into a neat pile and then pushed the swivel chair away from the desk.

'What's wrong?' Meg asked. 'I know that face.'

'Nothing.'

'Oh, and Ralph rang again, something about Ely Park's grand opening,' Meg said. 'You'd better call him back, it's getting embarrassing. He's probably thinking you're avoiding him.'

'For once he's right,' Danny said. 'Got six missed messages on my phone. It's never good news with him.'

'Aren't business partners supposed to talk to each other?' Meg said.

'We're not partners, he's more than made that clear,' Danny said. 'I'm just there as a "racing advisor", I think he called it. Basically to make sure he doesn't balls it up before the track has a chance to take root.' Danny no longer wanted to share his worries out. He forced a smile and beckoned her over. 'Come here, postie.'

She sat on his inviting lap and he spun three-sixty. She let out a surprised laugh. 'Don't need to ask if you've had your coffee yet.'

'Just buzzing from life,' Danny said.

'Don't you wanna check what's in them?'

Danny glanced over at the top envelope, all brown except for a dreaded window. 'Not yet, I'm in a good mood, let's make it last.'

Danny looked back at her. 'What?'

'Nothing,' she replied, smiling. 'Can't a girl look at her man.'

40

'Yes but it normally means something.'

'You know sometimes at night when I can't get a wink's sleep,' she said and then paused. 'I look at you thinking how lucky I am.'

'What to be set free from Rhymney and your parents?'

She shook her head.

'You're not worried about anything,' Danny said. 'To make you lie awake.'

She sighed, 'Even knowing I've got to get up first thing can be enough to keep me up.'

'Mammy Meg, Mammy Meg,' Jack cried from downstairs.

She kissed him on the lips and then parted from his lap. 'Probably a good thing, with that little dynamo about.'

'Do you want me to go,' Danny said.

'Nope,' she said. 'This one's got my name on. He's probably lost his Spider Man doll … again.'

'Don't call it a doll,' Danny said, 'at least not in front of him.'

Meg parted with a smile.

Danny sighed as he picked up the bundle of letters. Sifting out the ominously official ones, he was left with a postcard. It was a photo of a sunlit seaside harbour with yachts riding the sparkly green-blue waters. It looked like one of the fishing villages in Cornwall or Devon he used to go as a child.

That's odd, he thought, can't recall anyone who's away on hols. So he flipped it over to see if it was addressed to Silver Belle Stables. There was no address. It was blank. And so was the 'affix stamp here' box. The message box was left white too.

Danny couldn't quite believe what he was seeing.

He then squinted at the credits in tiny print at the base of the card. Photo: Lyme Regis, Dorset, UK.

He put it down on the *Racing Post* to lie next to the headline 'Bert Mills and Artemis Missing'.

Bert's boat hole, Danny thought, bloody hell! Was he alive? Was this his way of saying to those back home he was alive? Did Leo get the same thing?

41

Danny now had good reason to go round there.

He ripped open the only other promising envelope and read:

Dear Mr Rawlings,

Mooncraft Media is a small, yet progressive and innovative television production company looking to produce a short film about the day-to-day running of a racing stable.

The recent exploits and the story behind your exceptional steeplechaser Salamanca attracted us to Silver Belle Stables as a perfect fit for our subject.

Although a local company, we will look to syndicate the programme out to numerous media outlets and trade TV companies, with the possibility of selling rights to one of the big four channels.

As a local company we believe this represents a good opportunity to project a positive image of your yard to industry professionals and the wider public alike.

We very much look forward to hearing from you.

Yours

It had been signed with a squiggle.

Give them a bell later, Danny thought; probably get more exposure for the yard than that lame attempt on *Antique's Heaven* last year.

Danny wiped a sleeve over the fisheye camera on his laptop. Must remember to Skype Mum later, Danny thought. With a few owners on the books abroad at least part of the year, this video link enabled Danny to at least tell them to the face their pride and joy had gone lame or had colic.

His thoughts soon slipped back to the panic attack outside. It was sobering to think his career in the saddle could end in one terrifying moment.

Chapter 5

DANNY SAT LOW IN THE SADDLE, staring at the gentle upslope.

Through Powder Keg's eyes, it must've seemed more like a mountain to climb, compared to the flatness of the French provinces and then Gleeson's gallops.

She appeared to have settled in well at her new home, particularly once reunited with Zola in box two. That Shetland was clearly her best friend and only constant in her world.

She also seemed to have relaxed a bit here and was looking about, head and ears turning inquisitively, though her black neck lathered in sweat told another story.

It wasn't only his face that was left red after smacking Gleeson's tarmac the last time he'd dared mount her. His palms and elbows still stung.

This time he'd made sure to reach a thick covering of grass before climbing on. His stomach had tightened but those concerns were unfounded as she now stood there quietly.

'This'll open ya lungs, girl.'

But when Danny shook the reins, he soon realised this was to become more a blowout for him than her. Despite rousting and cajoling her as if it were the finish of the Gold Cup, she'd barely consent to break into a hack canter. She certainly made it look like an ascent of K2.

Soon as she began cocking her head and hanging to the left, he feared Toby had sold him damaged goods. But she was moving soundly enough, so he suspected this was more in the head than body. It was like a struggling relationship, going nowhere fast. Halfway up he gave her a few stern slaps down her withers to remind her who was now the leader of her herd.

As Danny eased off where the ground plateaued over the ridge, Powder Keg needed no encouragement in slowing to a walk. They skirted the far reaches of Silver Belle Woods and then the stone footprint where once the original country pile Samuel House stood proud over lush green slopes.

He felt deflated even before Powder Keg had run in his colours. Perhaps she reserved her best for the track, as when winning both her starts in French AQPS races, called bumpers in Britain as they were once known for amateur riders jostling for a decent position in the early skirmishes.

He drank in the vivid green of the slopes reaching the road far below, and mix of grazing and arable fields beyond. Sitting upright on horseback he filled his lungs and imagined the master of Samuel House doing the same there back in the day.

The silence almost sang to him, like when he'd shut the front door on the final lingering party guest at the yard's Christmas do.

Up there the January gusts brushing his face felt like the cool of a freshly turned pillow. The chemical smell of pesticide was also carried on the wind, nipping the back of Danny's throat.

Still, no worse than when they're out muck spreading, Danny thought, trying not to spoil the moment.

He glanced over at the brown field of harrowed earth, expecting to see Leo occupying both his time and his mind with the crop sprayer.

Instead his eyes were drawn to the herd of grazing cows in the neighbouring field, in particular the two Welsh Blacks lying peacefully on their side, stiff legs parallel to the grass. They looked like Jack's plastic farmyard miniatures after he'd flicked them over.

Danny knew something was very wrong.

He could pass over one dying for whatever reason, but two? What the hell had Leo been doing? Or perhaps he should ask what he hadn't been doing.

Bert's son always came across as an idle workshy oaf. On race-days Bert had to carry all the tack and kit around, shadowed by his hulk of a son shoegazing with hands in ripped loose-fit jeans.

When Danny sniffed the air again, he reckoned he now knew the answer.

'Don't want to exert you too much in one day,' Danny muttered sarcastically as he urged Powder Keg on. 'You do realise I've blown fifty big ones on you, you're making Leo look like a Trojan.'

He stopped shaking the reins when a distant banging then filled the air, bouncing off the valley sides.

At first he couldn't place it. His eyes swept the view and along the main road out, right up to where it was eaten up by the treeline marking the boundary of the Silver Belle Estate. He felt sure the noise was coming from down there. Until now he'd rarely ventured to that far corner of the estate. He could hardly ignore that racket. He didn't want Leo storming round claiming it was spooking the cattle.

Sometimes it got like the Somme down there when the rainy season set in, which was most of the year in these parts, often seeming like spring would never arrive. It wasn't conducive to working horses, even mud-loving jumpers, as one slip or misstep could put them out for the season.

No wonder they'd dug a ditch between the hedgerow and the road. Even that wasn't enough when the insistent Welsh rain appeared to set like plaster over the mid-Glamorgan valleys and once it slowly drained downslope, there was only so much the brook would take.

One morning last winter he recalled turning back to the yard with two primed runners in the van. Seeing the tops of the roadblock cones bobbing away, he knew there was no way out. That was a dark day in every respect, he recalled.

After the biblical deluge they'd had a few days back, Danny was reluctant to venture down there on this youngster but he had to find out what was making the racket.

He kicked her in the belly and hoped she'd surely be more willing to go downhill. However, much to Danny's bemusement, she refused to take the handbrake off and pick up speed.

'You *are* a character, Kegsy,' Danny said through clenched teeth. 'Give me a ray of hope, for Christ's sake.'

When he'd nearly reached the foot of the slope, he gave up trying for anything more than a trot. The banging was definitely louder now, like a slow handclap.

45

The ground here rode more like good-to-soft, Danny thought, must be porous rock round as the rain had clearly yet to filter its way down the slope. As Danny hopped off Powder Keg, he was glad of that.

The leaden skies made him squint for a better view. Up ahead he could just about make out a crumbling ruin swallowed up by the overhanging birches and rampant undergrowth.

Since Samuel House was razed to the ground, this derelict outbuilding had slowly become a forgotten relic.

According to his former boss Roger Crane, it was a barn to store feed for the cattle that once grazed this part of the estate.

Its flaky walls were now a cobweb of cracks, ready to drop from the frequent smack of the iron door on its frame, sending it the same way as Samuel House decades ago. In fact it was probably only the trees and vines holding it from becoming a useless pile of stones.

Every swinging clunk of metal on stone was like thunder out here and, while he'd normally find any excuse to get away from this dark corner of the estate and back on the beaten track, he wasn't going to leave until it stopped.

He looked for something to tie the door firmly shut before returning with strong rope. The thick vines were rooted in place and were going nowhere. He began to scour the ground nearby, boots flattening the ferns and weeds as he went.

He stopped and looked down at a patch of ground unlike all the rest. There was a light covering of earth framed by snapped weed stems and trampled grass. It had been disturbed though not by him. He looked back over at Silver Belle Woods and thought, one grave was more than enough for this estate.

Most of the stones had fallen at the foot of the wall. There were, however, several strays where he stood. They must've been moved by hand, Danny reckoned. He skated his boots to disturb the fresh earth some more.

Soon the thick treads of his boots scraped metal. It sounded like a hollow drum.

He stood back to see a pair of rusty iron trap doors. Around the lock across the middle, there was a break in the orange crust, as if the bolt had been shifted at some point since the rust had formed. Danny looked over at the stone barn. If he needed something hiding, Danny thought, that crumbling shell wouldn't provide enough shelter. He considered what he might find down there. A food store? A wine cellar? A cesspit? Stolen goods? A body? Bert?

He stopped thinking, tugged off his leather gloves and stuffed them in his jacket.

From the undergrowth he filled his palm with one of the weighty rocks and began to strike the bolt's side. At first it wouldn't budge; only serving to feed his curiosity.

As he gave the bolt more elbow, it began to inch free from the metal loops holding it fast.

He straightened, and opened his lungs. As his fingers gripped the door handles, he flexed his race-fit biceps and pulled. The doors parted to reveal the gaping mouth of a black hole. A rush of cold air brushed over him as if he'd opened a window. The doors now stood there unsupported, ready to be dropped shut again. He looked over both shoulders. He felt like an intruder on his own land. Below he could make out the first few steps of a spiralling stairwell. Only then did he remember he'd left the torch with Jack. Battery was probably low now in any case. He tied Powder Keg's reins to a nearby trunk. For the first time her apparent aversion to moving an inch was a help.

He then swallowed his fears and stepped into the hole in the ground. Just six steps in he could no longer see his guiding hands that felt the turning brickwork.

He'd now lost his bearings but the fear was back. He shivered, as if to shed his crawling skin. He stopped. From somewhere deep below, he heard a steady drip. He then heard a scream.

'Bert?' he called out instinctively into the blackness. 'Bert!'

Danny now had no option but to carry on for another twist of the stairwell. It felt like he was being drawn into some dungeon, never to return.

47

He then heard another screech and the scurry of claws across his path. Rats!

What the hell were the Samuels up to back in the day?

He reckoned he'd never dare come this far again, so he kept inching deeper underground.

He then stopped again. Ahead he could make out a dull green rectangle of light

He paused to allow his pupils to grow but his brain had nothing to reference this otherworldly glow. He felt strangely drawn by the light like a moth but stumbled forward as he expected another step that wasn't there. He reached out for the wall and managed to break his fall.

The drips grew louder as he turned a corner and stepped into a circular chamber with a domed ceiling. At the top there appeared to be a round grille, letting through intermittent light from gaps in the trees above. It was tainted green from the heavy weeds entangling the grille.

What was this place?

He could see his breath as he stood beneath the mint-green spotlight in the centre of the room and slowly turned. He stopped when he saw a patch of grey on the brown brickwork. He went over. It was a stone, set into the wall and inscribed with: *The Ice Room 1919.*

Must've been where the Samuels kept the crushed ice for their cherry sundaes and whisky on the rocks, Danny thought, life must've been such a stretch. He shivered again. *It's bloody cold enough.* He only wished he'd got a freezer this big.

He was about to leave but knew someone had recently gone to the trouble of locking this place. There's a reason behind every action, Danny reckoned, and began to search the darker side of the room.

There, lined up in an arc against the curvature of the wall, Danny made out several spherical shapes. He edged closer. They were ruddy brown and varying in size, ranging from beach ball right down to football. They looked a bit like eggs.

Danny shuddered at what could possibly have laid them and what might emerge when they hatched. He then pictured the dead cattle on Bert's side of the fence. Was there a link? Maybe these eggs were behind the unearthly rumblings that had shaken him and the Silver Belle Estate.

They were like from some alien movie. He felt a weird energy from them, or was his mind playing tricks in the silent gloom. Perhaps spacecraft had chosen his estate as a landing strip.

'Get a bloody grip, Danny,' he whispered.

He shook his head. In the darkness his imagination had hijacked his senses. Perhaps his ex, Sara, had been right, it was time to bin some of those UFO and conspiracy books he'd kept from his teens.

He was more ready to believe the balls were hot property. After all, opportunist thieves searching for a safe haven to store the loot could see this from the road. They'd surely come back to pick them up. Suddenly he felt it was time to leave. Perhaps he should take one back to the house. There were several here, so they shouldn't miss one.

Curiosity made him silently shuffle closer, careful not to trip over the uneven flagstones.

His heart was racing quicker than Frankel as he knelt in front of a medium-sized sphere, no bigger than a medicine ball.

With a lover's touch his fanned fingers, outstretched and trembling, caressed its cool and smooth surface. He could see the grille above in its shiny brown surface but his fingertips had left no impression. It also appeared to be as solid as a medicine ball. Suspecting they were stolen, he pulled his fleece down over his hand and began to rub the area he'd left fingerprints.

Suddenly it came for him with a low rumble, like a ten-pin bowling ball, Danny stumbled back as if escaping the clutches of a crazed killer. What the hell was this place? He ran for the black rectangle of the only way out.

He scrambled up the spiral stairwell a good deal quicker than on his descent. He heard and felt the whistling wind and hoped the trap doors wouldn't live up to their name. Being stuck down here in the cold and wet, waiting for the keeper of those . . . things, didn't bare thinking about. As he saw light reflected in the brickwork making the final turn he felt a shot of adrenalin spike his blood.

Almost there, Danny thought.

He leapt from the hole as if trying to board the final lifeboat. He then turned to see Powder Keg bucking. Danny rushed over and had only just grabbed the tethered reins when the filly's hind legs left the ground and kicked out, taking a chunk of bark from a nearby trunk.

Danny didn't panic, knowing that would only make things worse. He just quietly reined her in and then ran a calming hand down her face. 'There girl, shush now.'

Powder Keg's senses clearly picked up something Danny's hadn't. Perhaps there was nothing bad about her temperament, she merely lived on her nerves, cautious of new things. She was certainly sharp in the head and maybe he should treat her with more respect than anger.

Danny checked her over, running a hand down from her compact hind quarters down the mud-flecked support strapping over her hocks. He then walked her round in circles. Everything seemed in order, no sign of lameness. In fact she was moving better than earlier.

Danny smiled. 'Glad you're finally showing some life girl, want you bouncing for Ely's The Whistler Triumph Hurdle trial next week. It's got your name on it.'

The thought of a trespasser returning to his estate that night grounded his mood. He didn't want to leave but then had an idea.

He ripped off the top inch of tape from Powder Keg's near fore strapping and led his charge over to the trap doors in the ground. He pushed the doors to drop shut. He then knelt and pressed down the patch of tape over the crack between the rusty door and its stone frame.

He then pulled up a fistful of grass. Powder Keg showed her first palpable signs of interest. 'Not for you girl,' he said, scattering the grass to cover the tape. He hoped it would act as a makeshift seal. He would return at first light to see if had been broken.

Even before looking at his phone's screen, he knew there would be no reception up here. He cantered Powder Keg back, the way he'd come.

That morning he'd set out to see exactly what he'd bought but came back with more questions than answers, most of them unrelated to the filly beneath him.

On the retreat he found himself scanning the green fields, half expecting to see the scorched-black circle of where a craft had landed and caused the ground to shift when Ronny was being schooled.

All he saw was Meg and a few of the lads riding Indian file along the sand strip downslope back to the stables.

Keen to get far away from there, Danny shook up Powder Keg to lengthen her stride down the gentle slope from the ridge but she was still having none of it. Despite Powder Keg's best efforts, they finally made it back to the yard

He slammed the kitchen door with a rattle of glass. He found the card Mavers had left him as a parting gift. If you hear anything abnormal, Mavers had said, call this number.

There was nothing normal about that place.

As he knitted the card between fingers, he mulled over what best to do.

He could feel indentations on the cardboard. Initially he thought it was braille or perhaps embossed lettering. But when he inspected, there was the imprint of a pen mark. Stood there in the kitchen still spooked by the memory of the Ice Room, he didn't have the light or the inclination to find out what was written there. Instead he punched in the printed landline number on the card.

Meg came in blowing almost as hard as the wind outside. 'That'll teach me for taking Shock Value out, he's a right monkey. Needed to push his ears off just keep up with the others.'

'Get used to it,' Danny said, 'we've got another in the yard.'

Meg tilted her head donnishly.

'Powder Keg, she's a right madam and before you say I told you so, she's got more ability than quirks.'

She raised her hands. 'I come in peace.'

51

Danny looked at her distantly, mobile pressed to one ear and police calling card in the other hand. She came over.

'What's going on?' she whispered and looked at the card.

'It's a calling card.'

'Not that,' she said and held his hand still. 'You're shaking.'

'I'm not,' Danny replied. He pulled his hand free, and put it and the card in his waterproof over-trousers. 'Came down here for a better reception,' Danny said. Meg frowned. 'Not from you … the phone.'

'If I don't want to know, don't tell me,' she said. 'I'm taking the afternoon off, going into Rhymney to pick up my dance shoes, you know the ones I told you about when we were in Prague, managed to track the shop down but it was a failed delivery, so picking them up at the depot.'

'Yeah,' Danny said distantly.

'But I'll be wearing mangos for practice tonight,' she said.

It was as if Danny had left part of himself in The Ice Room. 'Eh?'

'You are listening then,' she said. 'Just checking.'

'Have the horses been fed and watered?'

'Told the lads to get it done,' Meg said, beaming. 'I could get used to being head lass.' She then left for the lounge.

Danny punched the call button but it went straight to answerphone. Danny cleared his throat. 'Hello … PC Mavers, this is Danny … Daniel Rawlings the jockey, you questioned me after the Welsh National. What it is, you told to call if I notice anything unusual, well, I have, something like a bunker just off the main Rhymney road. It's hidden by the tree line bordering my land and well, I discovered these weird … spheres, like eggs they were. I wouldn't normally ring but they're just off Bert's land too. Reckon they might be stol- … well, you'd know more about that, just thought you'd better see it. Anyway that's it, if you want to meet me there, I've got a half-hour break between first and second lots in the morning, say eight.'

Danny hung up. He always felt uneasy getting the police involved but felt just as strongly this could be the lead they were after.

Chapter 6

DANNY FELT AS LOST as he probably looked.

Surrounded by champagne-quaffing suits in the middle of this corporate tent he stood there wearing navy combats, black layered sweater and the ghost of a frown.

No one gave him a second look let alone attempt to strike up a conversation, probably to Danny's relief. He was only there for one thing and she'd been gone for what felt like ten minutes, though it was probably nearer five.

By then he'd given up trying to stop Jack from weaving between the several round tables covered in white cloths and canapés. His son flew around the tent, arms stuck out as wings.

Danny checked his watch. What the hell was keeping Meg?

He could see the tarpaulin walls of the tent were flapping. He knew Ronny The Rocket wouldn't be fazed by the wind. The last few chastening winters roughed out in the lower field would serve him well.

'He appears to be enjoying this more than you,' a voice came from Danny's right. He turned to face the tall, willowy frame of a man. Early fifties, Danny reckoned, with a full head of grey hair topping a thin, angular face. He wore tweeds from the cap on his head down to his slacks, and a wispy beard that appeared work-in-progress.

'Always good to see a new face on the pony racing circuit,' the man added. 'But I do know it from somewhere.'

'I'm a trainer. Danny Rawlings.'

'That's it!' the man said with a spike of excitement, as if finally completing a crossword. 'What luck to meet you here.'

Danny glanced at the red laminated badge pinned to the man's lapel. It read: *Rhodri Hughes – Chairman Welsh Pony Club.* 'I'm guessing there's not enough money in this to live on, Rhodri?'

'No, they don't pay the bills,' Rhodri said. 'I'm in property myself. They say never to mix business with a bit of pleasure, they lie. Days like this are a welcome distraction, what with the state of the housing and land markets.'

'Surprised to hear there's a dip, had three offers on Silver Belle Stables in the past few months,' Danny said.

'So you're thinking of packing up the game,' Rhodri said.

'Offers, I didn't accept, it's not even on the market,' Danny said. 'Guess the views make people jealous. Only armed bailiffs could turf me out of that place.'

'Still, coming here must be a welcome break from the routine.'

'Bit of a busman's holiday I guess,' Danny said. 'Just hope our boy does us proud in the second heat.'

'How do you rate your chances?'

'Well Ronny's as stubborn as he is speedy.'

'I'm afraid everyone in this tent will say the same,' Rhodri said. 'Shetland ponies are strong in mind and body, a hardy lot. It's what kept them from extinction when other breeds perished. In my eyes they're every bit as impressive as a thoroughbred.'

'But that's like comparing Formula Three with Formula One.'

'In every sport they all need to start somewhere,' Rhodri said.

'That's what I keep telling Meg.'

'And it's the same for these plucky little Shetlands, who were renowned for their racing abilities long before the thoroughbred galloped the earth. You have a lot to thank them for. Without them, you'd be out of a job.'

'Oh, get real,' Danny said. 'I can see you're a fan of them, it's hard not to be, but like you said, ponies don't pay the bills. And I train the best staying chaser in the land, so can't see me having to quit just yet.'

'The second best,' Rhodri replied, stroking his bristly chin, 'Artemis is the number one.'

Danny drew a composing breath. 'I know racing's a game of opinions but yours is wrong.'

'It's not *my* opinion,' Rhodri said.

Was this guy some wind-up merchant? He gave Danny the creeps.

'Look, whatever happened to Artemis at Chepstow that day, nothing would've got close to Salamanca, he was simply awesome and that's coming from the trade press.'

'I'm not judging them on that race.'

'Why not? It was billed as the big showdown,' Danny said. 'And anyway, if you look at their overall profiles, Salamanca matches Artemis in class and has even greater stamina reserves, that's his strength.'

'Ironically that could yet prove his very weakness too.'

Danny finished off the champagne to wet his mouth and to disguise a swallow.

'You see, I was at Chepstow,' Rhodri said.

'Why?'

'I fear Artemis was the casualty of a much bigger race.'

'They don't come much bigger than the Welsh National,' Danny said.

Not content with belittling Salamanca's ranking, Danny reckoned, Rhodri now set about dismantling his star chaser's CV. He pretended to look at his watch. 'Think I'll go look for Meg.'

'Daniel, they'll come after you next.'

Danny stopped from turning. 'Who?'

'I don't know who,' Rhodri replied.

Danny smiled and turned again.

That's five minutes of my life I'll never get back, he thought.

He was about to round up Jack when Rhodri called after him again, 'But I do know why.'

Danny couldn't leave without hearing this. He could do with a laugh to relieve some of the pre-race anxiety. He joined Rhodri in sitting at one of the tables.

'To understand the motives of these people, you must know their background,' Rhodri explained, back to stroking his patchy beard. 'And in some ways it's related to Ronny The Rocket and his rivals out there. Prior to being domesticated over seven thousand years ago horses needed both speed and stamina

56

as they do today. Except back then it was a matter of survival, to escape predators. You merely exploit this hardwired response every time you send a horse to the track.' Danny was intrigued as to why horses behaved like they did but none of this explained why he was in danger. 'It was only the turn of the eighteenth century that wealthy English landowners imported three Arabian stallions – the Godolphin, Darley and Byerley Turk. And they crossed them with seventy-four British mares.'

'But what's that got to do with Ronny?' Danny asked.

'The other breeds had already died out, leaving the hardy ones, namely the Shetland and Dartmoor ponies. Guess Darwin was right.'

'Because they were speedy,' Danny said.

Rhodri nodded. 'A recent horse genome project involving over a hundred scientists in twenty countries studied the DNA of many racing legends, both living and dead – from bones of past legends, to blood samples of modern-day greats,' he explained. 'There are over two-hundred genes linked to human athletic ability and the scientists expected as many for horses, but when they discovered a single gene called myostatin, also known as double-muscling gene in cattle, was found in such dominance among the modern thoroughbred, they were left dumbfounded.'

Suddenly Danny pictured the two dead cows in Bert's neighbouring field. 'Cattle you say.'

Rhodri nodded again. 'There are three variants of myostatin: the C gene which passes on speed to the progeny, the T gene for stamina and then there's a combination of the two. Sprinters with the combination C:C possess all speed or muscle twitch, middle-distance performers tend to have the C:T variant combining a mix of speed and stamina, while T:T is for out-and-out stamina, or energy production.'

'So Salamanca is pure T:T,' Danny replied. 'Better start calling Salamanca Mr T then, got more stamina than Mo Farah.'

'But even superstars of their day like Eclipse and Hyperion were bred to stay with the T:T variant. I presume you know both of them.'

'I've tried to forget the latter,' Danny sighed. 'Seems a waste of time for all those eggheads, shouldn't they be finding a cure for cancer or something.'

'Like I say, they have their motives.'

'But you still haven't said where Ronny The Rocket comes into all this.'

'There was an even more shocking discovery from the research.' Rhodri leant in close, as if to share a precious secret. 'The speed gene came from a single mare over three hundred years ago.'

'And?' Danny asked. 'Would've thought that was obvious, as you say, everything has to start somewhere.'

'But this *Eve* of today's thoroughbred population was British.'

'Guess that's why they're called the English thoroughbred,' Danny added.

'But, as I've said, the mares in Britain at the turn of the eighteenth century were mostly hard ponies like the Shetland.'

Danny laughed. 'You're telling me they crossed a giant Arabian with a Shetland. Intrigued to have seen that mating – were there a series of winches and pulleys involved?'

'The proof is there,' Rhodri snapped, clearly annoyed that Danny made fun of his pet topic. 'And they could trace it back to just one very quick Shetland mare, so without the likes of Ronny The Rocket, the modern thoroughbred wouldn't exist in its current form.'

'But why is all this affecting me?'

'There is currently a race taking place that is greater and with more far-reaching consequences than any taking place on the racetrack. Yet it remains blinkered from the public eye. A race to find the answer to one of the oldest conundrums in racing.' Danny swiped another glass of champagne from the tray of a passing waitress, no longer aware of Meg's lateness. 'For centuries breeders strived to produce the perfect specimen of a racehorse, some say they found it in the form of Frankel. But there's always room for further improvement.'

'Doubt it,' Danny said.

'They said at the end of the nineteenth century that "everything that can be invented has been invented", a possible reason for such a comprehensive research. As the C speed gene has now been isolated, a handful of companies soon set about formulating an equation to determine a racehorse's perfect trip even before setting hoof on a track. That conundrum has already been solved. A spoonful of blood from their horse is enough for wealthy owners and breeders to find a horse's optimum distance. The service will come at a price but they know money isn't a concern for most of their customer base of rich racehorse owners. Someday whole strings will be screened as a matter of course.'

'Never had any problem with form and pedigree in the paper, an ounce of breeding equals a pound of feeding,' Danny replied. 'I dunno, everyone wants an easy way out with quick fixes these days, from diets to Botox.'

Rhodri studied Danny for a moment. 'Tell me, if you could live your life over knowing what you do now, would you?'

In a flash Danny saw his fourteen-year-old self staring blankly out of the lab window in Double Chemistry, pricking the shiny wooden veneer of his desk with a compass, wishing he was anywhere but there, fantasising his very own Great Escape to a better life, or at least another life. But none of those dreams of the future involved shinning up drainpipes to get at an open first floor window to avoid a forced entry or handing notes over the counter in binges at city bars and bookies. Danny nodded. 'But then, one of my biggest mistakes was getting back with my ex, Sara, and if I hadn't, this little mite wouldn't exist.'

'In life we learn by trial and error,' Rhodri said, 'but in the shorter working life of a racehorse, there is little time to benefit from any mistakes. Need I remind you Salamanca was campaigned over a woefully inadequate two miles in his first season.'

'That's cos there was some speed among the female bloodlines of his pedigree,' Danny replied.

'And analysis of Salamanca DNA would've disproved this in hours, not a whole season,' Rhodri said.

'But the gap between big and small owners is wide enough as it is,' Danny said. 'As if racing's not a rich man's game already. Won't be long before the big boys offload their weaklings before they've even had a race to prove themselves. Where's the competition then?'

'Quite the opposite,' Rhodri said. 'That's why these tests won't break any rules of racing. They only determine the horse's optimum distance to get best results, not whether it has any ability. So there'll be no mass selloffs of unraced horses at the shallow end of the gene pool and races will become, if anything, more competitive as each horse will be producing his best over their best distance.'

'So what's your problem?' Danny said.

'Money remains the root of all evil and while the result of this race in itself won't break any rules,' Rhodri replied, 'the same cannot be said for any of the unlicensed firms that enter the running.'

'When will they complete this?'

'They already have,' Rhodri replied.

'So the race is over.'

Rhodri looked over both shoulders and leant in close enough for Danny to feel his breath. 'They're only halfway.'

'What do you mean? You said they've solved the conundrum. Race over.'

'For sprinters,' Ralph said. 'They've yet to formulate an accurate equation to decipher T:T dominant blood samples. But given recent events, it shouldn't be long now.'

'Artemis!' Danny put his glass down. 'They kidnapped Artemis for his T:T gene.'

'One of these companies clearly regarded Artemis as the perfect stayer to model their equation on,' Rhodri said. 'That's why I put Artemis ahead of Salamanca. These people don't make mistakes.'

Danny took another lingering gulp of his champagne and felt the bubbles tickle the back of his nostrils. 'My one runs over four miles, but he's no plodder.'

'Every horse can run four miles, including sprinters, even I could run that far before my knees went. It's more a question of seeing it out at proper racing speed, that's what sets the top few apart.'

'This is all a bit mind bending,' Danny said.

'Ignore me, remember these are just the theories of an old fool,' Rhodri said. Danny managed a smile but could see he wasn't that old and he certainly wasn't a fool.

'That's better.' Danny succumbed to an urge to stand.

Rhodri looked over both shoulders and said softly, 'I thought *you* of all should be aware.'

'So you believe Salamanca will be next on their list.'

'You did tell me Salamanca had just as much class as Artemis and even *more* stamina.'

'There wasn't any luck about you meeting me here was there,' Danny asked. 'This is why you are here saying all this to me now.'

'I've not *said* anything, clear?' Rhodri said, smile gone. 'And they're theories, remember.'

'What now?' Danny asked. 'Wait and see if they come for me or the horse?'

'For starters I'd stop stoking the Salamanca hype-machine in the press,' Rhodri said. 'They can read.'

A smaller hand touched his shoulder and then ran down his arm. Danny picked up Meg's sweet scent.

'Sorry I took so long.' Danny turned round to face her. 'There was a queue at the toilets, seems I'm not the only nervous rider.'

'Meg, I'd like you to meet someone,' Danny said. As he turned back, Rhodri was gone. He scanned the groups chatting away. There was no sign of him.

'Who?'

'Nothing.'

'You haven't had to make up someone to talk to,' Meg said.

'You okay?' Danny asked.

'Last time I felt like this was before my GCSEs.'

61

'You'll be fine,' Danny said. 'Remember it's just a trial for the Shetland Pony Grand National. It's not Aintree.'

'It'll probably feel like it on Ronny and it's important to me,' Meg said. 'I'm looking forward to this as much as leading out Powder Keg on her debut.'

'Can you put a leash on that?' growled one of the suited businessmen nearby.

Danny turned to see a dark streak down the man's pink shirt and grey trousers, and he was holding an empty glass.

Jack was no longer darting about. A look of shock quickly turned to uncontrollable bawling.

'Oh god, we're really sorry,' Meg said.

Couldn't have happened to a better person, Danny thought, nice one, son. 'Come here Jack, let's go see Mammy ride Ronny The Rocket, leave this gentleman to his drink.'

They left the tent and Meg shakily fastened the chin strap of her skull cap.

'Did you get a feel of the track?'

'It's like a merry-go-round,' she said. 'Makes Chester look like Newmarket.'

'Come on, Jack, let's get The Rocket ready for launch,' Danny said. Meg flung her leg over and walked Ronnie down to the start. Danny found a decent view of the finish and helped Jack onto a bale of hay in front of him. He just hoped he'd have something worthwhile to see there.

Meg was five foot three in flats and weighed in at eight stone two, stats Danny could only have dreamed about during his weight-curtailed career as a Flat jockey. He imagined Ronny would be equally pleased with those figures. He hoped his sturdy little legs would soon be a blur round the two laps.

The starter unwound his flag and they began to make a line of sorts.

Meg had Ronny near the back of the nine starters.

The Tannoys blared out, 'And they're sent on their way for heat two of the Shetland Grand National trials. It's Hide And Peek with Lucy Mayweather that gets a flyer and poaches a four-length lead as they hurtle at the first line of brush.'

62

'Come on Meg, get him going,' Danny shouted above a chorus of noise from friends and family of the rivals. He could see Ronny The Rocket had barely taken off from the launch-pad. Her arms were moving more than the pony was. It would've been better if she'd got off and pushed. However, her persistence paid off as he consented to go but they'd the leaders a good dozen lengths start.

The others quickly shifted up the gears and soon were at racing pace.

Seems Rhodri was right about the speed gene, Danny thought.

It was only then he spotted Meg bringing up the rear on Ronny. She kept working hard with her arms not to become any more detached from the field. If he had nothing to aim at, Danny knew Ronny would soon completely lose interest. It's a shame they didn't allow whips as a persuader.

'Make his mind up,' Danny found himself mutter. She sat lower and, with reins bunched in her gloved hands, pushed Ronny's neck, but still there was no immediate response. He looked up at a sky grey as a Yorkshire mill town, anything was better than what was taking place on track.

There were plenty of cheers from relatives and owners around him as they thundered by for the first time. By now Meg and Ronny were so far behind they received their own shouts of encouragement, led by Danny, as they embarked on a second lap.

Danny was impressed by Meg's persistence for such a small reward. He wouldn't be sure he'd push that hard. Either she was out to impress or believed Ronny wasn't trying nearly hard as her.

As the leaders rushed by again Danny could see Ronny begin to pick up speed. This was more like the Ronny who'd left Zola standing in the lower field.

Meg kept pushing with the vigour and zeal of Tony McCoy as they picked off the stragglers one by one.

Danny's cheers grew with every quickening stride. 'Come on, Meg! Go, Ronny!'

They were fifth clearing three out. He knew only the top two per heat qualified for the finals at Olympia.

Ronny skipped over the next and kept finding more on the flat, as if gathering momentum downslope. They could do this, Danny hoped.

On the final turn for home Ronny's tiny legs bounded on relentlessly, carrying them into second with the leader now in their sights. There was no flailing about Meg's limbs as she urged her lazy charge on, more an efficient simplicity.

Within a length from striking the front and Danny was shouting like a mad man, lost in the moment. Half a length in it. A neck.

As they crossed the line, Danny cupped his face. He knew his girl had been mugged on the line. 'Shit!'

A mother nearby covered the ears of her child.

The kid will have heard far worse at school, Danny felt like saying. Instead he apologised and then ran over to greet Meg and Ronny after the finish line.

Danny kissed her and patted him. 'You did great, both of you.'

'Bloody hell, Danny,' she said between breaths. 'It's harder than cantering them on the gallops.'

'Welcome to the world of race riding,' Danny replied, beaming.

'Except it isn't,' Meg said. 'It's under a mile over knee-high sticks. And I lost!'

'From where you were with a lap to go-'

'Don't Danny, I'm gutted … save it for later.'

Danny smiled inside. He'd now seen and heard enough. Not only had she shown strength in body and mind on the track, her response of disappointment in the face of defeat told him she had the competitive drive and innate desire in her for success needed to make it as a jockey. 'It's a qualifier and you qualified, job done.'

'Glad we did that at least.'

'You did that,' Danny said. 'Despite The Rocket here stalling on the first lap.'

'I couldn't have done it without this one,' she said. 'That last lap was such a buzz, felt like the real thing. Riding that low makes you feel like you're going faster. I want more, when's Olympia?' Meg asked, some life returning to her blue eyes. 'We'll need to book a hotel in London.'

'No, we won't,' Danny replied.

'I haven't gone through all that to skip the final. I've got the race-riding bug.'

'And I've got other plans for you,' Danny said.

Her face dropped like a mime artist and her pencilled eyebrows arched. She looked crestfallen. 'You know I don't like surprises.'

'You'll like this one.'

Meg ran a hand through Ronny's shaggy mane and stepped off. She then flung her arms round the Shetland's neck and beamed a smile. Danny hadn't seen Meg this happy since he'd asked her to move into Silver Belle Stables.

Perhaps he should believe more in her jockeyship. Her horsemanship was never in doubt, but he had never seen that competitive streak in her. The way Ronny picked up for her urgings from the saddle was impressive. And she was at it from the start, so there were no fitness doubts, probably from all the long days slaving at the yard.

'I think you should experience the real thing instead. You're too good for this.'

She looked at him. 'Eh?'

'It's about time we make use of your rider's licence for real,' Danny said, 'if that's what you want?'

'Want?' she asked. 'No want about it, I'd bloody love it … but I've never ridden under rules, just a few point-to-points between the flags at Ystradowen and Lower Machen.'

'Regulation fences are stiffer but you'll find the contours of racetracks easier to get the horse balanced than between the flags on a pointer,' Danny said. 'Anyway this'll save me finding a second retained rider for the yard.'

65

'O-M-G,' she added, and jumped on the spot. It was now Danny's turn to get a hug and kiss. 'You won't regret this, handsome. Bloody hell, this is epic! Proper bang tidy!'

Danny smiled. She always revealed her Welshness when excited.

Chapter 7

8.23 AM. EVEN FROM BACK THERE Danny could see something was different.

He jumped off Powder Keg and dragged her in the rain to the face of the trapdoors. The leaves and earth had gone and the strapping tape he'd stuck there had been torn in two. The bolt across the crack of the door's divide had been moved.

They'd come back for the goods, Danny reckoned.

He glanced over at the hedgerow and the glimpses of the road beyond. He was alone.

Had they already gone?

He leant down and pull the doors apart but stopped short of stepping in. Were they still down there?

At first Danny peered into the black.

Whoever it was they were trespassing, Danny fumed. He descended the stairwell more assuredly than last time; the darkening spirals had become less of an unknown.

Danny stopped one side of the opening to the Ice Room. He again heard the metronomic drips from high above but that was all. He inched far enough to at least see a semi-circle's worth of the inside. There were no movements in the dark, no shadows flicking up the brick walls. He now felt certain the trespassers had gone.

He stepped into the room and crept as far as the ethereal finger of green light in the centre. Suddenly, from somewhere behind, a shuddering slap on stone went right through him. He spun on the spot and stood there squinting in a shower of light and raindrops seeping through the circular grille high above. He hadn't felt this vulnerable since being cornered at the start of lunch break at school.

He heard another step. Louder, closer. 'Who's there?'

Instinct made Danny step back to keep his distance.

Knowing the footsteps came from somewhere between himself and the only way out, Danny felt a tightness across his chest. He began to shake. Flashes of Ronny's schooling session came to him. Was this another panic attack?

Suddenly a dot of light dazzled in the void. Then a figure came from the shadowy veil. Its head was aglow of radioactive green. *The alien-being had come back for its offspring!*

'Jesus!' Danny cried, eyes white with fear as he stumbled back to where the spheres had been. He wished he could've reached out and thrown one, put up at least some defence against this thing.

The stricken cattle outside came back to him in a flash. Was he about to share their final pain?

As Danny's eyes finally adjusted to the half-light, he gasped, 'Keyes?!'

'I took your message and came.'

Danny sunk his face in his hands and began to laugh.

'Who the hell were you expecting?'

'No one,' Danny replied.

'Then share the joke.'

'Just never thought I'd be so glad to see you.'

'You have something for me,' Keyes said, clicking off his torch.

'Where's Mavers?'

'He's been otherwise detained,' Keyes replied. 'It's still me you report to. This is my case and when something out of the ordinary happens up here, then-'

'Then I'm prime suspect,' Danny interjected.

'*Then* I want to see it first-hand.'

'How long have you been down here?' Danny asked.

'Not long.'

'Come look, they're over here.' But, as if he'd lost his keys, Danny kept returning to the exact same place where he'd seen the spheres, knowing full well he'd only find flagstones each time. 'Seems you won't see much after all, they were lined up over here, honest.'

He felt his face burn.

'What were they?'

'Several brown spheres, all different sizes,' Danny said, playing an imaginary concertina with his hands. 'They were right

68

here. Whoever dropped them must've come back and picked them up.'

'Balls,' Keyes said flatly.

'I'm not talking bollocks,' Danny said, 'I swear.'

'I would laugh but I'm this close to charging you with wasting police time. You do know both Mr Mills and Artemis are still missing?' Keyes asked. 'You say there were balls, big brown balls?'

'Anything out of the ordinary, I'm to call, that's what you said,' Danny said. 'I think this qualifies!'

The face Keyes pulled told Danny he found the story a bit too extraordinary.

'Bet you're kept busy being a trainer for a career,' Keyes said.

'It's a way of life, not a career.'

'Perhaps you need a break, a holiday.'

'I wasn't seeing things.'

'I'm just saying the light is funny down here, it can play tricks. This is the darkest spot and with tired eyes, well-'

'I touched one,' Danny said. 'You saying I've got tired fingers too.'

'What did you touch?'

'I dunno, but it came for me,' Danny said. 'Haven't been back here since.'

'We've had cases of thefts in rare bird eggs.'

'If you'd seen them,' Danny said, 'you'd know it wasn't a bird that laid them, unless they've cloned a pterodactyl. So what now?'

'I can't give a crime number as there was no crime,' Keyes said and began to head for the opening. He flicked on the torch again. 'There are no witnesses and nothing of yours has been stolen, I can't see anything more I can do.'

'Any news on Bert and Artemis?' Danny enquired as he followed, 'Thought there'd be a ransom demand or something by now.'

'We're still following up leads,' Keyes said. 'That's all I can say.'

69

Daylight made Danny blink as his pupils shrunk.

Now that Danny looked for it, he could make out the shadow of a parked-up saloon car, possibly a silver Mondeo, through holes in the hedgerow.

Keyes said, 'Well, you didn't think I'd drive through this slop.'

Seems like the recent rainstorms had finally filtered downslope, Danny grumbled. He circled the quagmire back to Powder Keg.

Danny made very sure DCI Keyes was away from the estate before returning to Silver Belle House.

He shut the door behind him and shivered as his body adjusted to the warmth.

As he walked through the kitchen, Meg emerged from behind the fridge door. She looked down at the tiles. 'Oh, bloody hell, Danny! I've just run a mop over that.'

Danny looked back and then down. He'd left a trail of red boot prints. 'Sorry, love. Don't know where they came from.'

'Your feet perhaps!'

'I meant where the red stuff came from.'

'As long as it's not blood.'

Stood on the spot, he pulled off his boots and studied their leather soles. 'Seems too bright for blood.'

'God, Danny. You've got the red stuff all up the back of both legs too,' Meg said. 'Where in hell have you … don't answer that, just go get cleaned up.'

Danny recalled falling back in the Ice Room. Was it some secretion from the eggs? But they were brown.

Could still be blood, he guessed.

He dropped the boots outside the kitchen door. He was about to mop it down again when he ran a sweaty hand down the back of his combats. His fingertips came back coated in a thin layer of red dust. 'What the hell?'

'What is it Danny?' Meg said, slicing open a packet of pink chicken breasts.

He knelt and touched the tread patterns. His fingers were shiny red. 'Has Jack found his powder paints again?'

'Not after the last time, I put them on the top shelf,' Meg said. 'Please tell me it's not some pesticide.'

Danny smelt his fingers and exclaimed, 'Odd.'

'Chemically is it?'

'It doesn't smell of anything,' Danny answered. 'But I still wouldn't put anything past Bert's son, their cattle are already dropping like cheap tents.'

'Well, whatever it is, make it disappear, Danny, I'm about to chuck these under the grill,' Meg said.

Danny looked at his ochre hands again. The shakes had returned.

Chapter 8

1.10 PM. DANNY COULDN'T TAKE THE FINAL STEP, like a bungee-jumper with cold feet.

He'd just heard whistling from the kitchen. Meg never whistled. He'd finished making plans with owners, then declaring horses for the week ahead, and had only come down to brew up a rewarding cup of tea.

He was left wondering whether there was more to Rhodri than just theories. Had Artemis' blood fallen short of perfection? Had the DNA hunters come back to the valleys for the next in line?

Standing on the staircase in the hallway, he removed his smartphone and silently edged to the bannister. He was facing the front door but the kitchen door was the other end, out of view from the stairs.

Slowly he craned the phone out over the bannister and used its glossy black screen as a mirror to see back the way. The kitchen door was open enough to show a man dressed in black facing the sink and rear window.

He didn't need to be an ex-burglar to know socks were quieter than boots on tiles. He slipped them off and rested them on the old carpet of the stairs. He was already out of his work gear after riding out two lots first thing that morning. Suddenly he no longer felt tired.

The Welsh slate felt cool as he crept soundlessly down the hallway. From there Danny could see it was a man. Where was Meg?

This intruder could've shared the same stylist as the one that stormed the home turn at Chepstow, Danny reckoned, but that's where the similarities end.

From here the figure looked to have a jockey's build, except for the love handles beneath a black sweater and white hair sprouting from the back of a matching woollen hat.

The intruder stopped what he was doing and stared out of the window. Danny then saw a flash of light shimmer down a blade. He glanced over at the knife block. There was an empty slit.

Perhaps if he stormed the room yelling the intruder would panic and flee. Danny was prepared to take the risk of a blade in his side.

But then, what if Meg crossed the intruder's path to freedom outside?

That was a risk Danny wasn't prepared to take.

Instead he slowly slipped through the gap in the door and navigated the kitchen table. An element of surprise was his only chance of disarming the man.

Danny caught the ghost of his own scared face in the window ahead. He needed to pounce before the intruder saw the same thing. He lunged forward and left arm hooked around the intruder's jowly neck. With his right hand, Danny gripped the wrist of the knife-wielding hand. The knife fell to clatter on the kitchen tiles. There was a groan as Danny forcibly pulled the man from the sink and, with little resistance, easily pushed him to the ground. He was about to throw a punch when the woollen hat came off. 'It's me! It's me!'

Danny looked at the face. 'Oh fuck! What've I done? You okay, Stony?'

'I was,' Stony croaked.

Guilt and shame made Danny hurriedly help his old friend to his feet and brush him down with his hands.

'I'm not an invalid,' Stony said, seemingly more hurt by his treatment after the attack.

Stony feelingly dropped his weight on a pine chair as he tried to gather his breath and composure.

'What the hell do you think you were doing?' Danny asked sharply, as if to deflect the blame.

'You said your door's always open,' Stony said. 'So when Meg pointed me to the kitchen, I let myself in.'

'I didn't expect it to be you.'

'I guess that now,' Stony replied. 'With a welcome like that, who the hell were you expecting?'

73

'I dunno, that's the problem.' Danny shrugged. 'There's a lot going on up here and not all of it good.' Danny picked up the knife. 'And what's this about?'

'Fancied some fruitcake, while it's still warm like,' Stony replied. 'Small slice that's all, Meg said so, at least I think that's what she meant, mouthed the word fruitcake at me.' Stony then stretched and felt each limb, but remained seated more likely out of necessity than choice as he looked over at the window. 'You've bagged a winner there. She's a better mover than me.'

Can't be Powder Keg, Danny reasoned, moving to the window.

On her own Meg was doing swirls round the forecourt mapping out what looked to Danny's untrained eye like a Viennese Waltz. 'She's got a dance comp coming up.'

'She stuck up five fingers over at me and that was three minutes ago, so she should be finished soon,' Stony said.

'You're lucky she normally sticks two fingers up at me if I interrupt her counting steps mid-routine. Want a swift whisky? Medicinal, of course.'

'If you put it like that,' Stony said and then groaned. 'Poor lass, surprised you're not out there with her, you're a jockey, so there's balance and poise.'

'But not the rhythm,' Danny said. 'What's your excuse?'

'They've got night classes down Cathays Community Hall where I go, but don't reckon my new hips would survive a Samba.'

'Forgiven?' Danny asked and handed down three fingers of single malt.

Stony's head went back and he downed a good measure. 'And forgotten.'

'But to be fair, it was an easy mistake,' Danny reasoned. 'I mean, burglar-black?'

'Alright, Dylan Thomas!'

'Eh?'

'I've been on a winning streak betting online, and these are my second luckiest clothes,' Stony explained.

'Why not wear your luckiest?'

'They're in the wash, got splashed by a car. Had to be a muddy puddle too and that bastard knew it!'

Danny smiled. 'Never seen you in this black hat and jumper combo.'

'My luck only turned for the better yesterday,' Stony said. 'Doubt if I'll even wash these until I have a loser.'

'But you're not at a computer now.'

'I've got a bet running at Exeter this afternoon, it still counts,' Stony said. 'Don't want to risk jinxing it, see.'

'There is treatment out there,' Danny said and smiled.

'I'll be the one smiling when it comes in. Ten-to-one I got.'

'Has it helped with your luck in love?'

Stony shrugged. 'I'm the pin-up boy own the community hall.'

'Didn't know they had "wanted" posters down there,' Danny replied.

Stony's smile had gone. 'I'm no expert on signs but there's a girl down that community hall I go that flirts with me. Well I say girl, I've seen her bus pass and I say flirt, she talks to me. Sheila's her name.'

'She okay?'

'Alright, quite ordinary to be fair, which is a positive down there,' Stony said. 'Aside from her fear of courgettes.'

Danny gave a confused smile. 'That's insane.'

'I know! Don't you think I told her as much?' Stony said. 'Of all the marrow family, the courgette is the least threatening.'

Danny laughed. 'Do you know Stony, I think you might have found your soul-mate there.'

Stony smiled and then brushed it off with, 'Nah.'

'Never too late to find someone, it'll happen,' Danny said and gave his friend a slap on the back but Stony recoiled feelingly.

'Don't know whether I want it to happen,' Stony said. 'Got a feeling the type of woman who'd want me, I wouldn't want.'

'Perhaps you're too choosy,' Danny said.

'I know, beggars and all that. Think it's more about me, I've made myself a very safe life, a routine I like and don't want to disrupt. She'd have to be a bit special, otherwise it's probably not worth it. Oh shut up, Stony, last thing you need this, probably got a million and one things to do.'

Danny flicked the kettle on. 'Think I've got time for a brew.'

Stony's reflection joined his in the window.

Exiting what looked like a fleckerl, Meg saw their gallery of faces watching her. She looked surprised by the existence of an outside world and stopped spinning, and dropped her arms. She then came over.

'Hi, Stony, you alright?' Meg asked, as she came in from the cold

Stony looked at Danny, who hoped their altercation really had been forgotten. 'Yeah, bit stiff, but this'll help.'

She added, 'They've arrived, Danny.'

'Who?!' Danny asked sharply.

'The film crew,' she replied. 'Who do you think?'

'Don't bother, Meg,' Stony said, finishing off the Scotch. 'He wouldn't tell me, neither.'

'Just make sure Jack doesn't get out,' Danny said and removed the letter from Mooncraft Films he'd kept safe in a kitchen drawer.

He opened the front door. A large truck had pulled up on the shale driveway.

A fifty-something portly man struggled from the passenger side of the cabin. He was everything Danny expected a director to look like and more. His purple velvet hat was tilted donnishly and his cravat was a swirl of colours, spilled over an equally garish waistcoat, like some tropical bird. He wouldn't stand a chance in Rhymney on a Friday night.

'Quentin Crawford, a pleasure to meet you, young man,' the man said.

Quentin, Danny thought. Yep, that fits.

76

'Danny,' he replied and offered his hand, more to shake off the one currently on his shoulder. He looked over at the plain white production truck pulled up alongside Silver Belle House.

Danny added, 'The stables are over there.'

'Super, darling,' Quentin said, already framing pictures with his hands. 'I think we'll kick off by taking some lovely panoramic shots before the sun disappears. Up there will be great.' He pointed beyond Silver Belle House, towards the ridge. 'What's the other side, boy?'

'More of the same … boy,' Danny said and looked over at the size of the truck. 'Didn't know it's going to be a feature film.'

'Wasn't it Coleridge who said, "He who is best prepared can best serve his moment of inspiration"?' Quentin said.

'Well, it'll take more than inspiration to get that thing up there,' Danny replied, pointing at the truck.

'We'll make it.'

'If you do, just watch for the stone footprint of Samuel House and the green slopes beyond are steep, they stretch down the road you came on where the rain collects, the ground gets testing.'

'Any other features of interest I should know about down there,' Quentin asked.

'Only if you're into old dilapidated stone houses or swamps.'

'Perhaps we'll leave that way,' Quentin said.

'I haven't got a tractor to pull you out,' Danny said.

'No, no, you're a busy man, I would rather get stuck and perish than impose on you anymore. Now, shall we?'

Danny also heard the subtext: 'shut up now, you're boring me.'

'We certainly don't gallop that way, the horses' welfare always comes first at Silver Belle Stables. They're the heart that keeps this place moving forward, I treat them like my children.' Inwardly Danny squirmed. He didn't want to come over as a walking ad for the yard. It had sounded better in his head.

'Especially Salamanca, I bet.'

77

'I'd risk my life for The Tank,' Danny replied. 'I know he'd do the same if he could.'

Meanwhile the TV crew were standing around like extras, seemingly awaiting Quentin to click his plump fingers.

'I'll leave you to it, if that's okay,' Danny said, keen for the yard and setting to be the star of the show.

'If you're sure,' Quentin said and his wandering hand again ended up on Danny's shoulder. Danny wasn't sure how to act around this old ham. 'We'll be as quick as possible and don't you worry yourself about seeing us out, we know the way.'

'Will you be doing any talking heads of me or my partner Meg or one of the stable hands?' Danny asked. 'You know, going through our daily routine or the horses.'

'That's for another day,' Quentin said.

'But you'll need to see the Tank himself.'

Quentin nodded to a slight man with short brown hair and holding a camera almost as big as his head. 'Graeme here will go check the lighting back there.'

With his gleaming chestnut coat and plaited mane, he knew Salamanca would look a picture bathed in sunlight. If only he could be sure he would behave in the hands of the stable lad back there.

Danny would've checked for himself but there was business to do. 'Won't you need to take motion shots, capture the champ at his best.'

'For now, we must make the most of the sun. The scenery will look simply majestic up there.'

'Don't blame you, normally *The Sun*'s just a newspaper around these parts,' Danny replied. 'This way.'

He then directed the truck's driver between the side of Silver Belle House and the schooling ring. He looked on at the truck's slow inexorable drudge up the rain-softened slope. Even the production crew managed to be keeping pace on foot. Suddenly the prospect of lightening the in-tray proved less tedious, so he turned and made for his office before the convoy had even disappeared over the horizon. He felt disappointed that

Quentin appeared more interested in the aesthetics of the valleys than the workings of the yard.

At least it was relatively painless, Danny thought, knowing these occasional invasions of his privacy were necessary to help keep the yard in the public eye. He only hoped this TV spot would do more for the yard than that lame effort on *Antique's Heaven.*

Back in his office Danny left his mobile on the desk, expecting a distress call from the production team sunk by the mud, but it stayed silent as he finally got around to sending private messages to Meg's friends on Facebook as a birthday party reminder. He then went to the master bedroom to check on Meg's costume he'd recently been sent by courier.

Danny heard the front door slam shut. Meg had already returned from clothes shopping at Cardiff's St David's with her girlfriends. He quickly folded up the costume and slipped it, along with the documents linked to her other birthday present, under a pile of folded boxers and socks in his drawer of the wardrobe. That was about the only safe place he knew as he didn't want to leave the delicate garment gathering dust in the loft.

He rushed downstairs to see the dent she'd made in his credit card. She dropped several bags on the hallway floor and shook her arms. 'It's hard work enjoying yourself.'

Danny didn't complain, she deserved the retail therapy for all the hard work.

'Had a good day, then?' he said. She giggled and then hiccupped. 'I'll take that as a "yes".' Danny helped her with some of the big colourful designer carrier bags. 'Surprised you had time for the pub.'

She hiccupped again. 'I'm not often a lady of leisure. Oh, Danny, it was a right laugh. Hadn't seen them for like, forever. We'll have to do it again soon.'

'Not that soon,' Danny said, checking one of the price tags.

'Call them my pressie from you,' she said, sobering up a bit.

'Too late,' Danny said. 'Already got yours.'

'Oh, yeah?' she said and wrapped her arms around his neck. 'Want to share it with me now.'

They kissed passionately. Their lips parted.

'Oh, before I forget,' she said. 'From the taxi I saw Bert's son roaming his fields with a rifle.'

Danny broke from their embrace. 'When?'

'Just now,' Meg said, even more sober now. Danny began tugging on his boots. 'Leave it, Danny, he's a farmer's son, it's probably his idea of pest control or something.'

'He was a bit odd *before* his dad went AWOL.'

'As long as he doesn't trouble us,' Meg pleaded. 'Don't go, please.'

'I owe it to Bert,' Danny replied. 'If the poor sod is alive, soon he won't want to come back to that place. Animals are snuffing it and they're the ones he knows I'll see, dread to think how the horses are kept behind stable doors in the yard.'

'Remember he's got a gun,' Meg said. 'I'm coming with you.'

'No, you're not,' Danny snapped. 'Stay here, Jack's having a nap. I'll be back soon, love.'

He slammed the door shut and then pushed it to check for sure it was secure. He then set about the ten-minute walk to Bert Mills' Sunnyside Farm.

He suddenly felt nervous about who or what he might find there.

Chapter 9

DANNY CRUNCHED UP THE SHALE DRIVEWAY. It was like walking on a bed of crisps.

So much for making a quiet entrance. He saw a curtain move. *And there goes any chance of sneaky look in on the stabled horses before knocking.*

On the pillared entrance Danny had noticed a shiny brass plaque with Sunnyside Farm and Racing Stables, and a three-quarter bronze statue of Artemis surveyed the driveway.

Surprised that hadn't already been lifted, he thought, given the recent spate of metal thefts, even war memorial plaques and lead off church roofs weren't sacred to them.

Years back Bert wouldn't have bothered with this architectural bling. When foot-and-mouth took hold and milk margins were squeezed, many similar farms had gone under.

Bert, however, had clearly eyed the racing successes of the then Samuel House next door and diversified into training jumpers from the old stabling block near the farm outbuildings. As with all new trainers, he just needed some equine talent and in Artemis, his prayers were answered.

The sweeping driveway was also similar to the one wending its way up to Silver Belle House but that's where the familiarity ended as Sunnyside Farm was more of an old farmstead than a groundsman's lodge. It was a cottage of grey Monmouthshire stonework, mostly hidden by a thick beard of green-red Virginia creeper, and small windows beneath a Welsh slate roof, remarkably modest given the exploits of his cash cow Artemis.

The Mills family was now just Bert and his son Leo. The cottage was dwarfed by several outbuildings, many an afterthought from when the farm was thriving, including a barn for the harvested crops, alongside the stables.

Danny remembered the week he'd stayed there riding out for free as a kid. Back then the stables had a sparkly newness about them. He'd never forget the first thoroughbred he'd ridden out at racing speed on these gallops. Bunking off an afternoon at school, it was as memorable as the first time he'd had sex and he'd confess it was almost as enjoyable.

It was one of those life-defining moments, sitting on the back of a three-year-old filly, a recruit from the Flat. Seeing the blurry trees rush by and feeling the wind brush over him. In every sense it took his breath away.

His weak pubescent limbs were mastering this graceful half-ton of muscle. The filly was respecting him, quickening for a shake of the reins and slowing for a tug. It felt dangerous. It felt more than exciting. He felt liberated at a time when he needed liberating. No more dreaming in the lab at Double Chemistry. And the bullies could no longer make him feel sad. That day he vividly recalled wanting to steer off the beaten path and gallop into the sunset.

By the time he'd unsaddled, Danny could finally see a future. For that to happen his father knew it needed to pay. Not long after, Danny found himself unpacking his kitbag alongside a similarly homesick kid in a shared bedroom at a yard in Lambourn.

Returning all those years on, he now felt similar anxiety as back then.

He doubted Leo was even born by then and the stable-dog Travis, who was always the first to run up and greet visitors with a flurry of barks, would have died years ago. This time around Danny was allowed to walk up the driveway in peace.

In fact the whole place seemed lacking in life, or any spirit, not at all like a working farm and stables. Grieving or not, Leo had questions to answer.

Danny slipped off a glove and knocked on the white paint of the front door. When there was no answer he waded through knee-high shrubs to peer through a ground floor window but couldn't see in for the white reflection of the overcast sky.

'Yeah?' a voice came from Danny's right. He looked over and then up. It was Leo, who must've got his size from his mother's side as he'd seemingly shot up to twice the size of Bert. His fat head and hulking frame probably made him look fatter than he was. He was breathing hard.

Danny stepped back into another shrub and then mouthed 'sorry'. 'Been out for a run on your land?'

'You're not looking for Dad, so what is it?' Leo asked. Danny could've asked the same question but didn't want to be manhandled down the drive so soon.

'Just doing my bit for neighbourhood watch, that's all – see if you're bearing up.'

'We're in the phonebook.'

'I know,' Danny said. 'But-'

'But you still thought to come round here snooping. Well, I'm on top of things, don't you worry.'

Seemed he'd also grown a mouth, Danny thought. 'I see you're okay now and I'll be on my way. It's just, I reckon I might know why your dad went missing and where he might be.'

Leo stepped back from the open doorway. Danny took the silent invite.

He was led through the hall. There was a cold soullessness about the place. He'd sometimes feel the same when coming back from a holiday. On the patterned tiles there was a coat rack, umbrella stand and numerous pairs of shoes and boots of varying condition; some needed throwing.

The kitchen was a hangover from the Seventies, with harvest gold floral wallpaper and gloss orange units. He regretted not taking shades.

Swanky Londoners probably pay a premium for this now, Danny reckoned, though he suspected Bert wasn't into kitsch or shabby chic. Since Bert's divorce clearly all the money had gone straight back into the business outside and not the nest.

'Living well, I see,' Danny said, flipping open a pizza box, among a collection's worth of junk food packaging. Inside there were mouldy crusts and dark streaky grease stains.

Danny peered into a rear porch area. There was a line of coat pegs and a clean boot-scraper. He checked, 'All the stable staff clocked off early then.'

'Until Dad comes home.'

'What if he doesn't?'

Leo's eyes widened and then narrowed, as surprise turned to anger.

'Didn't mean anything by it,' Danny added, palms up. 'Who's looking after the string out there, you've got twenty fighting-fit jumpers ready to go.'

'I'm feeding them, changing the bedding.'

Danny glanced at the kitchen table. Hopefully Leo was looking after the horses better than himself. 'You do know they're finely tuned athletes and need regular workouts.'

'They won't be running until Dad returns. I've shut up shop, just keeping them ticking over. It's Bert's name above the door, he holds the licence – I'm just babysitting the place 'til their master comes back.'

'Can I go check in on them all the same?' Danny asked.

'No!' Leo snapped and moved to cover Danny's route to the back door.

A simple 'no' and Danny might've walked away but that overreaction reeked of something to hide.

'No one's allowed to snoop about,' Leo added, as if realising the mask had slipped. 'Especially you.'

Danny took a moment. 'Where did that come from?'

'From the same man you seem so desperate to get back.'

'He's your dad, for fuck's sake. I lost mine too soon.' Danny just about managed to hold his voice from breaking. His dad always said, don't let them see any weakness or fear. They'll only grow stronger and more fearless. 'And if I knew there was even the slightest chance of seeing him again, I'd do anything.'

'I am.'

'Is that what you were doing out there?' Danny asked.

'I was patrolling my land, that okay is it?'

'Patrolling your dad's land,' Danny replied.

'Dad's gone,' Leo snarled. 'It's *my* land now.'

'Sure about that?' Danny removed the blank postcard from his jacket and gave it to Leo, who briefly glanced that way before tossing it on the table to rest between a can of cola and polystyrene burger carton containing a gherkin. 'Take a closer look.'

Leo glanced again.

'Look familiar?'

'Too familiar, it's Lyme Regis, went there every year as a kid, when my friends were jetting off somewhere sunny. Hoped never to see that shithole again.'

'Not the image,' Danny said. 'The postcard.'

'Why the hell would I?'

'I reckon it's a sign.'

Leo sniggered. 'From God.'

'From your dad,' Danny replied. 'You've just admitted it's the family getaway.'

Leo was shifting his bulk between feet. 'So? Anyone could've sent this.'

'With no post mark, no stamp, no text.'

'Maybe it was meant for me,' Leo said.

'But oddly there is an address: Silver Belle Stables,' Danny said. 'Funny that, seeing as it was hand posted. Tell me Leo, why would the sender go to the trouble?' Leo shrugged. 'Well, I've thought about it and do you know the answer that kept coming back, to make damned sure I knew this card was meant for me. So why send it? The pic of Lyme Regis is as good as Bert's signature.' Danny waved the postcard at Leo's face. 'This tells me he's alive.'

'Where's mine then?'

Danny searched Leo's brown eyes for any hurt from a possible betrayal of a father as good as disowning his only blood relative in favour of Danny, a distant neighbour and bitter rival. There wasn't even a flicker of emotion. It's as if he was reading off a script. 'At least say it with some emotion, Leo, as if you mean it. No, you don't really care, because you already know he's alive.'

'I've told the police all I know!'

'Is he staying here?' Danny said, waving the card again.

'I dunno!'

'No, that'd be too obvious,' Danny thought aloud. 'One of the first places the police would check.'

When Leo began to shepherd Danny from the kitchen, there was only going to be one winner.

'Wait, Leo,' Danny said, being dragged through the hallway. 'Where do we go from here?'

'I know where you're going.'

'I need the loo, then I'll go,' Danny said, gripping the bannister.

'Make a mess of your own,' Leo said.

Danny glanced down at Leo's freakishly large feet in potato-riddled grey socks, wrinkled and humming. He raised his left knee and stamped down hard. Leo was sent hopping down the hallway. 'You bastard fucker … bastard!'

Danny knew this would probably be his last time here legally and saw his chance. He fled up the stairs three at a time. On the landing there were four doors, all shut. In the first room there was an unmade three-quarter bed below posters of Vampire Weekend and Cardiff City FC.

Further along Danny pushed the door of a bathroom.

Fixed to the third door there was a brass plaque: RACING OFFICE. It was locked.

At the end he shouldered his way into a room the size of a master bedroom, with shocking pink carpet and whitewashed walls. The room was neater and even chillier than the rest of the house. The bed was made up, probably awaiting Bert's return.

Danny glanced back. He didn't see Leo, but could hear the creak of stairs.

Danny slammed the door shut and shifted the bolt across. That wouldn't buy him enough time, so he dragged both bedside cabinets over and pushed them against the door.

Danny checked the drawers of those cabinets. Nothing but a few porno mags and cracked reading glasses.

Danny turned to the mirrored wardrobe. His arm reached into its dark recesses.

There was a rail of musty jumpers and blazers on hangers, all earthy tones. They swung as he hurriedly slid them until he came across a coat that stood out from the rest. It was black and larger. He pulled it out and chucked it on the bed.

There was now enough space and light to see a shoebox on the floor, pushed to the back. He reckoned shoes were the last thing it contained, given the pile of them downstairs.

When he saw DO NOT TOUCH inked on the side, Danny went straight for it. He pulled the green box into the light and pranged an elastic band away. He pulled off the lid. Inside there was a bundle of envelopes held by a doubled-over band. Each one of the white envelopes had been crudely ripped open.

There was a fist banging at the door. He heard Leo's muffled voice, 'Let me in!'

He glanced over and then at his watch. He pulled the contents of the top envelope. It was a single folded sheet of A4 paper. In different newspaper typeset the cut-out letters had been glued on to read: **12 DaYs**.

He returned the sheet and then checked the fourth one down. **9 dAYs**.

They resembled what he'd seen on Keyes' smartphone

'I've called the police. They're coming. Let me in!'

Danny knew there hadn't been enough time to make the call. He was bluffing, for now.

Turning back to the contents of the shoe box he reckoned he was leafing through some creepy advent calendar counting down the days to Christmas. He knew Bert was a bit odd, but this? He skipped to the bottom of the pile. It read: **fInaL day**. Danny looked at the front of the envelope. The Sunnyside address had been printed using a label writer. The stamp had been franked with the date 28th December – the countdown had already ended. That was the day Bert was last seen.

Was this a countdown of a very different kind – a deadline in its most literal sense? What on earth had happened on Bert's **fInaL day**?

Danny saw something pressed up against one of the sides of the box. It was a police investigations unit card. Exactly the same as Danny was given at Chepstow. He delved deeper into the box and also saw a letter from Mooncraft Films, again matching the one he'd received.

Danny needed to sit on Bert's double bed. He slapped the lid down on this Pandora's Box. He was well on his way to filling his own, what with the police calling card, the invitation from the TV crew.

Perhaps the cryptic letters were on their way. Why had Bert bundled them all together? Did he think they were linked? Would Danny suffer the same fate as Bert at Chepstow? Maybe they would strike again at Ely Park's grand opening.

Danny's thoughts were taken by a loud crack of wood splitting. He jump to his feet and looked over at the door. There was the curved blade of an axe showing through a nest of splinters.

Shitting hell, Danny thought. He'd clearly underestimated the kid. Perhaps Bert was under these floorboards.

Danny ran to the only window and lifted the net curtains. It was a good fifteen foot down to a shaded concrete area leading to the stables behind the trainer's house. But there was nothing to hang off to lessen the drop or a drainpipe to shimmy down. Danny couldn't risk twisting an ankle with Ely Park coming up. He heard another shatter of wood and then the thud made by great chunks of door raining down on the bedside cabinet.

Danny pulled up the sash window and had one leg out when he felt the pull of a strong arm coiled round his neck. He was dragged back into the room and fell to the ground. He'd only just scrambled to his feet when another hand on his back pushed his chest to the wall.

Danny's cheekbone cracked against the wallpaper. He groaned.

Helplessly Danny's arm was then yanked up behind his back. 'Dad always said you were a wrong 'n,' Leo whispered near Danny's ear.

Danny groaned again as his arm was then levered further up his back. His stretched biceps began to ache.

He then felt the cold razor-edge of the axe blade against his cheek. 'Do you want this in your neck?'

'You've not got the balls,' Danny said, though he wasn't as confident as he'd sounded.

'Self-defence I'd say,' Leo replied. 'That's my excuse. This was forced entry. You've got form, they'll send you down for years, again.'

'Not if I'm dead,' Danny said, anxiously glancing at the shimmering blade in his peripheral vision.

Leo dropped Danny and then the axe with a thud.

Danny felt the pressure on his arm ease enough to break free from the arm lock. He turned to see Leo now studying the shoebox and its contents littering the bed.

Leo asked, 'What's this?'

If Leo was feigning ignorance, he deserved a clutch of Oscars for the performance.

'Evidence,' Danny replied. 'Clues to why your dad vanished.'

'Where did you get them?' Leo asked.

'I thought you'd already know,' Danny said. 'You see, police would've turned this place over looking for something just like that. Tell me why the hell they missed a bright green shoebox with Do Not Touch on its side.' Danny looked over at the mirrored wardrobe. 'It was facing me like a beacon, so I'm guessing it was placed in there after the police left.'

Loudly, the sprung mattress surrendered to Leo's heft. The letters slid closer to him, as if drawn by some gravitational pull. Silently he sat there, eyes seeking the floor as he began shaking his head.

'Well, if it's not you, is there a secret lodger or lover?'

Leo continued to shake his head.

'I want to find your father nearly as much as you,' Danny said, softer.

'What's it to you?' Leo snapped, now glaring up at Danny. 'You hated each other's guts, Dad always says so.'

Danny knew that healthy competition had driven a social wedge between them but they were hardly warring neighbours.

'It's true I'd never go on holiday with the man. I mean, Lyme Regis, come on.'

Danny swore the faintest of smiles creep across Leo's face. Was this the first hint of a bond? He needed Leo to open up.

'Look I'm here to find whoever took Bert, or whatever drove him to do this, as I'm scared they'll come after me or, just as bad, Salamanca.'

Leo shook his head again.

'What do you know, then?' Danny asked but was met by silence. 'No? Well I'll start, then. I know it was you on the track that day, in here there's a black balaclava and sweater to prove it.' Danny went over, slid back the mirror and pulled out the offending items. 'Funny, never had you down as a Goth. You can't hide behind one of these now,' Danny fanned his fingers to model the balaclava like a glove puppet.

'Don't you think the police gave this place a proper going over?' Leo snapped. 'First thing they did.'

Danny looked at the open wardrobe and the clothes in his hand. 'Not that properly, it seems.'

'Get out,' Leo barked.

'I'm guessing you're not into clothes shopping.' Danny looked at the black clothes. 'So who got you those?'

'I didn't.'

'Your dad, then.'

'He didn't, neither.'

'Leo, if you keep denying everything, you'll put lives at risk, including your *dad!* Do you really want me to hand them to the police, tell them where I'd seen them last, Chepstow.'

'Then I'd tell the police you'd planted them,' Leo said. 'You said yourself they'd searched that wardrobe, found nothing.'

'Why the hell would I-' Danny took a calming breath. 'You've had plenty of time to get your story straight.'

'There was no story,' Leo replied. 'Less I know, the less I lie.' Danny reckoned this was the first truth to escape Leo's lips. Leo added, 'And we weren't out to fool the police or the papers, they weren't the ones making our lives hell.'

'Then who?' Danny said, exasperated. 'Who was Bert running scared from?'

'That's just it,' Leo said. 'He never said, the less I know!' He'd picked up the axe, weighing its wooden shaft in his hand. 'Now get out or I'll leave you like that door.'

'Don't you see,' Danny snapped. He suspected this was his only possible link to Bert. 'They're after the make-up of their DNA. Working out what makes our horses champion stayers. We're in this together more than you think.'

'What horses?'

'Salamanca and your Artemis,' Danny explained.

Leo shook his head.

'Ask yourself what they've got in common, endless stamina and class.'

'Salamanca's been taken then has he?' Leo asked.

Danny paused while he tried to fill the hole in his theory. 'No, not yet, but he's next on their list,' Danny said. 'Whether you like it or not, we're the target in their race for a formula to map out a horse's career to reach its best potential before its even seen a racetrack.'

'And your problem with that is?' Leo asked.

'The end result might be good for owners, but we'll be the victims.'

Leo stood suddenly.

Sensing he'd long overstayed any welcome Danny rushed by for the door and then turned. 'You know where I am.' He hoped the invitation to an angry young man with an axe wouldn't backfire but, if Leo kept lying, he feared it wouldn't just be cattle dropping dead.

Danny left Leo slumped forward on the bed in a sea of death threats. He was convinced Leo was in some way involved, albeit possibly unwittingly.

He reckoned Leo would remain there sulking for a good while yet. So he quietly clicked the front door shut and paced round the farmhouse to where he remembered the stables to be, round the back. The winter sky was noticeably darker than when he'd arrived. It's as if someone had turned off a sidelight. In fact the whole place looked darker and dingier than the last time he'd visited as a kid.

Danny looked back at Bert's house, a black shape against the dark blue sky.

91

He removed his pen-torch and flashed light on the nameplate of the first box. It read: 1 ARTEMIS – bay gelding by Commanche Trouble out of Lead Story. Both halves of the stable door were shut.

Probably as a mark of respect to the yard's flag-bearer, Danny reckoned.

He moved on to box two with a nameplate *MARCHER LORD*. A large bay head greeted Danny as he looked over the metal V into blackness. He opened the door and entered. He was greeted by a big bull of a gelding with a belly to match. No wonder, as his feed and water were both fresh and brimming. Danny patted his strong neck and whispered, 'At least Leo's feeding you.'

But Bert's son clearly wouldn't stretch to working this one, or roughing him out in the field to keep trim. It seemed Leo wasn't lying; the yard had gone into shutdown mode since the master of Sunnyside Farm had vanished.

Danny checked the bedding. It had been changed. When he stood, he stopped and watched the gelding begin to pace the box. The strapping bay was box walking in circles, but it was more like watching a caged polar bear than a cage fighter, heading lolling and stride short. Danny knew this was a classic symptom of stress, or boredom, often brought on by loneliness.

If Marcher Lord was kept here much longer, he'd surely suffer mental or behavioural scarring long after his release, Danny felt.

But Danny had to move on, check the extent of the neglect. The box three in was, according to the sign, home to THE BIG SMOKE – a 9yo grey gelding. When Danny looked in he didn't need to be a trainer to tell this wasn't The Big Smoke.

Into the light came the most unremarkable little thing; a young bay with a small, compact body under her thick winter coat. She possessed the conformation of a juvenile hurdler, still to fill her frame. Danny reached out to run a calming hand down her nose.

'Okay, girl,' he said. He slowly gained her trust as she stepped fully into the last of the daylight.

As Danny rested his forearms on the top of the lower half of the door, he raised them sharply and grimaced. She backed away coyly. His fingertips felt the prickly edge to the door. She'd been crib biting, chomping down at the wood of the door. It was another stress symptom, often due to loneliness. Powder Keg would start whenever separated from her pal Zola.

Leo could've at least put a radio in with her, as the sound of voices would at least ease the sense of solitude.

As he flashed light in there, it was the shading of her ribs that first struck him. He entered and silently edged closer. When his fingers combed her winter coat, they snagged on the fur, matted and patchy in parts. She started nibbling his arm. 'Easy there Tufty.'

He could see her feed tray was empty and it smelt more like the farmyard nearby. She hadn't been mucked out for some time.

This was no way to keep any animal, let alone a thoroughbred. Like a vet, he flashed light into her eyes. They looked as sad as her demeanour.

Leo had lied about changing their feed and bedding. Danny now doubted the rest of his story.

Bert had juggled running a working farm and stables for years and if his riding was anything to go by he was methodical in his approach. This mess had happened since his son Leo had taken the helm. Danny was fuming things could get so bad this quickly.

Also he'd clearly housed her wrongly. This was more serious than merely changing hotel rooms. It could lead to being administered the wrong feed, or medication, leading to possible infections or allergies.

Leo clearly wasn't 'on top of things'. Danny knew one blow of the whistle to the British Horseracing Authority or Racing Welfare would soon have Bert's licence revoked and the yard temporarily in lockdown for lacking duty of care to the animals. It turned his stomach to see animals kept this way. If Bert hadn't died, he'd wish he had if he could see this.

Danny shook his head and then lovingly felt the filly's ear. Since Bert had gone, Danny suspected the yard wasn't just being run badly, it wasn't being run at all.

If she wasn't The Big Smoke, where the hell was he? A regular in Class Three chases, he was no mug and too valuable for a small yard just to get rid.

This filly, however, wasn't familiar to Danny, possibly having never set hoof on a track. By the look of her, she wouldn't for some time to come. 'We'll call you Tufty, that okay, girl?'

There's no way he was going to leave without her. Danny's legs reached over the reeking mix of shit and hay and led 'Tufty' out into the cold night. He stopped by Marcher Lord's box and, while that gelding was better nourished, he could still hear the clop of hooves. He couldn't let that box walker down by deserting him.

Why not save them both? He had two arms and two empty boxes in Silver Belle Stables. He'd only just tied Tufty to the railings of Marcher Lord's box when from the silence he heard a scratching. At first he reckoned field mice had also bedded into the fabric of this outbuilding.

But there it came again, from behind the closed stable doors of Artemis' box.

He froze there for a few seconds. It couldn't be, he thought. He shakily unbolted the door. Had he heard the ghost of Artemis? He splashed some light in there. At first he saw a room larger than the neighbouring boxes. Artemis clearly lived like the king he was. Then, from the far side, he saw a pair of brown eyes unblinkingly staring back. He pointed his pen-torch inside and immediately stared at eyes staring back. Artemis!

A cursory glance over at the farmhouse, he was relieved to see it was still black as soot. He rushed into the stable.

Up ahead there was a grey gelding standing by the right wall, head turned his way. He didn't move. Perhaps he'd discovered where The Big Smoke had gone. Even if it wasn't, he could be more certain this wasn't Artemis. He checked the feed trough. It was empty, possibly why Danny had heard scratching. He went over.

Danny flicked on the night lamp. He didn't care anymore if Leo saw the yellow glow from this stable. He was fuming, more than ready for a fight, axe or no axe. Someone needed to knock some sense into that boy. He'd clearly learnt nothing about looking after the yard or the farm, or maybe he hadn't grasped the work ethic.

With the door having been fully shut, an eye-watering stench hung in the air.

He returned to Marcher Lord's box and scooped a fistful of grain from that feed tray. The Big Smoke snaffled the feed from Danny's open palms.

When was the last time this boy saw the gallops, or even enjoyed a spell turned out having a pick of grass in the field? Even murderers were allowed fifteen minutes out a day.

Danny came back with some extra helpings. As he re-entered some of the grains slipped through his fingers. He bent down to scoop it up. In the warm glow of the lamp he noticed, mixed among the straw bedding, there was newspaper. That wasn't odd in itself but these weren't shreds of paper, but more like jagged cut-outs. Danny put one to the light. It was a headline with some missing letters. Danny immediately pictured the contents of the shoebox from the wardrobe of Bert's bedroom.

Was this more evidence? He pocketed the find and then put a soothing hand down the withers of the grey.

He sorely wished he could grow a third arm. He felt awful leaving this one behind. It was like having to pick a child to save from a fire. He knew the box walker Marcher Lord and crib biter Tufty tied up outside were more needy cases. While this grey gelding was on the scrawny side, he felt it was more his natural build, rather than malnutrition.

'I'll try to get back soon as I can,' Danny whispered.

He led the two chosen ones down the driveway. 'We'll soon have you both bouncing again.'

He glanced back and saw a curtain twitch. He didn't care if Leo saw, or even chased after him. That would at least show he thought something of the horses. As he met the black of the country lane he slid the pen-torch through one of the side loops in his combats holding his belt there. Its tiny bulb was enough to guide Danny across valley with the big gelding one side and Tufty the other.

Slowly Danny led them to Silver Belle Stables. They would pick up on rushed energy if he hurried them, Danny reckoned, and they'd translate that as a 'flight mode'. It was up to Danny – their new herd leader – to reassure them everything was going to be okay. Tufty even yawned when they turned into his stables. In a human that could be a sign of nerves but Danny knew horses found it hard to yawn if distressed given an increased pulse.

He housed them in the end two boxes. He fed and watered them both high-vitamin grain and fresh water. He also placed Meg's kitchen radio on low volume in Tufty's loosebox. At first light he'd make sure they were turned out in the lower field to run about with Ronny and Zola.

He returned to the house and, knowing he was too wired to get anywhere near sleeping, he passed the master bedroom, and headed for his office to double check the security cameras in the newly-filled boxes on screens fifteen and sixteen.

He could see Marcher Lord was still living up to his name by pacing his new temporary home. Old habits die hard.

Understandable, he guessed, given the stress of these unfamiliar surroundings and smells.

Soon his brain and eyes ached from tiredness. He knew the reawakening of Ely Park was just hours away, but he couldn't stop monitoring them, like a new parent listening out for the baby monitor by the bed.

He removed the newspaper clipping found in Artemis' box. But it wasn't linked to the headline-making horse. In fact the headline was unrelated to horseracing. There were two squares cut out, leaving the letters: More Bank Holi- Chao-.

Bank Holiday Chaos.

Danny could easily fill the gaps with the letters d, a, y and s.

He sat back and ran a hand through his thick, lush hair. He was holding the newspaper used to help make the mysterious letters counting down to Bert's disappearance at Chepstow.

Was it Leo sending them? Bert had described a person of Danny's description posting them. Was he deflecting blame?

If the letters had never left Sunnyside Farm it would explain why there was no stamp on the envelopes.

Had he also pushed that Lyme Regis postcard through Danny's door? If so, what the hell was his game? Was he trying to implicate Danny in whatever game they were playing? Leo would surely inherit the family farm and yard if Bert were to somehow disappear. Why would he try to scare his distant neighbour too?

Finding the mask and coat in the wardrobe, Danny could place Leo at the final lap of the Welsh National.

Danny poured a few fingers of whisky from a secret seventy-centilitre bottle of Glenlivet hidden behind past account folders in his computer cabinet, saved just for such an occasion.

He sat there until waking with a start. He checked the CCTV screen. 6.39 AM.

Screens fifteen and sixteen showed settled horses. He smiled and then wiped gunk from his eyes.

Danny returned the whisky and stuffed the newspaper cutting into the back of a drawer.

Chapter 10

The sun was playing hide and seek with scudding clouds,
throwing patterns of light and shade over the lush virgin turf. It
was fresh and cool on this landmark day.

Having walked the track and then the stands, Danny knew
the going and the turnout were both good.

Head groundsman Terry rushed by. He was thin as one of
his rakes. Apparently he was an intelligent man. His career,
however, took an about turn after getting laid off as a college
lecturer for getting laid with too many of his students.

Danny now stood among a growing number of paying
punters, near the grand opening ceremony stand, the entrance to
the parade ring and a statue of the Samuel family's great mare
The Whistler, who once galloped this very site some eighty years
back. It stood on the spot where Danny had unearthed the mare's
bones by accident from what was then called Trelai Park playing
fields. Ralph had regularly boasted of its life-like conformation;
hardly surprising as the bronze was reputedly cast on the very
dimensions of the skeletal remains.

Clearly no expense was ever spared on the Samuels even
to this day, Danny reckoned.

He was surprise and heartened by the number of young
families there. Most of the seasoned punters were most likely
studying form for the opener not far away now.

Soon the runners for the first would be saddled up and
arrive here from the pre-parade ring.

Ralph Samuel, owner and apparently part-designer of the
track, was beaming as he climbed the podium. Following close
behind was, judging by all the gold chains and regalia around his
fat neck, the local mayor.

Ralph wore a tailored black suit and cradled giant silver
scissors fit for a clown. It suited him, Danny thought.

Ralph tapped the mic with his finger. Gusts made him
repeatedly tame wispy strands of blond hair. His blue eyes looked

98

tired. The dark side of Ralph he'd been forced to witness in Prague had yet to resurface. Perhaps now that he had this pet project, the anger had subsided.

'This won't take long-' Ralph said and then waited for the reverb from the speakers to end. 'As I said, this won't take long, don't want to keep you all from the Salamanca Bar.' He paused for expected laughter that never came.

Kids are a tough crowd, Danny thought, relishing this.

Ralph continued, 'For over eighty years, Cardiff, the capital of Wales, has been a hotbed of sporting activity and achievement, yet in that time, since the tragic closure of its legendary racecourse on this very hallowed turf, we have been deprived of quality horseracing. Today, I'm proud and privileged to announce that this will change as we have finally risen that phoenix from the flames.' He paused to swallow. His cue card was shaking. Danny had never seen Ralph nervous. 'We hope it will become not only a window of excellence for the sport of kings in terms of equine talent and jockeyship.' Window of excellence, Danny cringed, which one of his business cronies wrote this drivel. Better than doorway of doom, he guessed. 'But also a place to socialise, meet and greet and, as we've already witnessed, get merry.'

Blimey he's plugging the bar enough, Danny noted, perhaps he'd overestimated the gate receipts.

'It now gives me great pleasure on this exciting and sunny first day of the re-born Ely Park to ask the Mayor of Cardiff the honourable Philip Wilson to do the honours and cut the ribbon to declare Ely Park open!'

As the bejewelled mayor holding the unfeasibly large scissors cut the red tape stretched across the entrance to the parade ring, the applause finally rang out.

Probably glad it's over, Danny thought. He would always despise Ralph for what went on in the Czech Republic but, for now at least, it was in his interest to put that bubbling hatred to one side for the good of this fledgling business.

As Ralph stepped from the stage, Danny was close enough to see his name badge: Ralph Samuel – racecourse chairman.

Danny could've added murderer and fraudster to the badge. He was about to collar the chairman when a woman's voice called from behind. 'Excuse me, Daniel Rawlings.'

'What have I done now?' came out of Danny as a sigh. He turned to see at first a plump forty-ish black woman in a blue nurse's uniform. She was pushing an oxygen canister and a wheelchair. Danny then saw her passenger.

Looking up was the centenarian Fred Myrtle. Although Ralph had swiped the bulk of VIP tickets with a view to making new friends and meeting Z-list celebs, Danny went out his way to invite this sole surviving jockey to have ridden at the original track here back in the Twenties and Thirties.

Danny still couldn't quite get his head around this fragile, withered old man had once done battle with legends like Golden Miller, Brown Jack and The Whistler. He was part of the rich history of the very fabric of this sight and his presence was like fitting the final missing piece to the jigsaw.

'Hello Fred, so glad you could make it,' Danny said loudly.

The ex-jockey was being fed oxygen through tubes from his nostrils yet every breath came with a metronomic crackle, like some of the seventy-eight records his grandpa used to play.

'Wouldn't miss this … for the world,' he said, little more than a whisper. His jaundice eyes smiled. 'You've made an old man very happy.'

Danny crouched down to eye level and placed his hand on Fred's gnarled fingers peppered by liver spots and said, 'All this was long overdue, I'm just sorry you had to wait. Just go easy at the bar and in the betting ring, d'ya hear.'

Walter's laugh was more of a wheeze. His carer leant over and said loudly, 'Come on, Walter.'

Danny had only just said goodbye when he noticed Rhodri over by the parade ring.

Nothing unusual in that, Danny thought, he was clearly into horses of all breeds and sizes. But what piqued his suspicions and made him stare for a moment at the chute linking the parade rings was the sight of the Pony Club chairman shaking hands with Ralph, still clutching those scissors.

Was he spreading his theories and conspiracies? Could he possibly have something to do with the vanishing of Artemis?

Danny's thoughts suddenly spun forward to Salamanca's bid for the Cardiff Open, a three-mile chase that in its heyday carried a bigger purse than the Cheltenham Gold Cup and attracted the very best chasers in the world. With Artemis out of the picture, Danny was confident that wouldn't be the case this time around.

The first race, a low-key two-mile four-furlong novice hurdle, came and went without incident, much to the relief of the actual course designer Danny and groundsman Terry. This was his first track layout and he knew any injuries would fill the headlines above even the most spectacular performance.

It was now show-time. In the saddling box Powder Keg was bouncing and so was Meg. She looked irresistible in those silks.

Like many high-profile races, the race was named in honour of a great from the past, particularly if they'd shone brightly at a certain track or a particular race, like Carey's Cottage, Reynoldstown, Hatton's Grace, Cottage Rake and Arkle.

Danny wasn't surprised when Ralph chose his grandfather's mare The Whistler.

She was a regular star name here back in the day, Ralph reasoned at one of the planning meetings. He would bloody say that, Danny thought.

Danny then campaigned for Salamanca to be honoured and after weeks of hinting and cajoling, Ralph finally consented to name a hedge not far from the toilet block after the chaser.

Danny stormed from there, shouting, 'A fucking hedge!'

In the saddling box Danny pushed the sponsor's plastic armband up his shirt sleeve. That acted as his pass to the parade rings in front of the Ralph Samuel Stand and also told the paddock watchers the horse's race-card number even before the rug was removed shortly before Meg got the leg up.

It was one of the few times Danny felt proud to stand in as a stable-hand and lead out the two most important girls in his life.

Knowing this opening fixture would be a sell-out there were a few bookies' pitches set up behind the stand, not too far from the pre-parade ring. Even from there Danny's sharp eyes could make out the opening betting show glowing orange on those electronic betting boards.

The unbeaten Northern raider Omnishambles was the warm thirteen-to-eight favourite, with the promising Wincanton winner Neigh Sayer next best in at seven-to-two.

They'd priced up Powder Keg at sevens.

A fair price, Danny reckoned, given she had useful form in France but punters were right to doubt whether she had retained that ability, whether she would translate it to the British scene and whether her lack of race-fitness would even allow her to.

Being the groom and handler for the day, Danny led Powder Keg to the pre-parade ring. Wearing Danny's colours of brown and green, Meg tucked her silks into white breeches that hugged her shapely bottom.

Danny reckoned she could star as a pin-up in one of those jockeys' calendars but doubt she'd be up for that. With everything still to prove, Danny reckoned she would much rather be seen as a serious rival to the boys in the weighing room than just some sex symbol.

In the parade ring, Danny glanced over at the stands. Already there was a healthy number booking their viewing spot on the terraces. Up above, the tinted glass of the panoramic viewing gallery would've impressed Danny had he not know it was Ralph's office and not a feature for paying members.

'Keep a lid on it,' Danny told Meg. 'Save your energy for out there.'

'I can't switch it off like a plug,' she replied, tightening the chin strap of her helmet. 'I'm proper bricking it, mind.'

'It's this girl's debut too,' Danny reasoned, placing a hand on Powder Keg's gleaming black neck. 'Does *she* look nervous?'

With such a valuable commodity, some part of Danny still had reservations booking Meg and not a seasoned professional for

102

her first ride. Being a Grade Two she couldn't even claim her seven-pound allowance as a conditional jockey who'd not yet ridden twenty winners. If she could keep her head he was convinced Powder Keg responded more kindly to a woman's touch and he could certainly vouch she had good hands.

He had complete faith in her. But then again love was apparently blind and could make fools of anyone. The peal of a brass bell told the jockeys to mount.

While giving her a leg up on the flighty filly, he caught sight of Ralph again. He looked serious as he talked to someone with his back facing Danny. They were on the shaded path between the main grandstand and the block of Tote windows and toilets.

Why the hell was Ralph hiding in the shadows just minutes before his beloved track hosts its first Graded event?

This grand plan, funded by the inheritance of the corrupt Samuel family, was the product of fifteen painstaking months in the making, yet he was lurking by the toilets.

Not a good omen for Ely Park's prospects, Danny thought.

He then saw Ralph point towards the stabling block beyond those outbuildings. What were they planning? He was glad Salamanca wasn't booked to run at this meeting.

He then caught sight of Meg's frowning face in his peripheral vision. He looked up. Powder Keg was pacing as if she had springs on.

'Where's Zola?' Meg asked as she double-checked all the tack was secure and wasn't pinching the youngster.

'With one of the stable lads,' Danny replied. 'He got upset being left on his own, so Jay's taking him home in the van.'

She frowned and then stroked Powder Keg's glossy black plaited mane.

'By the time this monkey realises,' Danny said, 'it'll be too late for her to ruin her chances, she'll have already run her race.'

'I dunno,' Meg said. 'She's brighter than you give her credit.'

'Guess I've not seen the best of her,' Danny said. He glanced up again and could see Meg was a ball of nerves.

'Don't think I can do this,' she said. 'Feel like an imposter. There's Barry Geraghty and A.P. McCoy just over there, should be asking for an autograph, not trying to beat them.'

'And they'll know that. Stand your ground if there's any gamesmanship out there, you're the improving jockey with a horse that has your trust. They may try to intimidate you, but it's just cos you're the unknown quantity, the dark horse. On the gallops I've seen this girl in your hands, she can quicken on a sixpence, use that tactical speed to escape any tight spots but that's unlikely with this one, she's a born trailblazer so you'll avoid trouble out in front, just point her and go. Above all there's no pressure, no one is expecting anything, including me. Remember all I've told you about pacing the sections of this track and remember it's like driving, the secret is to see the problems before they happen. If the unthinkable happens and it can in racing, you're bright enough to improvise. I trust you, Meg, as much as this filly does. Just try and enjoy this one, it's the Triumph Hurdle at Cheltenham in March that really counts.'

Of course Danny knew today also counted a great deal but he wouldn't let on for fear of scaring Meg any more. He hoped those words would help, though even he wasn't convinced by them. He ran another assuring hand down Powder Keg's neck.

'Can I get one of those?' Looking down at him she forced a smile and was then gone, cantering off down the sand strip alongside the straight to the two-mile starting pole. From that marker the runners would need to cover just over a lap and eight flights of timber.

Danny checked the *Racing Post* was still in his back pocket and then glanced over at the shady pathway where Ralph was still lost in conversation, gesturing every other word with his hands. It was a habit that irritated Danny, though it was probably more to do with the man behind the hands.

'If I chop your arms off, you wouldn't be able to talk,' Danny once flipped out at Ralph. That was said shortly before Danny was ushered out of the planning room.

He glanced at his Rotary watch. There was enough time to listen in to what was getting him so animated.

Leaving the parade he bumped into the hack Cameron, complete with that colourful silks-on-silk scarf of his.

'Any chance of that feature on Salamanca?' Cameron asked, 'Preferably sometime before the Cardiff Open.'

'Oh, I dunno Cam, things are a bit-' Danny stopped walking and talking. 'I will, but for a favour.'

Danny dug for the letter from Mooncraft Films. 'You seem to know who's who in media circles. Have you heard of these?'

Cam looked at the letter. 'Can't say I have. But I can make a few calls.'

'It's just they started a piece on the yard and haven't heard from them since.'

'Like some builders I've known,' Cam said and suck air between his false teeth. 'I'll try.'

'Well, if you could try real hard,' Danny replied, 'you'll get that exclusive.'

Danny left hurriedly. He wanted to get within earshot of Ralph but without being seen. So he swerved the glass-fronted owners' and trainers' bar in the Club enclosure off to the left and then circled the long way round the main Ralph Samuel Stand.

Back pressed to the cool rendering at the rear of the stands he closed his eyes and focused his senses on listening. From just around the corner, he heard Ralph say, 'So the mapping has already finished.'

'Almost,' replied another voice. 'We'll talk via that disposable Pay As You Go when we start on this place. If at any stage we find ourselves in too deep, we'll head for the shallows and you destroy the phone and all records. None of this ever happened. Clear?'

'Clear.'

Was that Rhodri? If so, seems there was more to Rhodri than just theories of an old fool, Danny thought, the bastards were mapping the DNA of Artemis. Shallows of what? The gene pool?

Danny realised they could yet be after Salamanca's blood. The heel of his boot chipped the wall in anger.

From just around that corner it fell silent. All that could be heard was the muffled commentary of the runners going to post from speakers around the racetrack. Surely they wouldn't come this way, he thought, but then neither would want to be seen together entering the betting jungle round the front, so they'd more likely split and go their separate ways. Shit!

He then heard the clack of leather on concrete grow louder. Danny pulled the *Racing Post* from his back pocket and rustled it open in front of his face. He heard the footsteps hurry by. Danny extended his arms and the newspaper far enough away from his chest to see the back of Ralph's black suit heading towards the Members' Enclosure.

He heard a cheer and then the auctioneer's patter of the commentator. He glanced at his watch. It had past the 'off' time.

Danny slipped through a fire exit at the rear of the main stand and sped up four flights to get a decent view high up in the terraces.

He blew out as he saw Meg extend her lead to four lengths with a flyer over the third hurdle at the start of the back straight.

She was following orders. That in itself put her above some of the freelancers he'd had the misfortune to call upon, just the once each time.

She maintained that advantage going into the second of four jumps on the far side.

Helplessly, Danny looked on.

Although disappointed he'd yet to bond with Powder Keg, his job was then to find the filly a regular jockey that would make that connection. Early signs out on the track suggested that search was over. For the first time, it was the well-being and safety of the rider and not the horse that filled his thoughts and fears.

As the field progressed rapidly down that stretch, the imposing oak trees and railway embankment provided the backdrop, much like it did eighty years previously.

When she pushed her charge into the fifth, 'Yes!' escaped Danny's lips. He rarely found himself physically cheering a runner on, preferring to suffer in silence. But with Meg up, the stakes were raised like never before.

Come the sixth hurdle, Meg inexplicably took a pull on the reins with a view to taking it short.

'What the hell Meg!' Danny shouted. Now was the time to press home the advantage. He'd seen her do it briefly as Ronny was hitting top gear in the trials, as if afraid to go flat out. He'd hoped she'd learnt from that mistake. Perhaps it was Meg getting tired. It was her first competitive ride. He grimaced as Powder Keg's stride stuttered from the mixed messages sent down the reins.

'Don't disappoint the girl,' Danny yelled, though it was for his own sanity, as, above a sea of cheers and roars, he could barely hear the words, let alone Meg now at the farthest point on the track. 'Press on!'

Powder Keg's belly still carried a bit of condition and skimmed the forgiving orange top bar of the flight of timber as they skipped over.

By now the advantage had been halved to two lengths. As if sensing her error, Meg flexed her elbows more as her arms moved in perfect tandem with the quick, flicking stride of her mount. Powder Keg soon picked up momentum again. She clearly had a racing brain.

The filly was close-coupled with a short, scratchy stride pattern. It wasn't graceful but it was effective, covering the ground well as she scampered to the turn out of the back-stretch.

'Attagirl, Meg!' Danny shouted as he saw Meg sit low in the all-out drive as she cornered into the home run.

There was still over half a mile to go. Had excitement led her to go for home too soon?

Powder Keg's French form told Danny she stayed two miles easily but as Rhodri intimated in the corporate tent, it's more about doing it at racing speed and at her current pace he now feared the filly would soon be running on fumes.

However, a glance at the jockeys on the second Omnishambles and third Neigh Sayer, both still taking a tug on the reins, suggested the pace hadn't been as frenetic as Danny had feared.

Perhaps Powder Keg's snappy action made her appear to be moving deceptively quickly, or maybe it was those distinctive go-faster marks on her body. More likely the chasers were simply in a different league to his filly, he began to admit. He'd soon find out.

Keep her together and organised, Danny thought, as if he could telegraph it to his girl in the saddle.

He saw her neatly give Powder Keg a tap down the right side of her neck.

That was to keep the horse on a tight line sweeping into the home run, Danny hoped, and not the growing signs of fatigue.

Powder Keg skipped over the first in the straight to maintain a four-length lead. French equine imports were generally taught to jump earlier than British and Irish counterparts, many sent over fences as three-year-olds, so it wasn't a surprise to see Powder Keg appear to know her job. After experiencing first-hand her sluggish antics in homework, it was still a relief she reserved her best for exam day.

With her air-cushioned persuader, she began to administer reminders with greater force and frequency. Seeing Powder Keg keep responding, Danny could almost cry. But the two dangers in behind, Omnishambles and Neigh Sayer, loomed up menacingly. Out in front Meg was a sitting duck.

He saw her look across to see Omnishambles cruise up besides, closely followed by Neigh Sayer, whose jockey Ryan Draper was now working just as hard as Meg. Meg didn't look out of place among them.

'Get second, keep going!' Danny screamed though he wasn't sure whether it was directed at Meg or Powder Keg.

By now she must've been feeling the burn and he wouldn't have blamed her for easing off and settling for third. But Meg was having none of it and kept pushing her mount on. From a mix of tiredness and greenness, Powder Keg began to drift off the far rail. Meg reacted by deftly threading the whip through to her right hand and giving her a few corrective slaps on the rump.

108

Powder Keg straightened her racing line but was now a neck down on Neigh Sayer in the battle for second. She began to rally, like Dessie in the 1989 Gold Cup. He was seeing a new side to both the horse and rider out there. He smiled.

Omnishambles was now four lengths up as he cleared the final obstacle. Danny knew that bird had flown. He also knew there wasn't only three-grand difference between second and third prize but the pride and confidence she'd take home from nicking runner-up berth.

'Go Meg! Go Meg!' He felt like he was back at the Shetland trials. It made him think how far she'd come in such a short time.

What a natural, he thought, as the pair embroiled in a titanic duel for the finish line. Draper's strength and fitness would surely tell close home but Meg kept defying expectations and was now back to just a neck down. A head. A short-head. A nose. They were level as they flashed by the lipstick-red lollipop stick of the finish line. Like in athletics, rule one was to run to a marker beyond the finish line. He hoped she'd remembered him saying it. At least from Danny's naked eye Meg had got Powder Keg's head down on the line.

After years of watching thousands of photo finishes as a jockey, punter, form analyst for a betting syndicate and now trainer, Danny could've had a PhD in separating a close result. Calling upon his photographic memory he reckoned Meg had edged it but it all depended on the angle of the finish line from where he stood in the stands.

'Here's the result of the photo finish for second place,' the judged said with a cut-glass accent over the speaker system, 'second was number six Powder Keg, third number four-'

Danny didn't need to hear any more and was now in the stairwell, almost floating with pride down the four floors. His heart was thumping more than if he'd been riding out there. He pushed the bar on the fire exit and slalomed between benches on the tarmacked seating area.

Over the gathering crowds, Danny craned to see Meg's beaming face as she walked Powder Keg along the asphalt chute to the winners' enclosure.

So intent was he on congratulating Meg he brushed past a police officer in a yellow fluorescent jacket. Danny looked back to apologise. It was PC Mavers. Danny acknowledged him with a nod but was blanked.

Probably ashamed he was back on events duty, Danny reasoned.

'So here's the result of The Whistler Triumph Trial-' the announcer continued but Danny had already tuned out. One sight of Meg's beaming face and it was his stride quickening. In the winners' enclosure Danny led her to the pole marked runner-up.

He looked up and they both smiled. No words were needed though Danny suspected she'd have struggled to get them out anyway. He could see from her pink eyes and cheeks she was overcome with emotion and exhaustion.

Danny then pretended to yawn so as to have an excuse ready for his watery eyes.

'You promised me an easy first ride,' she said and giggled. 'Talk about a rude awakening.'

Danny ran a hand down Powder Keg's neck as Meg dismounted feelingly.

'Wanted to throw you in the deep end, see if you'd sink or swim.'

'Now you tell me,' she replied but seemingly nothing could spoil her mood right now.

It was a gamble to let her loose in a Grade Two but Danny thrived on risk and this time at least it had returned a five-grand runner-up prize and a stable jockey bursting with confidence and zest for the game.

Among the on-looking gallery he saw Toby, whose face was serious and arms were crossed, as if to say, 'The filly would've won had she made her British debut for my yard.' Was it jealousy?

Ralph, standing alongside Toby, leant across and said something behind a hand. Whatever was said, it made Toby smile, uncross his arms and say something back.

Was it Toby mapping DNA? It seemed as if he needed the money.

Danny looked away. His mood wasn't going to be spoiled now. Knowing Meg, her female intuition would soon pick up if he felt anything was wrong.

She loosened the girth strap from Powder Keg and slipped off the saddle.

'Well, did I measure up?' she asked.

'For a first ride, you did her proud.'

'For a first ride?!'

Danny knew there was a fine line between confidence and overconfidence He didn't want her crossing it. Stopping fearing the opposition and the track could see the horse or the rider pay the ultimate price. But Danny knew she would rather talk herself down than up, so he put the bullishness down to exuberance rather than cockiness.

'You looked like one of the rest out there,' Danny said and placed a hand on her silky shoulder.

'Thanks, Danny,' she replied. Her chin turned dimply as if fighting back the tears.

'What's wrong?' Danny asked. 'You can't be disappointed with second, I'm not.'

'Nor am I,' Meg said, sniffling.

'They're happy tears then?'

She shook her head. 'Where's my mam and dad to see this?'

'It's a bloody cold day,' Danny said and faked a shiver. 'They'll have watched it on the box and no doubt toasting you now.' He gave her a warming hug.

Head above her shoulder, where he knew she couldn't see, he let his face drop slightly. He didn't know where her parents were but they weren't on track.

'I so wish they'd come,' she said. 'I've never done so well at anything in my whole life.'

'And once they see it's not as dangerous as all that, they'll be your first groupies,' Danny said and winked. He'd barely spoken to her parents. They seemed disapproving of everything in Meg's life, including him. He couldn't change the age difference but he could change their opinion. He could only guess the feelings of her parents when she told them about using her rider's licence. He guessed every parent's reaction would be different. It was like having a child enrolling for the army or police force, the risks are always there and the parent might not like it, but in most cases they'll only regret denying their kid's dream more. If you can't win, join them.

His thumb wiped a tear rolling down her soft cheek.

She cleared her throat noisily. 'Reckon we can go one better in the Triumph.'

'Think Omnishambles will have something to say about that,' Danny reasoned. 'One race at a time, Meg.'

'But both me and this girl will improve,' she said.

'I'm a fan of this place but Cheltenham is something else,' Danny replied. 'If ever you think we've got several leading chances going there then you've probably got none – it takes a very special one to win at the Festival.'

'But this one is special,' she replied defiantly.

'I know,' Danny replied, not keen to spoil her moment.

Powder Keg was blowing hard. This ought to put her spot on for her next run, he thought. 'Now go weigh in before all your good work goes to waste.'

In the unsaddling box Danny sat on an upturned water bucket and relived the race in his head.

From the speaker nearby, the judge relayed, 'Weighed in, weighed in, the result is now official, horses away, horses away.'

Chapter 11

'RIGHT, DO YOUR OWN BLOODY THING, don't know why I bother,' Danny said.

After yesterday's exertions at Ely Park he'd planned to keep the filly sweet with a relaxed canter. The little madam was certainly relaxed, Danny thought, as he tried to get her moving.

Still, she'd eaten up and seemed fresh enough. The resilience of youth, he reckoned, though he couldn't say the same for Meg. She was having a sleep-in this morning after the big day before, complaining of a stress headache and feeling stiff.

Danny suspected it had more to do with the empty bottle of cava in the recycle bin. A celebratory glass turned into session. Danny forgave her, just this once.

He gave up coaxing Powder Keg, resigned to walk with her the final half-furlong to the stream and brook.

The January air chilled his throat and lungs. Powder Keg's glossy coat glistened like chipped coal in the winter sun.

Her pink tongue lapped at the numbingly cold water wending its way downvalley to meet the Rhymney River, which forms the boundary between Glamorgan and its neighbouring county Monmouthshire, before flowing into the Severn estuary east of Cardiff.

Most Sundays his dad used to rise early to take him fishing on its banks downriver. At that age Danny found it a bit dull and he felt the same about the packet ham on sliced loaf washed down with warm tea from a flask but none of that mattered. It was the only time he'd have alone with his dad. Looking back, after a grinding week down the mines, he couldn't believe his dad had left his warm bed for the cold, gloomy riverbank. Only fresh air I'd get, he used to tell Danny, as he helped hook the bait.

It took forever to get his first ever bite, Danny recalled, and when it did finally came the sound of rushing water had made him rush for a wee behind the reeds just as his float began to bob and the disappear under the surface. Danny smiled.

The flow of the stream by his feet almost made his imaginings more real, as if he was back there.

A dry swallow made Danny break from the dream. He felt he deserved the drinks break more than the filly but he was just glad to rest up. He listened to the cawing of ravens up in the woods, thankful his city life was just a memory.

As Danny looked down, he noticed a fish lying on the surface. He watched it slowly float on by. He instantly recognised those red and black spotted scales on its side – it was a brown trout, a common catch up here, so thought little else of it

Suddenly Kegsy began to cough and splutter. Danny pulled her head from the water. 'Don't go choking to death on me.'

It was only then he saw the brown trout again. But when he glanced downstream he could still see the first one now some twenty feet on. He could understand a fish dying, but not two in the same stretch of water. It was like a grenade had been chucked in.

He sniffed the air again. There wasn't even a trace of pesticide this time.

Perhaps the damage had already been done, Danny reckoned, it would take a day or two for the recent rain to wash away all the chemicals Leo might've been spraying about.

In Powder Keg's own time, Danny returned to the yard.

Once there he put the filly away and predictably poked his head over the grille of Salamanca's neighbouring door.

When he found the door hung loose on its hinges he froze and then stormed in. There was nothing but straw bedding.

Don't panic, Danny thought optimistically. Meg's probably grooming him somewhere. After all he'd made it clear to staff both new and old it was a sackable offence for anyone that dared to ride out Salamanca.

It was then he could hear the light feet of Meg as she waltzed into the stable forecourt. He came out.

'Recovered then?' he asked.

'Care for a dance? We're alone.'

'Bit too alone,' Danny replied. Choppy breaths made it hard to reply. He feared another episode like near the schooling ring. 'Salamanca, where is he?'

She stopped spinning. 'Thought he was with you.'

'I was up over the ridge with Powder Keg.'

'And he's not in his box?'

'Do you really think I'd be asking,' Danny snapped.

'Alright!'

'They've come for him,' Danny said. 'I fucking knew it.'

'Who?'

'The bastards who took Artemis,' Danny said. 'Rhodri did warn me. Of course he was bloody right. Why the fuck didn't I listen?'

'The pony guy,' Meg replied. 'I don't understand.'

'They're mapping the DNA of champion stayers,' Danny replied. 'The blood of Salamanca is like the Holy Grail to them. Artemis' sample was clearly flawed, they wanted more. I can't stand here doing nothing. Drag the lads from stuffing their faces and get them out here, we'll cover every blade of the estate.' His raised hands came down, slapping his hips in anger. 'Why didn't I bloody believe him?'

'This Rhodri seems to know a lot,' Meg said. 'A bit too much. Will you name him when you call the police?'

'Who says I'll call *them*?' Danny said. 'They didn't believe me about those spheres up in the Ice Room, probably have me sectioned if I tell them about Rhodri's theory.'

'I'll back you up,' she said.

'They'll still think I'm as nuts as that one,' Danny said, glancing over at Powder Keg. 'It's all her fault, if she'd put any effort in we'd have been back in time.'

Danny stormed off, chanting 'Bastards!' He then shouted back and ran a hand through his already ruffled hair. 'If I find one of our lads left the door open and the Tank's bolted…'

'But that'll be good then,' she reasoned, 'we might find him.'

Danny rushed back to Powder Keg, who was still saddled. Although not right in the head, she was the only inmate capable of quickening and cornering Salamanca if he was still out there somewhere.

'Tell them to get a move on,' Danny called after her. 'And when you get back, best you take Powder Keg, she likes you.'

'They'll want extra for this,' Meg warned. 'They've ridden out three lots already.'

'I'll give them extra alright!' Danny replied. 'If they want more work, they'll be lined up at the foot of the slope over there in five, or else.'

'Calm down, Danny,' Meg said. 'Never seen you like this before.'

'Salamanca's never gone missing before.'

Meg left to get the part-timers before they clocked off.

Danny chose to partner Marcher Lord in the search, knowing it would do the box walker good to breath fresh air and stretch his legs.

He grabbed the largest saddle from the tack room and then unbolted stable sixteen, ready to tack up the beast of a gelding. As the door swung open he just stood there, saddle over his forearm. The box was empty. What the hell? Perhaps Meg had let him out for a pick of grass in the lower field.

He ran down all sixteen boxes to see if any others had gone but all the rest were occupied, including Tufty, who seemed relaxed enough listening to 'You're Gorgeous' by Babybird on Meg's radio.

Like police searchers in a body hunt, all six of them were mounted and lined up at the foot of the upslope, waiting on Danny's call.

Spaced equally, each kept a straight line as they trotted the incline, scouring every inch for even a sign left by a runaway Salamanca: a lost shoe, chewed up turf, a trail of blood.

They'd crested the ridge. Sat on a low-grade hurdler Danny looked over at the stone footprint of Samuel House and then down to the road and over to where he'd stumbled upon the Ice Room.

116

He hoped Salamanca would suddenly shoulder his way through a bush or leap over the dry stone wall marking the boundary. Instinct told him that was wishful thinking.

Believing they were no warmer to finding him, Danny sent the others back to the yard. He went on alone to complete the circuit he'd routinely cover with Salamanca, who was a creature of habit. He kept calling out for his chaser.

'Salamanca! Salamanca!' he kept shouting as he retraced the well-trod path, albeit in a much slower time on this low-grade hurdler. Rather than leaping the brook, he allowed this modest jumper to splashed though it. He then swerved the stone wall Salamanca used to tackle with relish.

His mind was racing. Salamanca was missing, along with Marcher Lord, but Tufty was still there. Were they playing games to mess with his head?

Increasing desperation fired his voice as Silver Belle House grew larger. He kept shouting but only echoes of his own cries came bouncing back off the valley walls.

When Danny returned to the stabling block, Meg had already retired Powder Keg from searching duties. The filly's small inquisitive head was stuck out of her box watching Meg hosing down the forecourt.

'Meg!' Danny shouted. 'We're not giving up that easily, I'll get the van out, search the roads.'

'No,' Meg replied.

'No?!' Danny fumed. 'I'll hear that as yes!'

Meg stopped hosing and turned to face Salamanca's box. 'It's like he never left.'

Danny followed her eyes over to box one.

Suddenly he felt like dropping to the ground, like a Wimbledon champion. Salamanca's bold head craned over the grille. Chomping down on his feed, it looked as if he had a beard of hay. 'Oh, there is a God! Thank you!'

At that moment he felt like properly blubbing. He rushed over and went in to greet his horse, even though it was less than an hour since they'd last been together.

Meg came and leant over the stable door. 'Sound as a pound he is.'

'Why didn't you call me?' he asked.

'I did,' Meg said, 'but the line was dead, you know the signal's bad up there. No lies now, what's going on Danny?'

'Mind games,' Danny replied. 'They're messing with my head and they're doing a proper job of it, scare me away from this place. They want Salamanca's blood.'

Danny scanned the room. 'Who found him?'

'I did.'

'How far did he get?'

'This far,' she replied.

Danny looked over at her. She just kept staring into the box.

'But he wasn't here,' he said. 'I even kicked the hay over there.'

'Well he was here when I got back,' she replied.

'Reckon one of the lads took him out, panicked and then returned him?' Danny said.

'Not one of them has left my sight all morning,' she replied. 'I take my head lass role seriously you know.'

'I'll never trust a freelancer, I know what they're like,' Danny said. 'I was one once.'

'They wouldn't nick Salamanca,' Meg reasoned.

'Wouldn't put it past them,' Danny said. 'A torch of mine got half-inched last year, so penned my name on this one.'

'Don't go pointing any fingers, Danny,' Meg reasoned. 'Word will get round you're a bad boss to work for. Anyway, with the big Ely meeting round the corner, we need morale up. Salamanca's back now, that's the main thing.'

'For now,' Danny said. His hand skated over Salamanca's glossy coat, searching for any needle marks, or cuts.

Meg said, 'If only they'd returned Marcher Lord.'

'What?'

'He's not there,' she confirmed. 'Tufty is still there but Marcher Lord isn't.'

Danny brushed by Meg to see for himself. In box fifteen Tufty was stood there relaxed, but her neighbouring box was still empty. 'Shit!'

Meg had followed him over.

'How the hell am I gonna explain myself out of this?' Danny asked. 'The Mills' hate me as it is, I've only gone and lost a horse I'd taken from them in the first place.'

'You'll have to ring Leo, explain you feared for their safety,' she said. 'You could ask him to join in the search. He might know where Marcher Lord likes to go, where he might have ended up.'

Danny looked distantly Meg's way, picturing the curtains of Sunnyside Farm twitching as he led Marcher Lord and Tufty away.

Perhaps someone had switched the horses' boxes. But why?

Were they planning a betting coup? As an ex-form analyst for a betting syndicate, Danny had read all about them.

He recalled that scandal at Leicester racetrack back in the early Eighties where Flockton Grey hacked up by twenty lengths in a sprint restricted to two-year-olds. The winning margin didn't seem so ridiculous when it later transpired the runaway winner was the three-year-old Good Hand, who naturally possessed the added strength and maturity to blitz the opposition and land the bets at ten-to-one. It was a man against boys.

Or the Gay Future coup where a young Irish trainer sent three over to race at Cartmel in Cumbria, exploiting the lack of communication links with that remote track. The racing punters believed Gay Future to be trained by Tony Collins at a small Scottish yard when in fact he was merely a 'ringer' for the real Gay Future, who was muscular, athletic and primed to run a career-best, being trained to the minute in Ireland for that fateful day on August 26 in 1974.

Collins had even entered two others on the same card, but had no intention of running either. It was all a ploy to disguise the betting scam. Trebles were placed on the three Collins' runners but, when the other two were pulled out, the money all went on single win bets on Gay Future. That helped prevent pull the wool over the suspecting eyes of the bookies paying out. When the real Gay Future turned up from Ireland, a top amateur then replaced a young conditional jockey booked for the ride and the horse was partnered to an easy win.

But with no runners in the coming days, how could the part-time staff repeat the coup? And anyway that coup was back in 1974 when there was limited security or technology. While Silver Belle Stables was also out in the wilds, he'd installed state of the art alarms and CCTV.

'That's it!' Danny said and looked up at the security camera attached to a bracket arm high in the corner, red light flashing.

'Doubt it picked up much,' she said.

'Why?'

'There was glass below it in the corner there,' Meg said, 'Brushed it up straight away don't want him getting an infected cut at the eleventh hour.'

'Bastard's smashed the lens,' Danny said. It was a good nine foot reach up there. They'd come prepared. Was this a professional job? 'Still worth checking the footage, paid enough for them, about time I got a return. There's one halfway up the side of Silver Belle House overlooking the courtyard. Like to see them reach that one.'

He sprinted to his office and studied the grid of security screens showing each stable plus the front driveway. He'd rewound them to twelve-thirty – the moment he'd returned on Powder Keg from seeing the dead fish float by.

Studying footage of the driveway he froze the film when he saw a large man all in black, face hidden by that now familiar balaclava.

Flashes of Chepstow came rushing back to Danny.

Leo had dressed for the occasion, Danny thought. He clearly hadn't wasted much time taking Danny up on his invite.

The milky black-and-white footage was jerky and grainy so Danny couldn't be certain if it was the same gear he'd pulled from Bert's mirrored wardrobe. He let the film roll. The masked man paced up the driveway and off screen to the right.

Danny's eyes flicked to the screen showing the stabling block. There he saw the intruder heading straight for box one and then box sixteen. He led both Marcher Lord and Salamanca away. As the intruder passed Tufty he barely gave the furry inmate a second-glance. Leo was clearly only interested in getting back the classy handicapper and getting revenge by taking Salamanca too.

This was like a professional job, Danny thought, there was clearly more to Leo than the lumbering country bumpkin he'd first seemed. Or was he following orders? Was he colluding with the DNA hunters?

Danny spun the footage on to 12.46 PM. The masked man was back. This time, judging by the strutting walk and hulking frame of the gelding alongside, he'd returned with just Salamanca. Had he chickened out, or had the blood sample been let? Either way Danny was a bit choked up that Salamanca had been returned, unlike Artemis.

He imagined where his horse had been taken for those agonising minutes. Was there a van parked up on the road?

Now more than ever he wished Salamanca could talk.

Instead he took some solace in Meg's words, 'At least he's back.'

Danny stopped the footage and the bank of inset screens returned to showing live feed. At least Tufty appeared settled since her arrival, though he couldn't say the same for himself.

Danny came down to the kitchen where Meg was tossing a salad.

'Recovered yet?' she asked.

'Guess so,' Danny said with a half-smile. His breathing and pulse had settle somewhat but his cheeks kept burning.

She kissed him. 'It's nice to see you with a smile.'

'Guess you don't appreciate what you've got until it's gone,' Danny said. He kissed her and looked deep into her sparkly blue eyes. 'Some things are irreplaceable.'

'Are we still talking about Salamanca?' she asked.

Danny paused. 'Yeah, who else?'

She play slapped his arm. 'Danny!'

Danny poured a cold glass of milk though he'd preferred something a bit stronger. 'Got your party frock yet?'

'Yeah, so excited, little black number, it's one of Victoria Beckham's range, really lush,' Meg said.

'Hope it's better than her music.' He then downed the milk and wiped away his white moustache.

'Spice Girls were the soundtrack to my youth. What's wrong with them?' she asked. Danny didn't bother to reply. 'Think the party will do you as much good as me, take your mind off all this weirdness.'

To do that he'd also have to finish off a whole crate of those Buds in the larder, Danny reckoned.

Chapter 12

DANNY SAT UP AND STARED AT MEG, who looked like she'd been vacuum-packed into the quilt, which hugged the feminine curves of her petite body, with only the tiny kicks of a foot breaking that mould, like a dog lost in a dream.

Perhaps she was reliving that ride on Powder Keg. She'd painted her toenails alternate red and white, the colours of her favourite Jive competition dress. The birthday girl didn't know it yet but she'd be seeing those colours again that evening.

He dragged himself from their afternoon nap. Getting up at five-thirty that morning, they wanted to be fresh for the evening. He left the curtains shut and shuffled to the kitchen in Union Jack slippers.

Danny put a pan on to boil some eggs. He could manage that. He turned to chop some cheese cubes to spike on sticks. This was her special day, so he'd forbidden her helping out with preparations.

It was hardly Michel Roux, mostly finger food that just needed plating up: chicken drumsticks, mini pork pies and vegetarian wraps. She'd insisted on just nibbles, probably to leave little scope for Danny giving the guests food poisoning.

He turned to check the pan and was surprised to already see ripples on the surface of the water, yet there were no bubbles to suggest it was coming to the boil. There was a low baritone rumble, like the sonic boom of an RAF Tornado.

'Bloody planes,' Danny said.

In the lounge he'd double-checked Jack hadn't popped the balloons or pulled down the banner he'd helped paint with Happy 21st Birthday Mammy Meg.

Danny then went to muck out Salamanca's box, any excuse to check in on his star steed, and was pleased to see he hadn't got upset by the planes. In fact he looked in great heart for his date with destiny in the Cardiff Open that weekend.

Danny stared into those mischievous brown eyes. At over seventeen hands, he could've eyeballed the mighty Mill House, yet he was well-proportioned, with a robust muscular build and immense hind quarters designed to drive him on. He would give the boy one more serious bit of work to put him spot on for Saturday.

Never one to be bothered about being fashionable, Stony showed up early. Danny reckoned his pal had taken to Meg but he suspected he'd turned up first more for the free beer. He was wearing a Hawaiian shirt.

'The Exeter horse lost, then,' Danny said, handing Stony a bottle of Monk's Secret ale.

'Yep, giving this shirt a whirl instead.'

'It looks like a winner,' Danny said but struggled to keep the straight face.

'Alright, lips!' Stony said. 'You know there's nothing more meaningless than a joke that's not funny.

'Ouch.'

'Where's Jack?'

'Put him to bed already,' Danny said.

'Thought it was quiet.'

'For all I love him, I'm also loving this. Listen.'

'What?'

'Exactly,' Danny said. 'Can answer calls from owners without Jack clambering all over me, nagging to play throw the monkey, again!'

'Throw the-'

'Don't ask,' Danny said.

'And where's the birthday girl,' Stony asked.

'Getting ready I think,' Danny replied. 'What's in the bag?'

'Oh, nothing,' Stony replied, cheeks turning pink.

'Meg's present, is it?' Danny leant over and picked out a hardback book.

'No! It's mine.'

Danny read the cover out loud. '*Wear The Cap That Fits!*'

'It's one of those self-helps if you must know,' Stony whispered.

'What a load of-'

'It'll help me,' Stony replied and snatched it back.

124

'If you're in a hat shop.'

'*This* is Meg's,' Stony replied, apparently eager to change the topic. His hand rested on a large plastic case, large enough to have boxed the 40" flatscreen TV in the corner.

'Bloody hell, Stony, that looks generous.'

'Cost less than that book,' Stony replied with a smile.

Now Danny's intrigue had really piqued.

'Swear my bladder's shrunk like the rest of me,' Stony said as he got up for the bathroom.

When he returned, Stony smiled and said, 'Trying to turn back the years then?'

'Eh?'

'There's a bottle of black hair dye on the sink,' Stony said. 'Don't want Meg to see any grey hairs, I understand.'

'It's not mine,' Danny protested.

'Popped in the bookies down Greyfriars Road the other week, lads confessed it's not same down there without you.'

'Dare say I'll be back,' Stony replied. He then removed something hidden by bubble wrap from the case and rested like a lap tray.

Danny craned his neck forward. Stony added, 'But I'd done my sphericals down that place once too often, finding "other interests" a damned sight kinder on the wallet.'

'Wouldn't happen to that Sheila you were on about?' Danny enthused.

Stony glanced up. Danny felt the light touch of Meg's hands on his tight shoulders.

When Danny glanced back, for a horrible moment he believed his ex-wife Sara had returned. Gone were the natural flowing blonde curls, Meg's hair was now black and straight. Even the black skirt resembled one of his ex's. The mere thought of Sara returning to spoil Meg's night had sent his pulse off the chart.

'Holy mother of,' Stony said, 'pearl.'

'Don't mind me,' she said. 'I went to Rhymney High, they didn't need lessons in swearing there.'

'It's a generation thing, love,' Stony said. 'Never in front of a lady.'

'Never been called that.' Meg forced a nervous smile and then looked down at Danny. 'Well? You like?'

He couldn't figure whether it was dread or desperation in her eyes.

Danny glanced at the open door. 'Can I have a word?'

As Danny ushered her out, he turned and said, 'Tuck in to the nibbles, Stony.'

'What's this about?!' Danny asked, eyes flicking to her hair.

'Fancied a change, no biggy.'

'You loved your hair,' he said. 'You said it was your best feature.'

'I've had the bottle some time now,' she said, her words echoing off the tiled floor and stone walls, 'and when you hadn't bought me a pressie, it confirmed something in my mind.'

'Eh?'

'That you've gone off me.'

'In your mind maybe!' Danny said. 'Not in mine. I don't believe this, I was only saving my present as a surprise, something to look forward to at the end of the party.'

She ran a hand through her hair. 'I thought you'd like it.'

'That's the problem,' Danny said in a strangled whisper, one eye on the door. He wished he'd turned up the music now.

'I can't figure you out sometimes,' she said.

Danny pushed the door shut. 'We'll talk about this later.'

'I'm not Jack,' she said, 'let's have it out now, don't want this hanging over me at my party.'

Danny pulled her closer. 'I love you the way you are … were. I don't want a Sara Mark II. Besides, you've made me prefer blondes.'

'I've told you not to mention the S-word in this house,' she said.

'You're the one trying to look like her clone,' Danny said, 'Why on earth would I need reminding of that cheating bitch and a failed marriage?'

126

'But?'

'No buts,' Danny said, 'isn't that what you tell me?'

Meg shrugged. He had never seen Meg this vulnerable. Right now she didn't even seem twenty-one.

Danny added, 'Meg, you don't need to try with me. I love your curls, even that stray one that falls over your face and you have to tuck it here,' he ran a finger behind her ear. 'I love that little beauty spot on your neck, even the way you leave cereal bowls for the cornflakes to glue on the sides.' He scrunched his nose. 'Okay, maybe that's stretching it.'

Meg let out a teary laugh. 'Why do you have to make everything a joke?'

'Cos I love the way your nose wrinkles up just there when you laugh,' Danny said. 'I also love the way you dance on your own, do that little thing with your mouth when you're reading.'

'Everyone does that, don't they?'

'What I'm trying to say,' Danny replied, 'I've never had a nine-to-five office job, but I do remember that excited Friday feeling after a shitty week of trying to go unnoticed by the teachers and bullies at school.'

'Where's this going?' Meg asked.

'Whenever I hear the door go when you're back from dance class I get that same feeling.' Her bottom lip began to go. 'So what I'm trying to say is, please, don't change, not for me anyway.'

She tilted her head and arched her pencilled eyebrows.

'We're good?' Danny asked.

'We're good,' she said and her smile lit her watery blue eyes.

'Phew, that was hard for me, I'm no lush.' He gave her a reassuring kiss on the chemically crown of her head. 'Now, let's get back in there before Stony thinks something's up.'

'Do you want another, Stony?' she said, smiling.

'Oh boy, she's a keeper, Danny, I've always said. Make it a Flapping Cassock if you will, ta, Megan.'

She left for the kitchen.

'So are you going to tell me?' Danny asked.

'What?'

'The bag.'

'Now that Meg's here, I will,' Stony said and leant forward. 'Been taking classes at night school.'

Danny smiled. 'What in?'

'Fine art,' Stony said. 'And before you say anything, it wasn't to ogle at some life nude model, not by the second lesson anyway. Wanted to try my hand at something new, makes a change from filling in betting slips down Raymond Barton's. Well I've got my first exhibition at an established public arena next week, so guess I get the last laugh,' Stony said and sat back as if waiting to soak up the applause. He then added, 'I say exhibition, it's a stall at the local arts and crafts expo,' Stony said. 'And I say public arena, it's the Cathays Community Hall, but still.'

'But still,' Danny said, 'didn't know we had a budding Rembrandt in our midst.'

'I'm still learning, like, but teacher reckons there's something about my work,' Stony said, 'and before you tell me what that *something* is, I'd like you and Meg to come pop in and see it.'

'I'd love to, but-'

'I know, I know, horses come first,' Stony said, 'Really I understand.'

'I'll try my best, Stony.'

'I guessed that would be the case, so I brought one up,' Stony said, tearing off the bubble wrap.

Danny looked down at a watercolour of a horse clearing a fence with daylight to spare. 'It's Salamanca.'

'Guessed it from the silks did you?'

'No from the horse, it's the spit of The Tank, even got the strapping on his legs. You did this?'

'Don't sound so surprised.'

'I'm not,' Danny said. 'Always reckoned you had good hands in the saddle.'

That made Stony smile as he shifted his weight. 'Shame my hips were no good.'

Danny was still smiling at the painting. 'Still, never too late to find my true vocation, eh?' grinned Stony.

'I'll definitely make the time to get down there,' Danny said. 'We both will.'

'Don't worry yourself,' Stony said, 'but you do know how many have bothered to stop and look at my works?'

Danny didn't know whether to guess high or low to avoid insult. He just shrugged.

'Thirteen,' Stony said. 'Do you know how many that is?'

'Thirteen,' Danny said and gave a look.

'More people have died from having a vending machine fall on them,' Stony fumed and sat back again. 'Did you know that?'

'I do now,' Danny said and smiled. 'I'll just call Matron.' He was secretly glad the old random Stony was back in the room.

'*And* the only compliment came from Basil from the bookies' and you know he's got a glass eye, well his other one's gone milky. He said he was impressed, but I found him later chatting up a life-size cardboard cut-out of Amanda Holden.' Danny opened his mouth but Stony added, 'It's your turn not to ask.'

'Perhaps keeping it small-scale is good,' Danny reasoned. 'Give you more time to perfect your craft. I'm guessing art critics can be harsh as racing hacks.

Stony didn't seem so convinced. 'Just want the public to see them.'

'It's the weekend tomorrow,' Danny said. 'Reckon the footfall will pick up then. Either way I'm glad for you mate, really I am.'

'Yeah, perhaps so, always the doubter,' Stony said.

Meg returned with a can and a glass.

'Don't worry about the glass, Meg,' Stony said. 'Only means more washing up.'

'Come look at this, Meg,' Stony said.

She studied the painting, like a budding Brian Sewell, but then said, 'What is it?'

'Salamanca,' Danny said, 'and here's the artist, Stony.'

'It's yours now,' Stony said and kissed her. 'Happy birthday, Megan. But you two love birds will be happy all year round, I'd put a bet on that.'

When the guests started to accumulate, he was the one that suddenly felt older. Most were friends of Meg. One of them had brought an iPod with a remote speaker and killed the Oasis CD in favour of some dance mix. Danny felt liking saying, 'Call that music?' but he heard those words in his dad's voice which shocked him to silence. What comes around, he guessed. It was Meg's night.

With the party in full swing, Danny struck the safety match and lit the twenty-one candles on the cake with the letters MEG HAPPY B'DAY iced over jam sponge shaped into a horse-shoe.

'Did they charge by the letter, B-day, honestly!' Meg joked nervously, all eyes on her. Danny explained, 'They couldn't get all the letters on.'

She then turned it so the shoe faced up to her. 'The good luck won't fall out this way round.'

As she cut into the cake, Danny waved the match but it wouldn't go out.

He rushed to the Belfast sink before the flame scorched his fingertips. He turned the cold tap but instead of gushing water, out flashed a ball of yellow-blue flames.

Danny became rooted to the spot, like a deer blinded by the dazzling light.

The taps were like dragon's nostrils as the flames licked the ceramic basin and spread up its sides back at him. Only then did Danny react, just in time to swerve a lifetime of pain and more permanent blindness.

'Fuck!' He backed off and instinctively turned the taps off. He blinked his burnt retinas repeatedly. He looked over his shoulder and called, 'Meg!'

Megan turned from slicing and dishing the cake 'Isn't it me that should have the surprised look. What's wrong, Danny … Danny?'

Danny opened his mouth but his brain also appeared frazzled. Was the fireball linked to the cattle and the brown trout dying? Had there been a chemical or oil spill?

He surely would have heard something on the local news. Unless there was an almighty cover up and Bert had been about to go public. Or was it Leo going trigger happy with the crop sprayer. Over the summer Danny recalled more than once looking on in disgust at the chemical fountains from the sprayer beyond the stone wall. Perhaps Bert'd flung himself off the Severn Bridge knowing the scandal was soon to break. He was a man of dignity, Danny reckoned, and would fall on his sword if he brought shame on the family name.

But pesticides wouldn't turn water into fire anyway, Danny reasoned.

'Danny, what is it?' Megan said. 'Your face is as white as that basin.'

Better than being burn-red, he thought. 'Huge flames came from the taps just now.'

'This isn't the surprise you promised, Danny?' she asked and went to the taps.

'Don't, Meg!' Danny shouted and lunged forward but not in time to stop her turning on the cold tap. Danny yanked her back to save her from the flames' reaches but all that came out was a stream of clear water. The music then died and so had the atmosphere.

'There were these massive flames, they filled the basin and came back at my face,' Danny explained.

Meg's confused smile quickly turned to an awkward frown.

'Honest, Meg!' Danny was now also aware he had an audience.

One of the faces said, 'I had a gran go that way towards the end.'

'Who said that?' Danny said. Without hesitation a teen with floppy hair and a nose-ring stuck a hand up. Despite having nearly been torched, Danny felt like he was in the wrong here. He pleaded to the sea of faces, 'I'm not going nuts!'

Meg gave him another meaningful look and then turned to her smiling friends. 'He's a practical joker.'

'None of you drink that water tonight, yeah?' Danny said.

The faces kept staring back silently.

Nose-ring guy waved a bottle of Smirnoff Ice and said, 'Shit, and I was gonna hit the water later.'

Stony joined in the laughter and then called over, 'Blimey, Danny, flames you say. That birthday cake must be good stuff, where'd you get it from, Amsterdam?'

'Let's get this party restarted,' the nose-ring guy said as he went back to the laptop on the table and clicked the downloaded music set-list. Ed Sheeran continued to strum away, much to Danny's relief. The atmosphere thawed.

'I swear on my life, Stony, there were flames. They mushroomed out and then came right back at me. I still can't blink away these orange and green blobs floating about here.' He stuck his hands out. 'Someone's trying to put the frighteners on me, make me disappear from this place and Salamanca, like they did sending Bert those threatening letters. Well they won't get shot of me that easily!'

Danny downed his bottle of lager.

'I'll drink to that,' Stony said.

'You'll drink to anything,' Danny snapped, feeling his own cheeks now burn.

Stony kept grinning. 'Fair point, well made.'

For the rest of Meg's special evening Danny felt very aware not to cramp her style and kept a low profile. That was easy as he felt exhausted and he was up at six but there was no way he was going up until the last stragglers had left. He was banking on his belated surprise present making up for the scene he'd unwittingly created early.

'Perhaps it needs an exorcism,' Danny said.

Stony glanced over at the nose-ring guy. 'Bit harsh.'

'Not him, this place,' Danny said. He sat and his right leg started to go again. He removed the police calling card and threaded it between his fingers.

'What the hell's wrong with you?' Stony asked, turning to face Danny. 'You've been like a fiddler's elbow all night.'

'People are out to get me,' Danny said.

'Listen to yourself,' Stony said. 'Sound like one of the winos on the street.'

'I'm serious.'

'Why would they?'

'I'm the trainer of Salamanca, the new king of the staying chasers.'

'I dunno, Danny,' Stony said. 'You know best, but I reckon you're being a bit paranoid myself. It's okay to be on the lookout, being remote up here in the valley with a family to protect. I would be. Do you know what I would do?

'What?' Danny asked.

'Get one of these down you,' Stony said, waggling a bottle of Monk's Whisper. 'Six-per-cent-proof will soon make you figure things aren't so bad.'

'But it is bad, don't you see,' Danny snapped, knitting the card quicker, like he was going cold turkey. He felt the indents left by a pen on the card, fingertips tracing the grooves like a blind man reading braille.

'Well call them, then,' Stony said.

Danny stood.

'Where you going now?'

'I'm doing what you said.'

'Doubt there'll be detectives there at this hour,' Stony said. 'Anyway it's party time.'

'I don't reckon it's detectives I'll be calling.'

'Just be quick about it,' Stony said. 'Feel like a museum exhibit here, need you to bump up the average age a bit.'

Danny slipped away from the crowd.

For once he'd locked the office door. With a cabinet's worth of Salamanca-engraved trophies in there, he didn't want them in the wandering hands of any drunks downstairs.

He put the card on the desk and pointed the bendy stand of the racing green lamp on it.

His face also homed in on its black-and-white surface. It was like a cheap business card. He tilted the lamp and then the card to change the angle of light but he still couldn't see what his fingers had felt just now. The indentations were too shallow to be picked out merely by the contrast of shadows and light. He was about to rip the card in anger when he again felt the pock marks left by the imprint of a pen. It felt like the ghost of a number, impossible to read. He wanted some space to think so went to the main bedroom.

He flicked on the bedside lamp. He sat back on the bed, deflated. He seemed to physically shrink, shoulders dropped and face buried in palms.

He hoped Jack hadn't woken up from the music downstairs. He looked up at the finger paintings and coin rubbings his son had proudly brought back from preschool. Danny was just as proud of them.

An idea suddenly sprung him from the mattress. 'Thanks, Jack!'

It was like it was written in invisible ink. Except Danny knew he wouldn't need UV light to see it. Instead he rushed back to the bedside cabinet on Meg's side. He rifled for her black eyeliner pencil and then tore a sheet from her writing pad. He overlaid the police card with the writing sheet and pressed it firmly down.

With the pencil, he then shaded over the card beneath. The first four numbers were zero-seven-seven-seven. A mobile.

For once he'd hoped it would get through to an officer, rather than an unsuspecting suspect. As he carried on shading, he wrote the full number, beside it were the letters SAL. Danny's jaw tightened. It seemed like Salamanca was already on the police radar. What did they know?

Danny was now convinced Rhodri was right.

He pressed the number on his smartphone.

'Danny,' a female voice answered.

'Who's this?' Danny asked cagily.

'We can't talk on the phone,' she whispered.

'Why?' Danny said. 'It's just me this end. Are you still at work?' He glanced at the computer desktop clock. 11.23 PM.

'Yes,' she finally replied. 'Are you near a computer with a camera? I can set up an encrypted video link.'

Danny was desperate for answers. 'Yeah.'

'In a minute there'll be a request your end to complete the video link,' she said. 'Click accept.'

'Don't you need my info?' Clearly not, Danny reckoned, as a grey box flashed up on to the screen. Danny clicked 'Accept.'

He was then faced a thirty-ish woman with flame-red hair and eyes as green as the grass outside. She smiled. 'Good to see you Danny.'

'I never said my name,' Danny replied.

'I recognise your face,' she replied. In the bottom right corner Danny then noticed the small inset box showing his face which presumably filled the screen her end.

'Why did I find your mobile number on a police calling card?'

She frowned. 'I don't know.'

From someplace off stage left, Danny heard a muffled banging. It sounded like a fist on a door. There it was again.

Then, in the background, Danny swore he saw the director Quentin Crawford wordlessly rush by.

'Did you come to the yard with the crew?'

'Yes,' she replied.

'Why didn't you come back?'

'We'd got enough to complete the job,' Sally replied. He was surprised by the lack of any time delay on this feed.

She must work for Mooncraft Films, Danny reckoned, no wonder she already knew the yard's number.

He saw her face blanch and fill the screen as she leant closer. Perhaps that was her intention – shield him from whatever was going in behind. He could also see the worry lines framing those alluring eyes, the freckles on her pale skin and the split ends of her hair.

The PC's speakers crackled with the sound of something heavy crashing to the floor. Were they under attack?

'What's happening?' he asked.

'Just stay away from here.'

Although she looked down the lens, it wasn't clear whether she was still talking to him or someone there.

The screen turned black, as if there'd been a power cut.

Danny slapped the side of the monitor. But when he moved the mouse the connection timer appeared: three minutes and still counting. He hadn't been cut off.

There were now grey shadows, like ghosts, shifting with the urgency of a Formula 1 pit-stop mechanic. It reminded him of cross-channel interference on the old family TV set as a kid. Except there couldn't be any interference on an internet link. This was actually happening. He was left wondering what the hell he was witnessing.

His face now moved closer. He could still make out a dark blue rhombus shape of the night sky in the background. It looked like a slanted rectangular window. A skylight, Danny reckoned. Through the window, he could make out several yellow dots of light. They were in a horizontal line against a black area.

Also among the stars he could see one was a good deal larger and green. There was a distant ringing. Was it a fire alarm? It sounded more like church bells. He leant closer but then saw his face in the picture-in-picture lower on the screen. That close-up of his face would be visible to Sally and whoever else was there.

He backed away from the screen and a hand came up to cover his face. He then pushed the off button on the PC's hard drive until absolutely sure it had died.

He pulled the leads out of the modem and wireless router. He needed to completely divorce himself from what he'd seen and heard. Perhaps it was too little too late as he imagined a frozen screenshot of his panicked face still on the screen the other end. A spark flew as he also yanked the plugs from the wall.

Not the electrics too, he whined.

Mooncraft Films had come under attack, just like Silver Belle House.

Who would hold a grudge with a small independent production company?

'That just happened,' Danny told himself as he sat there sombrely in the dark with the party happening just beneath his feet, yet he felt a world apart from the laughter, shouting and thumping beat of music and dancing feet.

This Sally and her workmates were escaping, but from what?

With Danny's image captured and plastered over the screen their end of that video link and the yard's address surely filed somewhere at the Mooncraft Media office, it was only a matter of time before he was tracked down too.

It didn't make any sense, he thought, none of it did.

Would they now come after him?

Soberingly, he knew there was only one place he could find that answer. But where was Mooncraft based?

His face made silvery by the moon and stars through the only window. He was about to draw the heavy curtains when he realised he'd seen similar out of the skylight behind Sally. Anxious about ground conditions at Ely Park, he'd regularly monitored the weather forecast maps and remembered thinking it was a change to see all the cloud was over the English side of the border. Was it a Welsh firm?

He noticed one of the stars in the video was large and green. He'd lived in Cardiff city centre long enough to know there was something similar on top of the Capital Tower – once Cardiff's tallest building, though in London it would be seen as a regular block of offices. The flashing green light acted as a warning beacon for low-flying aircraft.

Also through the slanted window behind Sally, he remembered seeing a line of glowing yellow lights along the black silhouette of what could be a long building. He'd also heard the distant peal of bells on the quarter-hour. He'd lived in Cardiff city centre long enough to be familiar with both.

On his meandering walks back from the pub and snooker hall, he'd seen similar illuminating the turrets of Cardiff Castle. If that really was the castle then Sally was speaking from somewhere on Cathedral Road, near Sophia Gardens cricket ground and backing on to Bute Park.

On his smartphone he called up Google Earth. It helped confirm they were established four-storey late-Victorian terraced and semis houses. From an estate agent portal he could see many were large enough to hold companies, while most of the residential houses were split into three or four flats.

He fished out the yellow envelope from Mooncraft Media. Like the postcard, the ripped envelope had no stamp. Being too wrapped up in the postcard, he hadn't previously noticed. His finger touched the top right corner. There was no trace of adhesive or saliva. This came on the same day as the postcard. He also suspected they had been delivered by the same hand but clearly not that of the postman, as it too wasn't stamped and franked. His photographic memory pictured the letter inside.

Removing the letter then confirmed his suspicions – Mooncraft Media was a *local company*. It was there in black and white.

At first light Danny would go recce the area.

Danny returned to the party. He really wasn't in the mood but it was the first time they'd shared her birthday together, so he made the effort.

He came over to join Meg at the fridge and gave her a lingering kiss. 'Happy birthday, Meg. How does it feel to reach the big two-one?'

'You should know,' she said and smiled. 'Or have you forgotten?'

'Eh, cheek,' Danny's brow wrinkled. 'Well, I had planned on giving you your present but I think the moment has passed.'

'No it hasn't,' she pleaded.

'I'll give it to you later, when we're alone,' Danny said. 'It's too big to reveal here.'

'Promises, promises,' she smiled and hand pressed his chest. 'I'll wait if I must.'

One by one the revellers staggered into the dark night, most via a hired mini-bus from Rhymney.

Once Stony had downed the last dregs of his six-per-cent proof, Danny helped him into a waiting taxi.

'See, told you I could drink them under the table,' Stony slurred and then parted with, 'Good party, that.'

Danny stuffed a twenty into the driver's hand and slapped the taxi roof.

Shutting the front door on the final lingering drunk he stood there for a few seconds, relishing the silence.

He entered the lounge, every surface littered with bottles and cans.

'We'll do most of the clearing up tomorrow, yeah?' Meg yawned. 'Is this what it's like to be a twenty-something?'

'I know what'll wake you up,' Danny said.

'Not yet, Danny, we don't want to wake up to this mess,' she replied bagging up cans and fag packets.

'Close your eyes.'

'Danny, you know I don't like surprises.'

'It's not so much of a surprise now,' Danny reasoned. 'In any case I reckon you'll like this one.'

He stood behind her and put his hands over her eyes. She giggled. Perhaps they'd tickled her face. Seemingly she was willing to obey him this once. As he led her into that cold night her slippers caught on the foot scrape but she didn't seem to care.

He directed her round the back to the stabling block. 'Not far now.'

'My hands are cold,' she said.

'You won't notice in a minute,' Danny replied.

'You've got me gloves?'

'No,' Danny said. 'And no more guesses.'

On the courtyard surrounded by stables he took his hands away.

Danny studied her reaction. The smile had turned into a confused frown as she stared at the line of closed stable doors.

'What?' She then looked around the courtyard, softly lit by a night light on each corner. 'Where? I don't get it.'

'Over there, box two,' Danny said.

'No point in playing what's in the box with me,' she said.

'Go over there,' Danny said quietly, not to upset the horses.

There was a dark shape at the foot of that door.

'Oh Danny, not clothes,' she whispered, picking up the crackly dust cover. 'You know I've run out of room for my dance dresses.'

'Just zip that,' Danny said, running pinched fingers across his lips, 'and unzip that.'

She peeled away the dust cover to reveal a set of red-and-white quartered silks with a matching cap pinned to the collar.

Her hand went to cover her mouth and her eyes widened. 'Are these?' Megan asked and pointed at herself. Danny nodded. 'How did you know to pick red and white?'

'Your ballroom gowns told me enough,' Danny said. 'I've registered the colours with Weatherby's and all the paperwork's sorted.

'But I've not got anything to ride them on,' she said.

He looked pointedly at the box two. 'By the stable door, go look.'

She squinted at the brass plaque there. Her fingers traced over the black lettering. '*Powder Keg – black filly. Owner – Megan Jones.*'

She turned. Her wide eyes glistened in the artificial light and her mouth opened but nothing immediately came out.

'Hope it's okay?' Danny asked softly.

'Okay? It's the best,' her voice began to crack, 'But, it's too much, I … I don't deserve this.'

'I'm pleased you're pleased,' Danny muttered casually, as if it wasn't a big deal. He didn't want to spoil the moment by bigging up the gesture, like laughing at your own joke. Secretly though he garnered just as much pleasure out of seeing Megan ecstatic, beaming with child-like excitement. 'Earlier you doubted my commitment to you, and I'll admit, I'm crap at showing it. Thing is, I believe in this filly nearly as much as I believe in you. I wouldn't sell her at a profit to anyone, not even the Queen. But she's yours, you deserve her. The filly deserves you.'

'Oh Danny boy, come here,' she said.

She wrapped her arms around him. 'As nana used to say, I could cwtch you to death, a proper Welsh hug.'

140

'Come on,' Danny said. 'Let's get in, house is going as cold as I feel.'

She ran a hand through her hair. 'And this'll wash out soon enough.'

Chapter 13

11.34 AM. DANNY HAD ALREADY LOOKED IN on Salamanca and penned a gallop rota for the first and second lots to leave with the four work riders drafted in. But, after a sleepless night and the resultant stress-hangover, Danny couldn't stomach any breakfast.

He went to let Meg know he'd be out if anyone called. He found her curled up on the sofa in a new pink onesie – a birthday present from her best friend Karen – nursing a proper hangover and cradling a big white cereal bowl full of chocolate raisins. She was also wrapped up in the final of Great British Bake Off Sky-Plused from the night before.

Her tired eyes were as pink as her onesie and fixed firmly on the screen, as if wearing blinkers. Her hand habitually dipped into the bowl. 'One of my five-a-day,' she'd told him while pouring them out in the kitchen not half an hour ago.

He wasn't annoyed she was unfit for work. After a tough year of early nights and mornings, he was just glad she'd enjoyed the evening. It's not every day she'd turn twenty-one and seeing her blue eyes light up on seeing Powder Keg and her silks was enough. Those eyes weren't sparkling so much now.

She was seemingly oblivious to Danny clomping into the room in boots, ready to excuse himself.

'I'm off out to do something,' Danny said quietly. He hated lying to Meg but keeping it that vague, it wasn't technically a lie. He'd just been economical with the truth.

'Mm,' she replied, too invested in whether the finalist's flan had risen. So Danny didn't labour the point and left the room on lighter feet than he'd entered. In the hallway he quietly zipped his black combat jacket and then clicked the front door shut.

He snaked his glossy lipstick-red Mazda 6, another gift from Salamanca, over Caerphilly Mountain down to Cardiff.

He parked up in the shopping centre multi-storey and then paced along the Hayes past St David's Hall. As he walked down Castle Road, he looked through the glass of a once-regular haunt

142

of his and was almost stopped by the sight of office workers in there supping coffee from big mugs.

Bloody hell, that was the Castle Keep last time I was here, Danny fumed, is nothing sacred?

Caffeine was the new drug of the masses, he guessed. Lager was his livener.

Across the busy one-way street Danny caught flashes of a man in the regalia of a Roman centurion, from feather-clad helmet, silver breastplate, red tunic and knee-high leather boots. Like the Pied Piper, he led a regiment of primary school kids and two teachers through the gates of Cardiff Castle with a face that said, 'I trained at RADA for this.'

Danny crossed the Millennium Bridge not far from the famous stadium of the same name and then banked right past a map of Bute Park and wrought-iron gates opened invitingly.

He then followed the path running parallel with the backs of the houses fronting Cathedral Road.

The pleasant greenery of this inner city parkland escape failed to calm Danny's nerves. He looked up at the houses. Most of the windows were lightened by curtains.

Danny barely noticed dog walkers and joggers sharing the path. He began to slow down but didn't stop. To stand and stare would no doubt set curtains twitching.

His eyes scanned over the roof. Jutting from the continuous tiled roof of the terrace there were several grand chimney stacks and period dormer windows, making the most of the park views.

Danny pictured the sloped window in the background of the video link.

Up ahead he could only see one skylight. It didn't sit well with the period features. He suspected it was there to allow light in but prying eyes out.

What the hell were Mooncraft Films up to? Enough for their number to be noted somewhere in the police investigation unit and to come under siege last night. Seeing Danny's face on their screen, would the raiders now come after him?

He felt certain the answers were four storeys up there. His furtive eyes left the skylight and traced down the black line of an iron drainpipe. The reformed burglar in him noted that three windowsills were within a leg's reach, perfect for taking a breather on his way up.

He pretended to check his watch and then turned to go back the same way. He glanced over one more time and clocked the roof of a greenhouse poking above the scalable wall of the skylight house's back yard. That would be a marker for when he returned under the cover of night.

*   *   *   *

10.55 PM. Darkness couldn't have come soon enough for Danny, who was well-versed in the art of housebreaking though out of practice, enough to put him on edge. He'd caught the fear. It was like the first time all over again. Had he still the bottle?

He didn't want to do this. He'd promised his mum no more. But, having seen the mayhem in that video link, he suspected those under attacked inside would no longer be there, or for that matter care about him dropping in.

As he gripped just above the bottom rung pinning the iron drainpipe to the brickwork, Danny hoped his muscle memory hadn't forgotten the skills that made him known as 'The Rat' among the gang he'd had the misfortune of associating with back in his wayward youth.

One last check he'd pocketed the penknife and a crowbar wedged in his combats.

Danny shimmied his way up the drainpipe with ease. He'd still got it. Keeping his eye in on the saddle had clearly helped both his balance and stamina.

He hoisted himself up on to the sloping tiles, knowing one slip would sent him slapping on the paving some fifty feet below.

With a wide stance and thighs tensed Danny took staccato steps up the tiled roof, navigating the many patches of slimy moss. His legs felt shaky like a new-born foal as he slowly neared the skylight.

144

He afforded the briefest of glances back over at the yellow runway of lights spotlighting the castle's turrets and the green star on top of the Capital Tower. He then looked down at the skylight. It all matched up. This was the one.

Using his penknife, he cut along the seal of the skylight and then loosened the raised window from its frame. He lifted up the window and then dangled his legs into the darkness. He took in a calming lungful of cold night air and then slowly lowered himself in.

From the outside it was a tall building so, as he hung there in the blackness guesstimating the drop, he sorely hoped it was four storeys and not three.

Silently he hung there, suspended until his arms ached. He was well-versed in the art of falling safely. It was an occupational hazard. But he felt lost in this void, with no way of programming his legs when precisely to brace for impact. He found it hard to let go. Release on a leap of faith into the unknown. He kept picturing the desks and cabinets behind Sally.

Plenty of sharp edges and corners to crack a knee or snap a spine, he feared, unless she'd sat in front of a green screen. Was she even real and not some CGI trick?

He pictured Salamanca prowling his box like a caged tiger, ready to pounce.

As with many of his peers in the weighing room, it wasn't the broken bones he was afraid of but the missed rides on the track. With the Cardiff Open just four sleeps away, he simply couldn't bear the thought of missing their date with destiny.

Feeling his arms give way, he quickly centred his balance and thoughts. He wanted to drop on his terms. He then let go. With no visual references, he felt a weird sensation, as if floating through space. He braced his thighs again but a right knee was first to break his fall before flipping back on his arse. He bit his lip. The pain was worse than stepping on a plug. Yet he hadn't heard a snap, so set about searching the place before his knee began to swell and a crowbar-shaped bruise appeared on his right buttock.

At first the light of his pen-torch picked out four long white desks. Danny suspected they had been in neat rows before the evacuation. He then turned and, dominating the right wall, was a large noticeboard. Clearly been a quiet month for Mooncraft Films, Danny reckoned, as he shone light over the largely blank sheet of cork.

At waist height, however, there were a row of A4 sheets. Danny went along the gallery. The first was a picture of Salamanca. Its date matched the same day they'd come to his yard. It was the next photo that suddenly made him forget about his knee and buttock. It was a photo of Artemis, standing proud in a similar side-on pose as Salamanca. Except a thick red marker had crossed out the champion stayer. What did it mean? Was he struck off their list? Was he dead?

Also pinned nearby were four maps. One Danny could see was an aerial satellite shot of Silver Belle Estate. Another was the same of Sunnyside Farm. Were they planning their best points of access and escape?

The third map was of the South Wales region, inked with several red marks like poker dots. How many yards were being targeted?

There was another map showing a coastline. There weren't any marks or place names on this aerial shot. Knowing his time there was precious, Danny found it hard to think clearly. He ripped the maps away and stuffed them in his jacket pocket to check out later. He'd leave the horse photos as he knew them well enough already.

Up higher on the noticeboard it was mostly cork. Looking closer he could see red thumb tacks, some surrounded by the remains of torn paper. From there they looked like a shaving nick covered in loo paper. Why rip and throw them and not those lower down? What could be more damning than the crossed out picture of Artemis? Perhaps there simply wasn't time to clear the whole board. It felt like a hurried, and not all that successful, attempt at destroying evidence. That certainly tied in with Sally's video.

Danny suspected there was a lot more to Mooncraft Films' side-line in DNA analysis.

He turned to the four long desks filling the room. It was more like a school canteen than an office, not that he had ever spent much time in either. As he walked along the first, his hand skimmed over the smooth surface.

Over the smooth surfaces, he caught flashes of lidless biros, coffee rings and snaking power cables. He recalled the shadows on his computer screen.

He couldn't say what he was looking for, but he'd been through too much getting here to leave with nothing.

This is hopeless, he reckoned. His next step made him think differently.

It wasn't what he'd seen that made him freeze but what he'd heard. A loud crack of glass shattering. He stood there silently in the dark, listening out for any reaction through the walls or the floor.

He slowly lifted the offending boot and then shed some light over what he'd trodden on. It was a framed photo. With his free hand, Danny picked it up.

Behind a white cobweb of cracks he could make out a family photo – two adults with a child in the middle.

It reminded him of one he'd had done with Meg and Jack to mark one year of their getting together, except this photo had been badly mutilated. There was a face missing, crudely cut out. From the big, shapeless body beneath, Danny could plainly see it was a man.

He unclipped the backboard and removed the photo. Instantly he recognised the 'mother' in this family group. It was Sally. Her child was beyond interestingly pale, he looked ill.

There was nothing written on the back.

He slid the photo in his jacket pocket. She'd clearly brought this reminder of her nearest and dearest as a memento to help her get through the working day. It was the only apparent sign of humanity in this clinical, sterile environment. But why had her spouse's image been beheaded? What level of secrecy were Sally and her colleagues working under?

147

Perhaps whoever had attacked this place in the video link were capable of hunting down loved ones and taking them, like they did with Artemis.

Danny sensed a hollow sadness in the room. Was it the darkness playing tricks on his mind? A chill crept up his spine. He looked up at the open skylight letting in floods of cold night air.

Just as he was about to leave he noticed a whiteboard not far from the noticeboard. He turned the torch on it. One-by-one he lit up the large red letters S-H-A-L-L-O-W. He whispered the word.

The large letters were inked messily in red marker, suggesting they were written in a panic and meant to be seen. Perhaps red meant danger but why 'shallow'? Was it a warning? A password?

He quickly set about scouring the rest of the room, torch sweeping like a prison searchlight.

Danny flipped open a cylindrical bin and sunk an arm into a snowdrift of shredded paper. He then felt the soft of crushed velvet and silk. He fished out a familiarly vibrant hat and cravat worthy of Carnaby Street in the Swinging Sixties. These were as good as fingerprints in placing Quentin at this scene. Why had Quentin chucked them? Was the firm in trouble and ran when the bailiffs came knocking? Or had he had a fashion epiphany?

Chairs were scattered randomly as if also left in a hurry. There was enough time, apparently, to clear the desks before escaping.

Danny then splashed light into the far corner. He made out what looked like a small TV studio. Was this the production suite where they were cutting the film of Silver Belle Stables? It was a good deal smaller and low-key than Quentin's persona. He now held little hope the promo would even be made, let alone well made.

Both the greenscreen and lighting lamps had a sparkly newness about them, as if they'd still to be used. Danny followed the cable from both. Neither were plugged and the nearest socket in the wall was well beyond reach. There was no sign of any extension lead. Danny doubted they'd ever intended using this equipment. Was it for show? Was this in fact a shell company? A room mocked up as a film studio to mask something far more sinister.

Even this part didn't look or feel right. It was more like a showroom at one of those DIY superstores he was dragged around by his parents as a kid on those painfully slow Sundays.

Suddenly he wanted out of there. He could still feel his knee and behind so went to the only door in the room. He pulled on the steel handle but it appeared locked from the outside. It was then he noticed the door was closer to him than the door frame. He then felt its cool surface. He flicked on the torch. It had been reinforced with steel plate. Danny suspected this wasn't one of the original Victorian features.

He retreated and climbed feelingly on one of the desks. He jumped up to grab the frame of the skylight. As he hung there again, preparing to pull his weight out of there, he heard a thud below and then the beat of footsteps up the stairs. Shit!

A shot of adrenalin gave his arms the boost he needed to pull himself from there in one swift motion. He no longer felt the fear.

Perched on the roof Danny shuffled towards the drainpipe but took an overbold step and felt himself go. His hands came down as brakes as he slid over the mossy tiles.

He felt like a mountaineer without spikes, tumbling down an ice sheet. The tiles then vanished, leaving nothing between him and a crippling four-storey drop to paved patio below. As he felt the pull of gravity his hands reached out for the iron guttering in a final grasp for survival.

Fingers hooked over, he grimaced as he felt the metal rim break the skin. The grimace grew when he saw the brickwork rush towards him as his body whipped down from the sudden change in momentum.

Then there was a sickening thud and groan. He hung there in the dark, slightly swaying like wet washing, waiting for the bricks up close to stop slowly revolving.

It wouldn't be long before the gutter or his hands gave up the strain.

Making sure not to look down at the dizzying drop he glanced over at the drainpipe a good six feet to his left. He heard the piping groan and then felt himself drop a fraction as it bowed under his weight. He felt his jaw and arms tighten.

As he slowly descended he heard the distant chimes he'd heard in the video. It was City Hall somewhere beyond the Bute Park treeline. Must be midnight, he thought, as he dropped the final few feet. He leapt the back wall of the yard and was away into the night.

Chapter 14

WHILE DANNY WAITED FOR THE PC TO WARM UP, he downed two fingers of Glenlivet in the hope of doing the same.

He took out the maps he'd ripped from the wall at Mooncraft Films' former base. There was definitely a red dot stuck on both their neighbouring yards, likes Xs on a treasure map. They were being targeted. He wasn't going mad.

He unfolded the fourth map of the unknown coastline. He put the printout under a light and then a magnifying glass but it had no points of reference or markings, except for what looked like a crudely sketched lighthouse. The coastline was shaped like an inverted L. The lighthouse looked to be on the mainland, unless he was looking at the coastline the wrong way, confusing which sides were land and sea.

Was it Quentin talking to Ralph in the shadow of the stand on Ely's opening day? If it was, they weren't planning a short film on what had become the fifty-ninth racecourse on mainland Britain. More likely they were planning to open a sixtieth somewhere on this mystery coastline he held close, perhaps west of Ffos Las racetrack to cater for the Irish horses and race-fans.

Danny downloaded a large map of the British Isles. The inverted L-shape suggested it was on the west side of Britain. He suspected he'd only need Wales but he didn't want to leave anything uncovered. He printed off the image and then placed it on his desk. With the unnamed map in his left hand and a fresh whisky in his right, his eyes slowly traced the coastline, rapidly flicking between the local and national maps in front of him. He set out at Chepstow on the south easterly border of the principality. He suspected South Wales would most likely be where he'd find a match.

He slowly moved westerly across the south coast, passing Cardiff, Swansea, Llanelli and then Ffos Las racetrack, now the second youngest in Britain after the ribbon had been cut at Ely Park.

He still couldn't figure out why they'd have a blank coastline, unless Quentin and co. knew every inch of it already.

On his journey round Wales he kept turning the mystery map from portrait to landscape in the hope of landing upon an identical match. He'd already covered Pembrokeshire and had moved up the west coast past Aberystwyth. He occasionally glanced across at the Irish coastline but nothing on the desk came close to resembling the bays and estuary on the map in hand.

He'd now travelled beyond the Llŷn Peninsula, Anglesey and the Menai Strait and the northern resorts of Prestatyn and Rhyl. His neck tightened as he neared the northerly end of the Welsh border at Queensferry.

Wales was the only country in the world with a dedicated path covering its entire coast, nearly nine-hundred miles he'd read somewhere. He pinched his tired eyes. Right then he'd felt like he'd actually walked most of it.

He was about to fold both maps up when, just over the Welsh border, he saw the inverted L in the British map.

Lancashire!

More specifically, the area just north of Blackpool.

That was no lighthouse, he thought, it's the Blackpool Tower.

But they'd already got Aintree and Haydock up there, he thought. Perhaps they were planning on reopening Manchester racetrack in Salford. Danny once saw a TV segment on the racetrack which raced there up until the Sixties. It was now student digs and playing fields. Its fate had startling similarities to Ely racetrack. Perhaps, seeing the success of the reboot of the once-famous Cardiff races, they were planning to do the same near Manchester.

He wouldn't put anything past Ralph, who would stoop to anything in restoring the Samuel family's once great wealth. Kidnapping racehorses would most likely be on his radar if the money was right.

It was time to pay the racetrack owner–manager a visit on home turf.

Chapter 15

RALPH'S OFFICE WAS MORE LIKE A PENTHOUSE, larger than any single person could ever need and lit by a glass wall offering a panoramic outlook over the whole of Ely racetrack, something the small crowd of paying punters below could only dream about. Apparently all this topped Ralph's wish-list to the architect even before the first brick had been laid.

Having come from a long line of landed gentry, Ralph clearly wanted to show he was lord of this manor.

Today was a much-lower profile meeting, an aperitif to the upcoming Cardiff Open meeting at the weekend.

Ralph had taken the time and effort to colour print an oil painting Danny recognised as once hanging in the dining room of Samuel House.

It was Ralph's late grandfather Philip Samuel, who founded the original Ely racecourse but the picture was obviously commissioned before his fortunes changed for the worse. He was now pinned on the wall by the office door with his fleshy face peppered by pinpricks. It was then Danny noticed three darts fanned out on the filing cabinet nearby.

'Sit down,' Ralph said and eyed the leather chair opposite. 'I wasn't going to tell you this now but as you're annoying me-'

'This isn't good news is it,' Danny said.

'I'd never lie to you,' Ralph said.

'Well *that's* a lie for starters.'

'Ely Park is on the brink.'

'We only opened the gates last month,' Danny said. 'Even you couldn't have fucked it up in that time.'

'With all the fixed costs, I fear I won't be hitting my targets this year,' Ralph said and ran a hand over his side parting.

'Wouldn't be so sure,' Danny said and glanced over at the dart board.

'That just helps ease the stress you understand,' Ralph said.

'Handy with the tungsten then?'

153

'Having something to aim at helps focus one's eye,' Ralph replied. 'The course will barely break even.'

'But that's good for a first-year business,' Danny replied, 'I've seen Dragon's Den.'

'It's good says someone with nothing riding on it,' Ralph barked, 'other than your bloody horses that is.'

'You're forgetting, or choosing to forget, I *need* a local track, have you seen my fuel bills? It attracts new owners too.'

Ralph rolled his eyes.

'Not just me, all the local yards. A growing racecourse nearby, it's a winner for everyone – if the sea rises, so do all the boats.'

'And *you're* forgetting this wasn't my hare-brained scheme. I could've sold this to developers or become the richest landlord in Cardiff,' Ralph stood and began to pace, as if his feet were getting itchy. 'But when my inheritance could get sucked dry by all this,' Ralph raised his hands to the air, probably born of frustration at the track he'd become chained to. 'Then you'd think differently and want out.'

Danny said, 'We all knew this was a marriage of convenience and you've got jitters, want a divorce.'

'That's more up to you,' Ralph said. 'As we both know you've got something on me.'

'More than just *something* – if the police hear the Prague tapes, the fate of Ely Park will be the least of your worries.' Danny closed in and with little more than a whisper, continued, 'Guess I wear the trousers in this marriage.'

Ralph held his ground and said, 'But if I even get a sniff you're about to go grassing to the police, I'll get to you first.'

'Is that a threat?' Danny asked, knowing the answer.

'I'm guessing you've listened again to my confessional in Prague,' Ralph said, 'then you know what I'm capable of.'

'So where do we go from here?'

'Nowhere,' Ralph said. 'For now, we try to make things work.'

'Who were you talking to by your grandstand?'

Ralph was doing a good job of looking confused.

'Let me jog your memory,' Danny said. 'It was moments before the first Graded race staged at your sacred track and his name was Quentin.'

'I haven't the faintest idea what or who you are talking about,' Ralph said.

'Strange that,' Danny said and then raised his eyebrows. 'He's the director of Mooncraft Films. If he's after doing a short film about the racetrack, I seriously wouldn't bother. He came up to do the same at my yard and nothing came of it.'

'Whoever this Quentin is,' Ralph said, 'I have never met him, nor am I ever likely to.'

'Don't give me that,' Danny said, 'You were chatting in the shadows on race-day. I thought it was odd at the time. After over a year of political and planning disputes and construction headaches, the moment to enjoy the fruit of your labour in the Triumph Hurdle trial and you were chatting by the toilets.'

'Think what you like.'

'I do and I thought him to be a bit of a shit personally,' Danny said. 'And you seemed to be getting on with him.'

Ralph frowned. 'What the hell do you mean by that?'

'Opposites attract, that's all,' Danny said and then put on a sarcastic smile. 'And don't deny you know him, I also saw you chatting and laughing by the parade ring.'

Ralph paused and then smiled, 'That's Gerald.'

'Fat guy,' Danny said. 'Wouldn't be allowed in to the Premier Enclosure with those clothes.'

Ralph kept nodding. 'He had the potential to throw some business my way. What did you expect me to do – shout him down?'

'What kind of business?'

'You helped design the course,' Ralph said. 'Not manage it.'

'Like you say, it's your business not mine, so why slope off when the flagship race was about to start?'

'That's the Cardiff Open,' Ralph said. 'Not some hurdles trial for Cheltenham.'

'Come on Ralph, that Triumph Hurdle trial was the feature race on the card and the Press were everywhere,' Danny said. 'There's a reason why "first impressions count" is a cliché. Good reviews for that meeting would encourage racing folk from up and down the land to travel beyond their local track to Ely Park.'

'Again a potential opportunity had arisen,' Ralph snarled.

'Mapping DNA?'

'What?' Ralph asked. 'Were you eavesdropping?'

'Guess the walls have ears,' Danny said. 'So I'm right.'

'No, I'm afraid you or your spies have been the victim of Chinese whispers.'

'So what was it about?'

'He's from Lancashire and I'm Glamorgan, we were merely remarking on the similarities.'

Danny paused. 'I found a map of Lancashire.'

'Good for you,' Ralph said, as if talking to a small child. 'Have a gold star.'

'It was pinned on the wall at Mooncraft Films,' Danny said. 'You don't know what you're getting into. Bert certainly didn't. Be careful.'

'When am I not?' Ralph then pursed his thin lips as if to suggest that was all.

'What has Toby Gleeson got to do with all this?'

Ralph replied mockingly, 'Ooh I know, what has Toby Gleeson got to do with all this?'

'I bought Powder Keg off the fella. If you're planning to join forces and buy the filly back, good luck with that project as she's no longer mine to sell.'

'All these conspiracies, paranoia is a wicked illness Danny.' Ralph's fist then came down on the finely-polished maple desk. 'You're insane! Get help!'

'I'm not the one chucking arrows at my dead grandpa's head.'

'Wish I could've done it while he was alive,' Ralph replied, glancing over at the dartboard. 'He was nothing but a curse.'

156

Danny was now looking down from this goldfish bowl to the racetrack. 'All this was effectively handed down the family line without you having to graft for a day and you have the cheek to complain, you should see how the other half live, *mate*. Might then see you've got it darn sight better than most of the poor punters down there. And look at this place, you're living in a palace, like some dictator.'

'I wanted to put my stamp on the Ralph Samuel Stand,' Ralph replied.

'And your name,' Danny said.

'It's my money on the line.'

'And where did that come from,' Danny replied. 'The face on that dartboard, reneging on a bet.'

'Bet you want to do the same?' Ralph said, holding the darts. 'Easy to stick up a mug shot of your late pa.'

'At least mine didn't squander the family fortunes and then kill and swindle to give you all this.'

'I haven't the time for this "my dad's better than your dad" bullshit. Now, if you've come here for an argument, you've got what you wanted, leave!'

'Tell me one thing and then I'll go,' Danny said. 'All this touting for extra business – are you being greedy or needy?'

Ralph sat on his tall-back leather swivel chair. He then turned the monitor to show Ely racetrack's website. In bold white text on a red banner across the top there read: Pre-book and, if Salamanca loses in the Cardiff Open, we'll refund all tickets. Ralph tossed a flyer showing the same offer.

'Have these been sent out?' Danny asked.

'Of course,' Ralph said. 'The meeting's almost upon us. With Artemis and Bert off the scene,' Ralph said. 'Salamanca will be a cert, you said as much to the press.' He opened up the *Racing Post* to page six. 'Rawlings Confident Ahead of Ely Test.'

'When was this offer decided?' Danny asked in disbelief. 'It must've been a week or two back to get this up on the website and have these printed out.'

Ralph nodded.

'What if they found Artemis and Bert in the meantime – he was declared among the initial entries months back and Leo has kept him in at the five-day stage, probably hoping it would encourage his father if in hiding somewhere,' Danny said. 'Perhaps the film deal will lure him out. Rumours going round the weighing room there's a contract tabled for a feature length on Bert's life, if there's to be a Hollywood ending of course.'

'If he did emerge I'd be the next in line to kidnap the bastard,' Ralph snarled. 'Artemis winning would mark the beginning of the end for this place.'

'Maybe Quentin, sorry Gerald, assured you Bert would never return.'

'No assurances were made on any front.'

'Apart from giving all gate receipts back if I fuck it up,' Danny snapped. 'How could you do this without even putting it to me? As if there wasn't enough at stake on Saturday!'

'Bookies do it all the time – money back offers if the favourite gets beat.'

'You're not a bookie.'

'You must win.'

'I'll give it my best, I always do.'

'You must win!' Ralph repeated, louder. His fist came down again with a thud. Enough for a framed photo to topple over. His finger pressed the *Racing Post* article.

'Certs get beat, Ralph. You of all should know that, The Whistler here in the Thirties, remember the Pathé footage?'

'I believe it's a risk worth taking,' Ralph said.

'It's a risk we didn't need to take. Most turn up on the day, the place would've been brimming with punters from the city, valleys and beyond, South Wales loves its racing.'

'But we need to know for certain it's a sell-out, don't you understand,' Ralph argued. 'Our accounts are empty and you think *you've* got bills to pay. The accountants believe we'll be forced to call in the receivers if we don't get a full house at this final meeting for five months. This instant cash flow will save us.'

'Save you more like.'

Ralph replied, "'I need a local track, save on fuel bills, attract new owners", isn't that what you said?'

'Don't you think I've got enough on my shoulders without having the future of Ely Park, too?'

'Put it on Salamanca's shoulders, they're broad enough, right?'

Danny said. 'I could easily scratch my runner, go to Newbury or Cheltenham next month. I wasn't the one to come up with this,'

'You will line up and you will win,' Ralph said, 'I trust you implicitly.'

'Even without Artemis, there's still a few possible headaches in the field,' Danny reasoned. 'What about the Bulgarian beast? That jockey will want revenge on me winning on the Continent.'

'He won't trouble you,' Ralph said.

Danny's eyes narrowed. 'What have you done? What did you say to him?' Ralph didn't immediately reply. 'Did you threaten him?'

'No threats,' Ralph broke his silence. 'Exactly the opposite.'

'What?!'

'I made him an offer.'

'Bribery! I've heard of owners, jockeys and trainers fixing races but a racecourse chairman! Ralph, take a bow.'

'Keep it down,' Ralph said, 'it's race-day.'

'Do you want the BHA to revoke Ely Park's licence before you've even filed your first tax return? Is that what you want?'

'I'm trying my best to save this place.'

'No offence but I won't be nominating you for Cardiff Businessman of the Year.'

'He said no,' Ralph said, 'so what's the problem?'

Danny was now pacing between the filing cabinet and the glass wall. 'You really don't understand this sport do you? Just cos he's got some morals doesn't excuse your stupidity.'

'He said no!'

159

'How much?' Danny asked, as if to find out the final bill at a fancy restaurant in Cardiff Bay.

'Forty.'

'Grand!'

Ralph nodded.

'The reserves can't be that bloody dry.'

'I'd only have stumped up after he'd delivered, or not delivered in this case. Would've paid him with some of the gate receipts.'

'And there would've been enough?'

'I could now,' Ralph said. 'Before the promotion flyers went out, pre-bookings for the Cardiff Open meeting were at best twenty per cent in all enclosures.'

'That's because that Ely Park website is right out of '94 and your telephone booking team is called Joyce,' Danny replied.

'And a month on and we're fully booked,' Ralph said triumphantly, 'turning people away in fact. Everyone wants a freebie.'

'So I won't even have any home support, most willing me on to lose to get their cash back. Do something like this again,' Danny said. 'Two words: Prague tapes.'

'And you dare take the moral high ground,' Ralph said. 'You're as bad as me.'

'I'm no murderer,' Danny said. 'Listen to your confessions on the Prague tape and you'll know we aren't the same.'

'The thing about killers,' Ralph said, 'when you've killed once, it stays with you, but it becomes easier by the kill, you almost become conditioned to it.' Danny didn't like where this was heading. 'Ironically the killer almost feels dead inside towards those gone and the families left behind.'

'Think it's best I leave now,' he said and did as much. He went for a walk of the track.

With the Cardiff Open just days away, he wanted to feel the underfoot conditions for himself. Official going descriptions were sometimes as inaccurate as weather reports, with parts of the courses holding water more than others, depending on the rock type.

With a world-class drainage system built in, the Welsh winter would do well to ruin this newly-laid turf.

Good-to-soft, Danny reckoned, soft in parts down the home stretch.

On the infield he noticed the frost sheets were out. They were white and rumpled. From there it looked like the stubborn remnants of a melting snow cover.

Danny checked his smartphone for the five-day forecast from the Met Office. At no point was the temperature set to fall below six degrees.

What the hell was the groundsman Terry up to? Unless they were out there as a precaution. Either way they didn't look clever. He emailed Ralph to say as much. This place needed to look a picture for when the national and trade media returned en masse.

It was starting to get dark when he'd returned to his Mazda. He could hear a hiss of air. Danny kicked the tyres. There was some give in the back driver's side. Danny crouched and could hear the air louder from down there. He removed the spare from the boot and began to change the tyre. The final nut was proving difficult to tighten. He reached into his back pocket for the pen-torch but winced at touching his tender buttock.

Where the hell was it? When the answer came, a shot of adrenalin made him bolt upright.

In a flash he was back in Cathedral Road. As he pictured hanging there in the dark he again heard the thud from below. He now realised it hadn't come from the owner of the flat below but his own pocket. The torch had fallen from his trousers. His arse was aching that much he hadn't noticed the torch was missing until now.

That wouldn't normally make him change his plans, but this particular torch had been indelibly inked with D. RAWLINGS.

If whoever attacked the top-floor offices that night returned, they'd now have a name to put to his face on the screen in the video link.

He left the car parked up and headed across town to Cathedral Road. He felt like he was seriously pushing his luck returning to the same place but, if those inside had taken the time to rip off evidence from the wall, he certainly wasn't going to leave any incriminating evidence in there.

Chapter 16

DANNY BRIEFLY LOOKED SOMEWHERE IN THE DIRECTION of Bute Park but saw nothing, only the faded yellow lights of the castle turrets and city centre beyond. He feared an evening dog walker or an insomniac might make out his black shape up there on the roof. He wouldn't blame them for thinking he was either up to no good, or suicidal. And it would only take one call.

What would his excuse be? He locked himself out when he didn't even live on this road, or he was a roofer doing a night shift. He couldn't pick out any movements in the dark down below, so cagily turned on the spot.

Only gravity had kept the skylight down, both the seal and lock were still broken. That probably meant the owners hadn't returned since his last visit.

He lifted the window wide and carefully lowered himself to once again hang there in the dark. This time he knew it was a mere four foot drop and didn't hesitate in letting go. His knees acted like shock absorbers as they bent on impact.

In the grey-blue light from the window above, he set about feeling for his missing personalised torch.

'I told you not to come,' came from his right.

Danny stopped searching and jumped to his feet. 'Sally?'

'I warned you.' Her voice shook, either from rage or fear.

'I had to,' Danny replied.

His enlarged pupils could make out her blue face and lips remain motionless, as if pulled from a frozen lake.

The room's strip lights then flickered on. First thing Danny saw was the gun in Sally's hand. She was stood by the switch between the TV studio and the reinforced door. She looked down at the gun Danny was eyeing. 'You can never be too careful.'

She came closer.

He asked, 'How did you get in?'

'Front door,' she said and looked up at the open skylight. 'I don't need to ask you the same.'

He could now see the noticeboard had been stripped of the remaining maps, along with the photos of Artemis and Salamanca. Perhaps they were relevant after all.

'Are you wondering why they'd taken the pic of your horse?' she asked.

Danny shook his head. 'I'm only concerned they'll take the real thing.'

'We played them like pawns in a game you could never win,' she replied coolly. 'We valued those horses greatly in meeting our goals.'

'So you did take Artemis,' Danny said. 'And Bert was some unwanted by-product. All for this prized DNA code.'

'We helped him disappear,' Sally said flatly. 'Our goal was never Salamanca.'

'Artemis then?'

'When I first came to Wales,' Sally said. 'There was a bunch of touristy leaflets on the table of my rented apartment. One read, "Visit the beauty of Wales". Well, it turns out that beauty isn't just skin deep.'

Danny looked over at the whiteboard that still hadn't been wiped of the word SHALLOW.

'That was our code to all workers to abort,' she replied.

'What did they know?'

'Up here it was our job to study results from data. We wore gloves as if this were a laboratory. Our hard-drives were taken to be crushed routinely, so not to leave electric fingerprints for the police or valuable data for rivals. It was like working for the secret service. Our orders were to leave this place as an empty shell, exactly as we found it. We were contracted to complete a job and the only clause in bold was like some Stalinist gagging order.' She too glanced over at the whiteboard. 'When that was written, we were already in too deep, about to head for the shallower waters.'

'What was the data?'

'Telling you would seal both our fates,' she replied. Danny hoped that was a joke, but she'd only raised the gun not a smile.

'Must be one hell of a secret,' Danny said.

'One of national importance.'

'You can trust me.'

'Shouldn't it be saying that, Danny, you did get my number from the back of a police calling card,' Sally said. 'I've told you all I know, I worked here as one of the number crunchers, not out in the field.'

'Don't give me that,' Danny said.

'It was protocol,' she said. 'No one knew what the other was working on, a bit like working for GCHQ in Cheltenham.'

'Where did you move from?'

'Lancashire.'

'You moved with Quentin Crawford then,' Danny replied, recalling the topic Ralph and Quentin had supposedly been discussing at the grand opening of Ely Park.

'Quentin?' she asked.

'Gerald then,' Danny replied, recalling the fake director also had a fake alias. Danny wondered if it was Gerald in that defaced family photo he'd stumbled upon when last here, now lining the inside pocket of his jacket. 'He's your lover.'

She laughed. 'Employer ... former employer.'

'If you were fired by Mooncraft Films,' he said. 'Why the hell would you risk coming back? I saw your eyes through that camera over there, you can't fake that kind of fear.'

'There was no Mooncraft Films to be fired from.'

Danny watched as a seam of light running along the gun's barrel came and went as it shook from her laughing.

'Why the studio then?' Danny asked, pointing to the area in the corner with the lighting and cameras.

'That's more of a smokescreen than a greenscreen. From there I'd update our business partners with regular progress reports.'

Danny recalled the secure link she'd set up in his office. 'What kind of partner are they for you to hide behind an encrypted link?'

'We had plenty to lose if all this got out,' Sally said. 'But they are bigger than us, farther to fall with a reputation to ruin.'

165

'Why was our chat encrypted? What damage could I do their reputation?'

'You're nothing special,' she replied. 'Yet more protocol.'

'If you were in too deep,' he said, 'it'd take something powerful to draw you back, to take this risk,' Danny added. 'Something that meant a lot personally, emotionally, something irreplaceable. What were you looking for when I dropped in?'

They then stood there in the silent depths of night. She appeared to be sticking to the gagging order.

She replied, 'I could ask the same of you, this isn't the first time you've dropped in.' She looked up at the broken skylight. 'I felt the cool night air. The seal was broken when I arrived before you. The maps on the board over there are gone, including the aerial shot of the Silver Belle Estate.'

'That doesn't place me here,' Danny replied.

'But this does,' she said and held out Danny's personalised pen-torch. Like the gun, its shaft gleamed under the strip lights.

Danny fished out the family photo and showed her the bargaining gift. 'Guess we both came back for something.'

'You found it!' she said excitedly. 'Hand it me now!'

'I guess defacing loved ones was also protocol,' Danny said.

Danny couldn't figure out why she was so desperate to have back the mutilated photo. It wasn't for her faceless partner and she could take a snap of herself easily enough. That left the pale child. 'I'm sorry.'

'For what?'

'He died, didn't he?'

Her wet eyes began to sparkle and her bottom lip quivered as she said, 'Leukaemia.'

She was at least part human after all, Danny thought.

'My little Harry,' she croaked.

He then edged forward and placed the photo on the floor at the midway point between them. His eyes never left hers as he backed away.

She rushed forward and swiped it from the floor. She completed the exchange by rolling the pen-torch over to Danny, who made sure he'd pocketed it deeper this time. While down there he saw a credit card sized piece of paper she'd also left there.

'Good,' she said. 'You asked what they'd done to Bert, the answer will be on the other end of that line.'

'Already got one of these from the police,' Danny said.

'I very much doubt that,' she said. 'Look at it and then ring it.'

Penned on the card, Danny saw another mobile number.

'You sent those threats,' Danny said.

She nodded. 'A countdown to the day Artemis would be taken.'

'So he beat you to it,' Danny said.

'With our help,' she said. 'He disappeared from the public eye and all the threats.'

'But it's you who sent the threats,' Danny said. 'Why then help him?'

'Because they were empty threats,' she said. 'We just wanted him off the scene and we soon saw, much like yourself, his weakness was his star horse. Pawns in a game, Danny. We simply gained his trust after faking a short film of his yard,' she said. 'And then suggested he should fake a kidnapping on a very public stage.'

Danny recalled the Mooncraft Films card in the shoebox.

'Where is he?'

'The answer is on that number. *You* must call.'

'Why don't *you* ring it?'

'Like the rest of the team, I don't want to risk being implicated in the disappearance,' she said.

'Bollocks,' Danny said. 'This is a trap, whoever is on this number must be involved and you want my number to appear on their phone records. You seem fine with me being implicated.'

'How is that possible? Remember this is all news to you, having played no part in it. Just say you were responding to a tip off and let the police do the rest. If anything you'll be the hero. The man who set Bert free. He won't press charges.'

'How can you be so sure?'

'That's a direct line to Bert.'

'Why now after all this time?'

'We have all we want from him,' she said.

'What do I tell Bert?' Danny said. 'That it's safe for his return.'

'Just say the word "shallow", then hang up.'

'What if I go to the police?'

'With what?'

'This number for starters.'

'Like I said, it'll be disposed of by then.'

'They'll find the safe house.'

'Where is it?' she asked, tilting her head slightly, so her red fringe flopped down over her forehead. 'I haven't said.'

'But Bert will.'

'He was there out of his own volition. This faked kidnapping was his saviour, so he believes. He jumped at the chance.' She glanced at her wrist. 'If you have a conscience, you'll set Bert free. He's relying on you.'

'Where will you go?' Danny asked.

'Do you honestly think I'd tell you?' she said. 'While Bert is emerging from hibernation, the rest of us will be doing quite the opposite, scattering like bugs searching for a dark place. Bert has been briefed to check in at the police station, explain he'd suffered a breakdown due to pressures of training the champion.'

'Ex-champion,' Danny corrected.

'By then he will have disposed of the phone we'd given him. I trust you can play along with this story, it's in your interests if you want the easy life. Oh, and I wouldn't leave the front way after me, if you don't want to be placed here. Nice doing business with you, Danny.'

'Business?' Danny called after.

But with that, she was gone, leaving Danny with a tangle of thoughts and theories.

He flicked off the light and then pulled himself up through the skylight.

As Danny nervously glanced back he nearly lost his footing again. The skylight remained shut.

Recalling how he'd been launched from there like a lifeboat last time he'd been there, he walked the tiles slower with a wide stance, as if taking to an ice rink.

Feeling his legs shake, he reached out and clung to one of the giant chimney stacks.

It was then, down in the park, he spotted two orange dots glowing brightly. Two people had lit up. He prayed they were teens. At this hour no sane adult would be hanging about.

While they were there Danny couldn't make his escape. And he couldn't stand up here all night, so he took a calculated risk by spotlighting them with his torch.

In the white circle of light he could see there were two hoodies sitting on the back of the park bench.

They all froze from guilt; Danny stuck on a roof, kids puffing away in a padlocked park.

Shielded by the steadier of the chimney stack, he kept the light there, hoping to flush them out.

They fled like frightened foxes into the night, perhaps scared their parents would find out. Danny replaced the torch and refocused his efforts on getting down with skeleton intact.

He stopped where he saw a dark hole in the guttering, the mouth of a drainpipe.

He crouched to lower his centre of gravity and then inched down the shiny slate, shuffling like E.T. He then lay flat on his stomach. Parallel with the edge of the roof he reached over the guttering clogged with a decaying sludge of leaves. He could feel the sturdy iron pipe clamped to the wall.

As he swung his legs over the edge he was grateful he'd been watching his weight in the build-up to Salamanca's tilt at the Cardiff Open, gripping the ironwork for his life. He didn't dare look down as he slowly descended; feet and hands desperately searching for the struts holding the pipe to the old brickwork.

169

Whenever he felt his arms burn, he'd use the slender gap between pipe and wall as a foot-hole for the tips of his boots. This support acted as stirrups, holding him steady while he allowed the blood to return to his biceps.

He dropped the final five feet. As he cleared the back wall, he saw the park trees ahead light up. Someone behind had flicked on a light.

As he fled the scene, he tore up Sally's card. If the police stopped him now, he didn't want to be done for two crimes. He poured the pieces into a park bin, relying on his photographic memory instead.

He jumped the ornate Bute Park gates and kept up the pace as he crossed back over the Millennium Bridge.

Casually he pulled his mobile from his jacket and punched in the number. When the rings stopped he said, 'Shallow.'

He sounded louder at that ungodly hour. As Sally had hinted, there was no reply, just the sound of the dial tone again. Presumably Bert had heard enough. One word was all it took to set him free.

Chapter 17

THAT'S NOT BLOODY BLACKPOOL TOWER!

Just minutes ago, sitting there at his office desk, Danny had recalled Ralph and Gerald had been discussing the similarities of Glamorgan and Lancashire at Ely's grand opening.

He'd immediately set about discovering just how similar they were, typing the two counties into a search engine. Thousands of results came back, from the War of the Roses associated with Lancashire to Welsh male voice choirs of Glamorgan to the closure of coal mines in both regions.

Maybe the red dots on the Glamorgan map were former pits, he guessed. Danny recalled Sally describing the beauty of Wales as more than skin deep.

Perhaps those ghost mines were being readied to be reopened, like the rebirth of Ely Park.

Danny clicked on the 'search news' link.

To help filter the results Danny added Gerald to the search box.

He clicked on an archived article from the finance section of the local paper. Businessman Gerald Wately, who recently acquired the metal recycling plant in the Canton area of Cardiff, has diversified his portfolio by setting up the production company Mooncraft Films.

Danny then narrowed the search to within the last twelve months.

Seeing the results of the new search his jaw dropped slightly. There were pages of links to internet and newspaper articles from both Lancastrian and national media covering recent earth tremors across the Red Rose county.

Suddenly Danny's damp palms gripped the sloping leather arms of his office chair a little tighter.

Was he about to relive the unsettling turn he'd suffered by the schooling ground?

That morning when he was convinced the ground had shifted beneath his feet. It was only when Meg, who was sitting on Ronny at the time, had laughed it off, he blamed himself. He had since become convinced it had been some fit or panic attack. Was the answer on the computer screen? Had he found the link between the two counties?

Any ease in anxiety Danny felt from discovering it wasn't a potentially career or even life-ending disease was quickly reversed once he read on.

He clicked on a BBC article. It appeared there was a first quake not far from Blackpool on April 1 which read 2.3 on the Richter scale. Danny checked the date of the article June 2; this was no April Fool's joke. Reportedly there then came another tremor further up the Fylde coast that measured 1.4 on May 27.

Was that an aftershock? But the UK didn't lie on any major fault lines. So what the hell was causing these? Then he began to make the link himself.

He searched: 'causes Lancashire earthquakes'. His eyes lit up as the screen filled with relevant results.

Apparently these quakes were the likely result of a process known as fracking, where a potent mix of water, sand and chemicals are blasted into fissures running through shale rock deep underground. The pockets of gas are released and then extracted to the surface.

He then searched for: 'fracking Lancashire' and widened it to January 1 – five months earlier. According to a trade magazine on energy and environment, several companies had applied for the licence to test drill designated sights in Lancashire to discover the extent of shale gas deposits under there.

There was a list of those companies in their failed bid to secure the tenure from the government. Among them one name made Danny stop reading – Gerald Wately.

Danny whispered, 'As they say on Crimewatch, also answers to the name of Quentin Crawford.'

He returned to the map of the Lancashire coastline.

That's not bloody Blackpool Tower!

More likely, that sketch of a large metal structure was the location where they'd granted the licence to drill the test fields.

Gerald had clearly given up on that dream to be a pioneer in British shale gas exploration and instead turned to recycling as

172

his road to riches. So why had he kept the map pinned to the notice board.

Danny then returned to the map of South Wales, dotted with red. Holy crap!

Seemed Gerald hadn't given up on the dream. No wonder Danny had felt the earth shift beneath him.

Danny turned the search closer to home. Sally had described her secret was of national importance. When he discovered South Wales was sitting on one of the largest sources of shale gas in Europe, with a potential £70 billion windfall lying there waiting to be tapped, he knew she hadn't exaggerated.

By the keyboard, he looked again at the *Racing Post*'s front page hogged by Bert's beaming face taken at yesterday's news conference beneath the headline: Artemis Back on Ely Trail.

Danny sighed.

With Mooncraft Films seemingly wound up, he knew there was only one place Danny might corner the ringleader Gerald Wately. He searched for the Cardiff address of Onyourmetal Ltd.

Chapter 18

DANNY SPIED THROUGH THE WIRE FENCING.

He then rattled the towering gates, crowned by razor barbs and two whirring CCTV cameras pointing his way. There was also a sign: ONYOURMETAL Ltd.

Didn't skimp on security, Danny noted, seemed there was something more than scrap metal in there.

He felt for the hoof-nipper, pushed deep in his jacket pocket. That's where the makeshift wire-cutters would stay, as if he left his mark here there'd be an excuse to look back over that security footage.

Up ahead he could make out a large warehouse with a Portakabin nearby. Off to his right there was a line of several large metal containers and a forklift truck. Poking out of the nearest was a car chassis, a cooker, some piping and rusty iron panels.

From the outside looking in, with working capital being used and a store to house stock, Onyourmetal didn't appear to be a shell company.

With all the recent metal thefts, perhaps they were just anal about security.

Danny shied away from the cameras. He then dialled the phone number on the company's website. He didn't mind it showing up on their records. He wanted Gerald to know he was on to him.

As it rang, he slipped the phone in his pocket and came back into camera shot. He stood there eyes focused on the cabin window, waiting for a shimmer of light or the flick of a shadow. Any sign of life.

From the ringing in his pocket he could tell he'd got through. He could also hear a similarly faint ring come from the cabin.

Seemed like they'd locked up and gone home early.

Danny then tracked the wire fencing round to a secluded side path, regularly looking up for a break in those barbs, like metal spiders on a thread. On the other side there were tall, thick ferns, presumably to hide whatever business was going on there. He noticed the razors were overhanging his side of the fencing to ensure no one could swing themselves over. Once in he could quite easily find the momentum to clear them on his way out.

He came upon a wooden public footpath sign but Danny saw it as an opportunity. He felt the rough splintering wood and wished he'd brought gloves. He slipped his jacket off and tied it round his waist and faced the fence.

He'd spent his working life balancing on toes in stirrup irons, so he was like a seasoned free-solo climber finding footholds in the diamond-shaped gaps of the fence.

When he neared the barbs he untied his jacket and slung it over them as a safety net if he messed up. He reached behind for the wooden footpath signpost and then leapt across. Quickly his strong thighs wrapped around the pole to hold him there. He shimmied his way to the top and balanced there, with his weight on the main post and using the top of the sign for balance.

On three he leapt over the barbs into the wall of ferns. The clatter of snapping branches broke his fall to the ground. He checked for lameness, just a few cosmetic cuts and nicks. He then quickly climbed up the fence to unsnag his jacket. While up there, he snipped some wire with the hoof clippers.

They wouldn't miss a few inches, he thought.

He rustled through heavy foliage and then crouched in the shade, finding his bearings and his breath. He felt confident he was alone there. Any reputable guard dog would've been hanging from his arm by now.

Whether it was his intuition as an ex-burglar but the place felt dead. He didn't even bother to cover himself or his tracks as he crossed the open space in broad daylight.

He felt it wasn't in his interest to go knocking the door of the cabin. If anyone was there lying in wait, they'd have more questions than he had. If it was empty, there'd likely be a camera, given the rest of the security here.

Instead he tried the padlocked doors to the warehouse. He bent the finger of fence-wire into a hook and began to work the lock. When it clicked he dropped the heavy mechanism to the ground and rolled the metal doors apart.

There was a high flat roof and panelled walls, all metal. Probably a by-product of the company, Danny reckoned.

Stepping in there the clap of his first footfall bounced off the walls. It was like walking into a giant kettledrum.

When Danny's eyes adjusted he was surprised by what he could see or more like, what he couldn't see. He'd expected a great mountain of metal scrap ready to be crushed and reformed. But all he could distinguish through the grainy gloom were six white towers rising from the ground, each wider at the base than the top. They were like ghosts stood there silently in the centre of this closed space.

From outside the fence it looked like a fully functioning metal recycling plant. Inside told a very different story, Danny thought, one he was intrigued to uncover.

Squinting, Danny edged closer. What on earth?

With each step he felt it get colder. Something about this place made his skin crawl. Perhaps it was that burglar's intuition again.

Danny had only just made sense of these otherworldly shapes when there was a flurry of footsteps from behind. He hadn't even time to turn when he heard and then felt an almighty crack on the back of his skull. He saw the roughened ground come rushing up at him and then blackness.

*   *   *   *

Eyes shut and face stuck to the rough concrete, Danny was about to cry out when he suddenly recalled his final memory. He lay on his side, probably as he'd landed. He wasn't sure how long he'd been like that. He could still sense daylight from the open rolling doors.

Staying perfectly still, Danny could hear footsteps nearby, pacing back and forth. Whoever it was, they must still have the weapon that made his head now thump like all his worst hangovers rolled into one.

Tension made the tiny muscles around his eyes start to bubble. Suddenly the pacing stopped somewhere behind his back.

There was a groan as Danny felt arms sit him up. There was no way the attacker would do this unless he was convinced he was dead, Danny presumed.

For now he felt it best to play along and didn't put up any resistance as he was then dragged like a rag doll several yards though it felt like more to his arse. Then the attacker's arms hooked under Danny's sweaty armpits and hoisted him up enough, so only the heels of his boots provided any friction. Danny's back was pulled against the chest of his carrier and he could feel their heartbeat. The man was either unfit or in a panic. He sensed they were now making better progress but, fearing their destination, he suspected that was no good thing.

Several times Danny was tempted to put up a fight, but knew he'd soon be knocked down again, even if he'd managed to stand in the first place. He'd let his head flop forward, so his chin now rested on his own chest.

He was dropped unceremoniously to face-plant the tarmac.

Danny thought the area behind his shut eyes would explode.

Bright pink eyelids and the movement of cool air told Danny he was outside again.

Where the hell was his body being disposed? When he heard a motor fire up, he pictured the line of metal crushers and then feared the answer.

He'd wished his remains to be buried alongside his brother not recycled into part of some industrial machine. He then heard the rumble of tyres grow louder. He felt a sharp prod in two places on his left arm, enough to bruise. It then backed off. Danny lifted his arm off the ground slightly as he sensed it come again, too angular and hard for human arms. Danny was now picturing the forklift truck.

Hoisted into the air, Danny let gravity take his floppy arms and legs. He felt another rumble and had a good idea where he was going. Mentally he was already preparing to voluntarily jump off the metal arms into the crusher and then use the heavy goods inside as a climbing frame out of the container. But when he opened his eyes and looked down, he saw it actually contained very little, just a few small scraps. He panicked and rolled over but the arms of the forklift were now reaching out over the metal crusher, suspending him there. He waved at the glass of the driver's cabin reflecting his tormented face but the forklift's teeth began tilting forward to offload. He began to feel the pull of gravity and desperately gripped the metal arms keeping him there, but they soon began to slip through his grasp and he felt himself go.

He saw the sharp, twisted metal strips littering the iron floor. Like a pilot, he searched for the best place to crash-land.

With an echoing thud, he managed to hit the floor feet first like a cat. He was glad of some give in the iron shell.

Calling upon one of the wall as a crutch, he looked up at the black shape of Gerald peering in against the white sky.

Danny asked up, 'What are you waiting for? Why not just leave me here for dead? You're relishing this, sick fucker.'

'I could feel your pulse under your arms, Danny, you were only making a fool out of yourself by playing dead. Still, no need to play any longer,' Gerald said and smiled.

'You took Artemis, didn't you, Sally told me as much,' Danny said, words rattling this filthy iron coffin. He held his side. It felt like he'd popped a hernia. 'And then tried with Salamanca.'

'Enough about your four-legged friends,' Gerald scoffed. 'There is a much bigger prize up for grabs.'

'I know the license to drill Lancashire went elsewhere, so you set your sights closer to home, and began mapping for shale gas in Wales. But you didn't bother wasting any more time or money applying through official channels here. It never did you any good before. There are other ways to get ahead in this race, eh Gerald? Just turf out poor sods like Bert and away you go. Who needs rules and regulations? Better for you if it's a free-for-all, dig up the valleys and be done with it.'

'I may well have misjudged you Danny,' Gerald replied. 'It seems you in fact know a little too much.' He then disappeared behind the lip of the crusher.

'Where are you going?' Danny shouted, 'That day you turned up at the yard as film director, Quentin Crawford, it was the land and not the horses you wanted to survey.' Only his echo came back. 'I'm not finished!'

'I think you are,' Gerald replied distantly.

The metal floor began to shake from the loud roar of an engine warming up.

At first Danny heard the clunk of metal on metal. He then looked down to see a rusty section of piping slowly being rolled towards him by the ten feet of wall on its inexorable path, taking everything with it.

Shit!

Gerald wasn't using scare tactics. He meant Danny dead.

The place reeked of oil as he desperately searched for scraps. He picked up a five-by-one metal strip and propped it up against one of the fixed walls as a makeshift ramp out of there.

As soon as he placed a boot on the steel sheet he felt a sinking feeling as it gave under his weight. There was no chance he'd get the height needed to reach for the lip of the container.

Think, Danny, think!

Shouting would do no good out there; the only person in earshot wanted him crushed. He froze for a second when an idea hit him.

With his hands he bent the sheet like a wobble board. He'd use that to his advantage. He gauged the length of the metal sheet and then waited for the metal walls to slowly grind closer and closer.

Given he had just one attempt to get out of there alive, he remained remarkably calm. Perhaps subconsciously his mind was aware the fight or flight impulse would do more harm than good down there.

Like a tsunami there grew a collection of debris being picked up and carried by the unrelenting walls, from the springs of a mattress to a stripped shell of a car engine.

Against all survival instincts, he then waited there gripping the metal scrap waist high as the walls came for him.

His eyes shot between the moving walls, eight feet apart … now seven. It was almost time. He crouched and held the metal sheet level, about a foot above the floor. When the walls caught the ends with a clunk, Danny made sure to push the centre upwards, ensuring the metal bowed skyward.

As it began to form a humpback, Danny tested one foot on the highest point of the centre. He then put his weight on the makeshift bridge. Mercifully it took his weight.

With every second he grew taller and the walls grew nearer, but as the metal began to creak under the stress, he feared the breaking point was near. It became a game of stick or twist, life or death.

Or perhaps the ends would ping away from the walls. Either way a fall now would mean a slow crushing end.

The lip of the container's wall was now within grasp. He had just one chance and made sure to tense his race-fit thighs. Priming the muscles, he launched himself from the metal plate and desperately stretched his arms and fingers.

As he felt the drag of gravity, his fingers had extended enough to hook over the rim. They tightened their grip as his body and face slapped against the wall. By turning his head in time he'd saved his nose.

While he hung there, he saw the shadow of the other wall creep up his side of the container, as if being cornered by Death himself.

With jerky movements he adjusted to get a firmer grip and then, with all his might, he pulled himself up and then over the wall.

As he fell the ten feet almost gleefully, he heard a loud snap of the makeshift bridge giving out inside the can. Gerald would soon return expecting to see a mess of flesh and cracked bone. He would be disappointed.

Danny didn't have the time or inclination to realise just how close he'd come to being squashed alive. He sprung to his feet and appreciating he'd already pushed his luck too far, didn't go back for a closer look at the six towering ghosts.

Instead he escaped the way he came, easily clearing the outwardly pointing barbs as he swung himself over the border fence. He now knew Gerald wasn't just a metal dealer.

Chapter 19

ELY PARK'S CHANGING ROOM. Cardiff Open Steeplechase
T-minus sixteen minutes.

Four races in, the smells of newness like paint and wood
polish had succumbed to a heady mix of deodorant, leather and
man-sweat.

The atmosphere was electric in there, showers and sauna
were steaming hot, jockeys were changing and laughing
nervously and the aproned valets were a blur as they loaded
saddle cloths with lead weights, polished riding boots and hooked
up tack along with coloured silks for the riders. The clear-storey
windows had all clouded up.

A wall-mounted flatscreen was showing the Channel 4
team already analysing the runners and riders for the feature.

Danny placed a small black box under some of his smelly
socks in the side compartment of his kit bag. Should be safe
enough there, he thought.

He then went over to wish the best of British to Bert, who
was busy unpacking his kit bag in a lonely far corner.

He thought he might regret releasing Bert from hiding
shortly before the final declaration stage of the Cardiff Open. But
secretly he was glad Artemis was among the seven runners due to
line up for the big one. He felt it would be something of a win by
default without the champ in opposition. Though he'd never let on
to Ralph, who, staking the gate receipts and the future of Ely Park
on Salamanca winning, wouldn't feel the same way.

Before Bert had strapped his back protector secure, Danny
caught sight of the veteran's muscled torso.

He'd clearly used his time away from the game well,
Danny thought begrudgingly.

But how many races are won or lost on a six-pack, he
argued, it was aerobic fitness that counted. That's why most
mornings – come rain or shine – he'd jogged a lap of the cross-
country course on the estate before taking Salamanca back over
that same ground.

'What the bloody hell happened, Bert?' Danny asked. 'Or have you sold your story?'

Bert turned and sat on the bench, pulling on his white breeches. 'It all started with this threatening letter, saying they'd take Artemis and if I went to the police, they'd skin me and my horse alive.' Danny sat down beside. 'One by one the letters arrived, except these were counting down the days till they'd come get us. So, before it was time, I thought it best to jump before I was pushed. In my darkest hour I even considered parking up by the Severn Bridge and leaving a letter; scary, thinking back. But when the heavy fog was forecast I thought of a plan that would get my disappearance in all the papers, the kidnappers were sure to get wind that way.'

'Your son was out there on the track,' Danny said. 'I paid him a home visit and saw his costume.'

Bert sighed. 'At least he managed to do something right. For a quick getaway, he'd parked up the horsebox on the stretch of land near the start of the home-straight on the outside of the track. As the tapes rose, he'd already snapped away a segment of that removable plastic railing for us to lead Artemis away in that peasouper,' Bert was now buttoning his yellow and blue silks. He then tugged and pinched his gloves to a comfortable fit. 'Leo drove us to my car a few miles away, I couldn't as I'd had a drink to calm the nerves you see. He then returned to the yard before the police had chance to contact him with the bad news. I went to the one place I knew like home, Lyme Regis, crashed at a pub.'

'Where the hell did you the keep the horse in a pub?'

'Nowhere. Leo took the horsebox with Artemis in it. I reckoned he'd get too upset leaving the familiar sounds, smells and sights of home. Anyway, I didn't want being pulled over on my way to Dorset by a patrol car in a van marked with the stable logo. Leo was back in time to take the call from the policeman. We agreed he should put him in Marcher Lord's box, just in case police did a stocktake of the horses. Mind, they wouldn't know a horse's arse from its elbow. He's a good kid, Leo, heart in the right place and wouldn't hurt a fly.'

Danny felt his face where he'd had a close shave with an axe. 'Maybe not a fly.'

'You know what the road to hell is paved with, Danny,' Bert said. 'He only meant to please me by taking Salamanca that day, get you back for taking two of ours.'

'If you'd seen them, Bert, one was circling his box; another was biting the stable door. It was like *One Flew Over the Cuckoo's Nest* there.'

'Believe me, when he called and told me, I won't repeat what I said, but he hung up knowing I was far from pleased.'

Danny could believe that. Leo had returned Salamanca to his box in the time they'd taken to search the Silver Belle Estate.

'Why the postcard?'

'In the press you were talking up Salamanca as the all-time great and somehow Artemis was now the fallen champion. I quote, "The king was dead long live the king,"' Bert said. 'And for your record, Arty and I weren't beaten at Chepstow, we took voluntary retirement.'

'They twisted my words,' Danny said. 'Since when did you believe the papers?'

'Either way, I risked a one-off visit to see Artemis, and pushed that through your letterbox as a nudge and a wink to you that I was still about, waiting in the wings for my return.'

'Why leave it blank?'

'Couldn't trust you wouldn't go bleating to the police,' Bert replied. 'The plan was working, I was lying low for the threats to go and then I would be back from oblivion, just like this place, to pick up as I had left off – thankfully in time for this, feels like a retrial to get justice for Chepstow.'

'And were you ever holed up at that holiday cottage of yours,' Danny asked.

'Nope, too obvious, first place both the police and the kidnappers would check,' Bert said. 'I called in a favour from the local landlord as back-payment for training fees he owed for a filly of mine, Seven Dollars, not fit for being a morning hack let alone a racer that one, but somehow forgot to tell him as much.'

'Tufty,' Danny said. 'She still had her winter coat when I rescued her.'

'That's her,' Bert confirmed. 'Probably a good job, I wouldn't leave my worst enemy with Leo and a pair of clippers.'

Danny could believe that too.

Shame Leo had focused all his time on keeping Artemis sweet, Danny thought, the kid clearly knew which one paid his keep.

'It's good that she's on the mend,' Danny said, 'grew a soft spot for that one.'

'You can have her,' Bert said. Danny looked sceptical. 'No catch. That landlord certainly ain't having her back. She's probably only worth seven dollars, less than a haircut.'

'Wouldn't be so sure,' Danny said. 'Reckon she could scrub up well that one and I've still got a box going spare.'

Bert had seemingly mellowed since his return to the scene. The barrier between them appeared to have crumbled.

'Friends?' Danny asked.

'Ask me after,' Bert replied curtly, hands refusing to let go of his whip and goggles. That was more like the Bert he knew.

'I take it you haven't gone to the police with all this,' Danny said.

Bert shook his head.

'Then how can you trust I won't.'

'You would've done already.' Bert leant close and added, 'And thank you.'

'For what?'

'I think we both know.'

'No we don't.'

'I wouldn't be back here in time for today without you,' Bert replied.

'Why'd you reckon that?'

'Think deeper,' Bert said and smiled knowingly. He then left for the scales and his horse.

Danny frowned. How could Bert know it was Danny making the call to set him free? Surely he couldn't recognise his voice from just one word.

On his way to the parade ring, after weighing out, Danny repeatedly said, 'Shallow.'

Don't think I've got a lisp, he thought. Paranoia soon left him when he remembered his neighbour Bert would've had his mobile number on file in case of an emergency.

When he spotted Salamanca above the heads of the other connections on the far side of the parade ring, Danny was back in race-mode.

Mounted up on Salamanca he was then led round the ring quietly by Meg, every move covered closely by a personal TV cameraman. Danny looked over at Bert, who was getting the same special treatment over the other side of the ring.

Understandable as they were the stars of this show but in racing, stars didn't always shine. He just hoped, for the sake of the racetrack at least, both would bring their A-game.

Danny looked at the imposing specimen that was Artemis and couldn't believe he'd led that half-tonne powerhouse across valley, believing it was the six-year-old Marcher Lord.

Inspecting his chief rival leave the ring and gallop off down to the start, he now looked as fit and as fresh as the jockey on top. There wasn't an ounce of excess flesh on the bay belly of Artemis, who had also won best turned out. He'd clearly done plenty of work since Danny had led him away.

'Go get 'em cowboy,' Meg called out as she let go of the reins and slapped the giant rump of Salamanca, who was remarkably settled for a race-day. Almost subdued, Danny thought.

Since winning the Welsh National in a hack canter, perhaps he'd been too easy on him. It was too late to do anything about that now as he let the gelding stretch those thick chestnut legs and huge lungs of his on the way to post.

Although now a seasoned pro at this jumping game, Salamanca was allowed a good look at the practice fence. As he lingered there, Danny's pounding heart made the collar of his silks tickle his neck.

He looked over at Bert, whose steely eyes suggested he was not only racing for pride, but a place in the history books and a reputed six-figure Hollywood film deal.

For a moment Danny's focus was stolen by the frost covers further down the straight, not far from the family and picnic enclosure on the track. Typically Ralph had done nothing about the email he'd sent at the grand opening. They were bright white, like the ghostly shrouds he'd seen in the warehouse of Onyourmetal.

Perhaps Terry hadn't found time to gather them up, unless they were to cover up a bad patch of ground, or some other eyesore.

The two-hundred-to-one outsider of the party, Old Habits Die Hard, was heading the field as they kept turning like a school of fish. Danny suspected the no-hoper was out to grab some of the limelight by pressuring Salamanca for the early lead.

His stomach tightened as he waited for orders to feed through the gap in the railing on to the track proper and face the starting tape. It seemed forever until post time arrived.

The remote third favourite was the Continental-raider Troyan Pass, who had reportedly made the trip over specifically to exact revenge on Salamanca. Although the 'Bulgarian Beast' had something to find with Salamanca on their Czech form, Danny could only see problems surrounding him at this late stage in the prelims and that one ranked highly among them.

He bet Ralph was regretting the invitation to pay all travel costs to encourage foreign raiders. Unsurprisingly that offer was made before the one about refunding tickets if Salamanca got beaten. The fate of the whole track weighed on Danny's shoulders. He shivered. He was just glad Salamanca was blissfully ignorant.

He glanced over at Troyan Pass' rider Andrey, who eyed him back. Danny wasn't going to be intimidated. They were on his patch now and would have to beat him. There was no way he was going to beat himself.

'Lead them out!' the starter ordered, perched on his rostrum. It was time.

Danny straightened Salamanca to face the orange elastic stretched across the track and walked him in.

He pictured the Chepstow rout and suddenly an assuredness took hold of his limbs. He knew horses were much like humans in that they responded well to confident people. Any positive signals he was about to transmit down the reins would be picked up by his charge.

With Salamanca never far from his mind, Danny had designed Ely Park to be a proper jumping test and had therefore placed the first fence just half a furlong from the three-mile start. He also knew a birch-parting mistake there would unsettle any rhythm and in turn potentially set the tone of the jumping display as a whole.

As the tape rose, it was imperative to get some space and, with stamina assured, Danny rowed Salamanca into an early lead.

Soon, above the distant cheers of the crowd in the stands, he could hear the rumble of hooves up his inner and recognised the orange and mauve quartered silks. As he feared, Old Habits Die Hard was determined to be a nuisance. Danny hoped he wouldn't needlessly affect the result, like a lapped distance runner impeding the overtaking leaders.

Danny took the inside route, like a railing dog from trap one, and soon stretched the advantage. The first fence was taken cleanly by all. As they negotiated the first bend, Danny wouldn't give up the white plastic inner rail for anyone.

Unlike the other runners Salamanca had already been given a few spins around here with Danny doing the steering in safety tests. He hoped both of their added track-craft would give them an edge.

Everything was going to plan. As they turned to face the home-straight for the first time, Danny saw a stride some way out and asked for a big one. Sitting back on his haunches, Salamanca pushed the spongy, watered turf, sending them soaring through the air, a flashy leap reminiscent of the late, great Desert Orchid. When Salamanca reunited with the earth, he began to run away in the hands of a buzzing Danny, as if the exuberant jump had made the gelding feel the same way.

188

Even accounting for this shorter trip, Salamanca couldn't maintain this gallop with the choke out. Again he recalled Rhodri's words about the key to staying the distance was mostly to do with, 'seeing it out at proper racing speed'. Right now Salamanca was travelling above and beyond even a proper racing speed. Immediately Danny's confident hands reeled in the reins like a cattle wrangler with a lasso. Riding a good deal shorter kept a tighter leash, helping to prevent Salamanca from going faster. Like a dog walker using a retractable lead.

Back to galloping in the straight line of the home stretch, Danny was afforded a work-in-progress glance over his right shoulder. It was enough for his photographic memory to pick out the whereabouts of his chief rivals, namely glimpses of the blue cap of Bert, who was sitting quietly on Artemis back in the pack, seemingly content to observe this early sparring.

Another slick leap and Danny had five fences out of the way. He was about to run a rewarding hand down the thick glistening neck of his charge when panic suddenly spread over him like wildfire. Every part of his body began to shake. He bit his tongue. A film of cold sweat covered his face. The feeling of terror simply wouldn't go. He began to tilt off-balance. His athletic arms and hands felt numb, as if they'd just been cut free from a plaster-cast.

Had he been right all along about the collapse by the schooling ring? Was this another panic attack? Had his energy drink been spiked? This can't be happening, Danny cried, not now. Get a bloody grip!

As the sixth fence grew larger, instinct made Danny sit lower. He then gripped the reins even tighter, kicking his toes deeper into the irons. Stability was everything right now. Salamanca consented to go in short and pop the fence carefully. That was more than enough for Danny while he worked out what the hell was happening.

He looked down to see if the girth strap had worked loose and was flapping about, or part of the tack had snapped. Everything seemed in order.

He glanced back to see the chasing pack hadn't closed the gap. It's as if nothing had happened. Or perhaps they'd all experience it. Heading for the turn to go out on a second lap Salamanca rallied without being asked. It's as if the red loop of the lollypop stick triggered something inside, but there were no prizes for finishing first this time around.

The Tannoys blared, 'Going out on their second circuit our leader Salamanca appears to be hanging wide, as if he's heading for the paddock exit, but Danny Rawlings manages to keep him in check.'

Danny took a quiet satisfaction in that he was in fact intentionally steering a wider line in search of a faster strip beyond the span of the sprinklers, about seven horse widths out. Somewhat bemused, the chasing group kept a tighter racing line. Danny wasn't fussed about surrendering the lead again as he knew the ground they'd saved would be deeper.

Cornering the second bend Danny glanced across at the white sheets on the inner. He then pictured the six white ghosts in the Onyourmetal warehouse. They seemed to be haunting him.

Suddenly back from a reverie he was surprised by the existence of a seventh fence – the first in the back straight. Having put it there, he shouldn't have been.

Focus, Danny, bloody focus!

Danny asked for another short, tidy leap but Salamanca's ego was having none of it this time. His powerful frame left the ground a stride early. Danny sat back and wrapped the reins round his gloved hands to hold on tight. This could be a bumpy ride. He saw a blurry brown line of birch fly beneath them. They landed steeply. Reclined in the saddle, Danny was ready for this. He pulled with all his might to keep Salamanca's head from kissing the turf.

As they impacted the soft ground the other side, the gelding's sturdy legs refused to buckle under the half-ton burden. When they landed running, Danny was shunted forward, smacking his face above Salamanca's withers. He spat out a mouthful of mane and suspected a tooth as well. Any initial relief from staying on was wiped away by the sight of Artemis cruising upside.

From the other side of the track, he heard a distant roar from the Ralph Samuel Stand. This is what they'd come to see – the best at their best.

From his peripheral vision he caught Bert looking over. Danny was in no mood for any sledging. Instead the back of his glove brushed over his nose and lips. He glanced down. The leather was shiny with blood. He couldn't feel the damage yet.

It seemed nothing could distract Salamanca, who, like Danny, was now in race-mode, as if a switch had been flicked. It felt like the horse simply couldn't give a damn, impervious to all distractions, head down, galloping on regardless of those around, whereas Danny's brain had been left back at the first fence in the home stretch. It certainly wasn't Salamanca that needed blinkers.

Confusion soon turned to anger in Danny as they strode on to the eighth and the ninth regulation fences. He was back in front but at what cost. Bert seemed happy to let Danny regain the lead, cut out the donkey work for a bit longer.

Coming to the tenth fence he hoped for a big leap to re-establish some clear daylight over the rest. The way Salamanca responded and attacked the barrier suggested they were back on the same hymn sheet. From the big screen near the stands, he could see they'd already shrugged off the bit players. Even Troyan Pass couldn't go the gallop. It was now the two-horse race the racing and wider public had hoped and expected.

This is where it begins, Danny reckoned, let battle commence.

Over the next two fences Salamanca and Artemis sized each other up as they winged the walls of birch as if it was some kind of exhibition. Even from this far side of the track Danny heard the gasps in awe from the sell-out crowd. They were enjoying this more than Danny, who knew anything less than a win would leave his stable star ending his career known forevermore as the second best and the track in financial ruin. Either of these steeplechasers would be a standout in most other generations but knowing this wasn't nearly enough for Danny, who needed it proving in film on the track and ink in the history books.

He glanced over at Bert, whose alert eyes glared back. Danny detected some desperation there. His neighbour and rival wanted sweet revenge all right. This was a silent exchange; they both could see their horses were moving well within themselves, neither to be asked a serious question yet.

Danny knew only too well Salamanca could gallop at this pace for over a mile beyond today's distance, so he made the first move to exploit that undoubted stamina. A shake of the reins and a meaningful slap on hindquarters was enough for Salamanca to get the message and lengthen that raking stride. He'd stoked the engine room. His immense lungs opened up to fill a huge ribcage and rapid jets of steam shot from flaring nostrils as his muscular frame begged to be fed more oxygen as the thunder of hooves pounded the turf. Danny felt like he was riding an express train.

He knew taking a few lengths out of his great rival meant little as Artemis had as much tenacity as he did quality. He was still glad to retake the lead and three laser accurate jumps down the far side helped them go far enough clear for Danny to no longer hear the thud of hooves in behind. Danny wondered for a moment whether Bert had done his vanishing act again. He could, however, pick up the crackle of anticipation from the thronging stands far away as this reawakening of the Cardiff Open took shape.

It was left hand down again as they banked from a wider pitch and again rallied well. He afforded another glance back and almost smiled when he saw Bert hard at the pump, trailing some three lengths back.

For the first time Danny felt confident he'd got his last possible danger against the ropes as they turned to face the three fences and four furlongs. A slick jump at the first here could deliver the knockout blow. The rest were tailed off.

Only another seizure could rob them now.

When Danny looked up he feverishly snapped away his second goggles. He looked harder. Up ahead it was as if one of the ground staff had painted several black lines across his side of

192

the track leading up to the take-off board of the final fence, shielded from the eyes of the racing public and media in the stands.

Had trip wires been laid? Had the ground opened up to swallow them?

The shakes were back but this time he knew it was no panic attack. He let slip the reins but managed to gather them up as they briefly flapped about.

When he kept pushing and shoving with his hands, he felt his arms go weak. He swore the cheers turned to yells and screams from the stands.

Oddly he felt Salamanca change his legs, now leading with his off fore. Danny had never felt him switch his lead leg or stride pattern once in full flight. The gelding then tended to lug left. Had he gone lame?

No, he believed, this was the track, not the horse.

He looked again at the dark lines in front of the fence and to the nearby white sheets on the infield. The newly-laid turf of Ely Park had yet to establish and bed in. It would easily split apart near the epicentre of an earth tremor. They weren't hiding bad ground, Danny reckoned, but more drill holes, another of Ralph's plans to raise a quick buck.

Briefly he lifted his head from vigorously rowing Salamanca on, like an Oxford captain. Among the lines of bookie pitches, he swore he saw a few electronic betting boards topple over.

Several strides off the final fence, Danny could see the link. Almost upon them, he could also see clearer the dark lines on the ground. It looked like a cattle-grid. Danny felt sure both of them would be fired into the wall of birch if Salamanca caught a hoof in any of those cracks.

Danny looked over to see Artemis come through against the far rail and take a lead going into this sixteenth and final fence. There were no cracks over there. Would this prove Salamanca's downfall?

A fence repairer standing on the other side of the rail clearly hadn't seen it or had been paid to turn a blind eye. Another one of Ralph's minions, he reckoned.

So much for home advantage, Danny fumed. No amount of practice could've helped prepare them for this.

Yards away from the orange take-off board, Danny began to push on with all his might, asking Salamanca for one of his best trademark leaps in a bid to clear the several cracks lying parallel to the fence and then the five feet of bristly twigs, he would need to be completely synchronised with his horse.

Three-two-. But with a final glance down Danny saw they weren't cracks in the turf but the shadow of the white plastic railings in the wing of the fence, cast by the low lying winter sun off to his right. The shadow on Artemis' side would be off the track, out of sight from the face of the fence, Danny realised too late.

He wanted to pull back and abort, but it was too late for playing it safe by putting in another short stride, as the mixed messages would send them out of synch and fire them into, rather than over, the wall of birch.

Danny saw flashes of Dayjur when he inexplicably threw away a famous victory in the Breeders' Sprint by jumping a dark shadow across Belmont Park in 1990. He now hoped Salamanca would view these shadows the same way.

Salamanca duly left the ground two strides early, a few foot before the first shadow line. He'd clearly seen them.

Soaring through the air, Danny shut his eyes and hoped they wouldn't land anytime soon. He only breathed out when they'd finally reconnected with the lush turf and set about clawing back the deficit on Artemis, who'd wasted less time in the air.

As he began the furlong run-in, his arms and legs felt the burn as they moved, back in complete synch with Salamanca's formidable galloping action. Like an old married couple, Danny knew all of Salamanca's traits and foibles. He also knew his qualities and, seeing Artemis on the far side, he slipped his whip through to his right hand. Since the earth tremor, he'd felt

Salamanca's tendency to drift left. Not only did he not fight it, he gave a few sharp cracks with the whip to encourage it.

Ploughing a lone furrow on the near side, Salamanca was holding something back, with only the cheers of the crowd a reminder there was a race on. He needed a target to aim at and when Danny intentionally drifted towards the far rail, suddenly Salamanca's ears pricked and stride lengthened again. He'd reignited Salamanca's winning spirit. Like when he'd swim front crawl down the Lido, Danny regularly turned his head to the side to see Artemis coming back to them. Salamanca had clearly seen there was work still to do and took aim at the leader. A half-length. A neck. When they'd drawn level, he stopped looking over. He wanted Salamanca to have his undivided attention. Head down, his face kept brushing Salamanca's mane as he vigorously kept shaking the reins, asking for more when he couldn't be certain of the answer.

As they flashed past the finish line, the sell-out crowd were a wall of sound. Danny sat up in the saddle and straightened his back to get some air in his aching lungs. He wasn't sure whether Salamanca had sustained the finishing burst to win comfortably or Artemis had responded to rally back up late on. He glanced over at Bert, who was still relying on Artemis' bold neck to keep him on.

Danny found the courage to look up at the big LCD screen in the middle of the track showing a freeze-frame of the line. Before the judge had called it, he joined in the cheers and his fist punched the air. He didn't need to be an experienced judge of calling photos to know he was a good neck up in that still shot. He snapped the goggles away and waited for Bert to catch his breath. He knew it takes two to make a race and most of that roaring crowd would no doubt make a return visit to Ely Park on the strength of this showdown.

He reached over and offered a gloved hand to Bert, who accepted and then raised Danny's arm aloft as they walked in tandem back over the finish line to the appreciative cheers, some showing their allegiance by wearing scarfs of green and brown or yellow and blue.

'No excuses,' Bert said, now holding his side with a wince. 'We left it all on the track and you still won.'

'Racing's the winner here,' Danny replied graciously.

'After you,' Bert said as they channelled into the asphalt path to the winners' enclosure behind the stands.

Danny could barely hear the clacking of hooves above the cheers still ringing out from the racegoers seemingly magnetised either side of the path's railing.

He looked back to see the white frost covers. He wasn't surprised the track's owner Ralph and groundsman Terry were nowhere to be seen. Standing in his saddle he could, however, see enough of the store barn beyond the Tote offices to know the steel sliding doors were ajar. Perhaps the earth tremors had sent them into hiding there.

In the winners' circle Danny was greeted by a beaming Meg, who was ready with a yellow water bucket to give the winner a well-earned drink and wash down. Sat high up on Salamanca he couldn't reach to hug her, so kissed her raised hand instead.

'You were bloody brill,' she said. 'I've got a lot to learn.'

'Did you feel the ground shake, Meg?'

'Not this again,' she said. He dismounted and unsaddled. 'I watched the race up there in Ralph's office.'

He recalled a few of the toppling betting boards. Perhaps they were bookies preparing to pack up after another costly result.

Either way, after years in the saddle, he could pick up even a slight change in the going, so he didn't need confirming he'd felt something out there.

The trade press will have a bloody field day with this, Danny thought. He grimaced as he imagined the headlines: Salamanca Shook Up Controversial Cardiff Open or New Track's Big Day Ends in Farce.

By winning, he'd inadvertently helped secure Ralph's finances from the gate receipts of that ticket offer. It now seemed a potential scandal like this was a greater threat to Ely Park's future. He knew there was a minor fault line near Swansea, but nothing that could produce anything like this, an hour away by

196

motorway. The turf was away from the coalmining areas, so it was unlikely to be a sinkhole.

Danny weighed in and picked up the small black box from beneath his socks. It now smelt pretty rank, so he took out its contents and left the changing room. He then fought off stiffening legs to climb the stairwell to Ralph's penthouse. The door was locked.

Danny knocked, waited and then knocked harder. He'd clearly given the green light to Gerald to begin fracking on the track's infield. Danny had just felt the aftershocks.

Still in his loosened green and brown silks he flew down the steps two at a time and made for the open barn.

On the war path, Danny wiped cuts of grass and specks of mud from his sweaty face. He spotted Ralph and Toby sharing a pint in the bar on the Members' side.

Toby stopped talking.

'Here's the hero of the hour,' Ralph said, smiling.

'I know,' Danny snapped.

'Modesty never hurt no one,' Toby said.

'I know everything,' Danny added, staring down Ralph, whose smile had gone.

'Not here,' Ralph said.

'What's this?' Toby asked.

Danny opened his mouth but Ralph beat him to it. 'We were chatting earlier about something, not important.'

Right now Danny wished it was Ralph's face on that dart board. He turned to Toby. 'All it was, Ralph was wondering why Powder Keg had improved massively since joining my yard, yet couldn't even make the track when you had her. I said, "that's just racing", and do you know what he said, "no, it's cos Toby treated the filly like shit, you got your horses beat in more way than one". Apparently these days you found them an easier target than hitting owners, horses can't fight back.'

'He's joking, right?' Toby asked Ralph, face reddening.

This time Danny beat Ralph to the draw. 'Why would I joke about that? I'm sure he didn't mean much by it.'

Danny glanced at Ralph, who grinned back as if to say, 'is that the best you could do?' He clearly didn't know Toby that well.

As Danny walked away, he was surprised it took four seconds to hear a thud and a groan. He glanced back to see Ralph on his knees holding his jaw in place, and Toby, who was holding his fist as he walked away, still clutching his pint of lager.

Danny quickened out of there.

Seemed it was about time Terry got a lecturing, Danny thought, about why he rolled over and let Ralph get his own way. There was probably a backhander involved.

As Danny set about hunting down the head groundsman, his phone buzzed in his breeches. It was a text from Cam: 'Got answers, meet me in store barn now!'

Good boy Cam, Danny thought, the hacks aren't all bad.

Perhaps he'd also find Terry there.

Loudly, he peeled back the metal rolling doors enough to slip through. Worryingly they had been left unlocked. Health and Safety would go ballistic. Danny suspected Terry's career would soon take another about turn.

Danny flicked a switch near the door and strip lights high above flickered on.

He then weaved between a tangle of mowers, a tractor, earth compactors and debris clearance equipment, and white plastic railings, alongside black barrels with flammable stickers. It made his store barn look neat.

Why the hell wasn't Cam sticking a Dictaphone in his face after the Cardiff Open? Was this a trap?

The daylight seeping through the gap in the doors grew weaker with every step. He heard the click of scurrying claws over the stone floor. This was a new-build, Danny thought, they didn't hang about.

'Cam!' he shouted but all that came back was an echo. 'Cam!'

He noticed a pile of unfolded frost sheets. They were black.

He then spotted sections of metal scaffolding lined up against the wall opposite. From online images, Danny recognised them as parts of a dismantled fracking drill tower.

Perhaps those white sheets weren't frost covers and had been removed from that cobweb of metal to hide the holes they'd drilled on the infield of the racetrack. He could now picture the innards of those white ghosts lined up in the Onyourmetal warehouse. It seemed they were recycling scrap metal not for the good of the planet but to build those frames to destroy it.

As he ventured further in he heard a quiet dripping.

'Cam,' he called out again. 'Cam!'

As he turned a corner into a clearing, he felt his blood run cold. Up ahead he saw a man sitting upright by a wooden crate. His head was back, revealing a deep gash across his neck, below was a sea of dark red. His hands were held together in front of him by plastic ties. Danny nearly puked up his energy drink. He didn't need to see the body's face. The blackened silk scarf hung lower around the neck and the red burn mark above the cut told Danny enough. He stopped shouting Cam's name.

While the rats had fled for cover, the blow flies remained there circling.

Cam's orange Press pass was lying in a pool of blood, along with several coins and a bloodied hanky. He'd clearly put up a fight.

Danny's phone tickled his thigh. There was another text. 'My blood is on your hands!'

It was sent from Cam's phone but he now knew the texts weren't from the man himself. Being one of the pushier scribes, Danny feared Cam had asked a question too far in search of answers.

Danny's cries bounced off the high corrugated roof and the walls far apart.

From beyond metals doors, he heard an engine fire up. Danny knew there wasn't the time to go back the way and circle the barn, so he tackled the assault course of machinery to reach the back doors.

Adrenalin masked his aching limbs as he jumped the last of the replacement timber hurdles and yanked open the door. He saw a silver Vauxhall Vectra skid away in the muddy ground.

With Jack being looked after in the racecourse crèche and Meg with Salamanca, Danny was okay with chasing after the murderer.

Sally had said they had got all the results needed from Sunnyside Farm but she hadn't mentioned his estate. If there was unfinished business, he had a good idea where they were heading.

He sprinted to the horse carrier and shifted the gear stick. He put his muddy boot to the floor. With no precious cargo in the back, Danny wanted to see what this 4.5 litre engine could do.

Chapter 20

LEAVING THE CITY BEHIND, Danny had also lost sight of the Vauxhall. He didn't mind as he could never keep tailing them on the steep climb up Caerphilly Mountain. On the downslope the other side, Danny used the three-ton weight of the van to make up some ground lost. He took blind bends at speed, hoping for the best.

Danny was desperate to get back to the yard but was forced to slam on the brakes at the mouth of the woodland leading on to both the Silver Belle Estate and Sunnyside Farm. There was a line of red cones. Another roadblock. Except for once there hadn't been rain in days. Danny knew this wasn't floods and there was no chance they'd be resurfacing as there were hundreds of busier roads infested by pot-holes.

He looked over at the fields to his left and right. There was no Vauxhall Vectra-shaped hole in the thick hedges either side. Cam's killer had clearly wanted the woodland secure, placing the cones behind the car before driving on.

Danny rolled the van at a diagonal to make his own roadblock. He didn't want any unsuspecting driver to stumble upon whoever was lurking in those dark woods. He rummaged in the glove compartment for a penknife. He didn't want to go in there empty-handed.

On foot he swerved the cones and under the twitching roof of skeletal branches, he felt the air cool and the light fade.

About fifty yards in it felt like the clock had been turned on two hours.

Rounding a bend near the woodland's dark heart, he saw the red brake lights of the Vectra. Perhaps the full beams were to warn oncoming traffic daring to ignore the cones, probably also guarding the north mouth of the woods. As the road continued to turn, the white light made the wall of beech trunks up ahead all silvery and through the rear window it also picked out a black shape in the passenger seat. The driver's side was empty, door wide open.

Had the driver gone for a piss in the woods?

The engine was purring as it ticked over, ensuring the battery wouldn't run flat. Why had they stopped there? Were they waiting for Danny to catch up?

Danny was in no hurry to find out. Instinctively his pace slowed.

Knees bent, he crept closer. Resting on the dashboard he saw a gun. He ducked behind the car, shielded from the rear view mirror.

Glancing down the passenger side, he saw Sally's face fill the wing-mirror. She wasn't staring back. Before she did he ducked for cover again.

From there he could hear *99 Red Balloons* beating from the car radio.

Leaning against the car Danny held his breath not to choke on the red ghostly swirls from the exhaust. With the driver's door stuck out, Danny made the most of the blind spot.

As soon as the driver was back, Danny knew they would make their escape. He fished for his penknife in his jacket and stabbed the rear tyre.

He presumed the engine and radio combined would drown out the hiss of air and, with the car still supported by three pumped tyres, he reckoned she wouldn't detect any subsidence. He was equally sure they wouldn't be leaving the woods as quickly as they'd arrived.

Danny darted for cover of tree trunks and thick vegetation. He then waded through the thigh-high brambles, weeds and fauna to reach the edge of the wood bordering his estate, not far from where he'd happened upon the Ice Room.

His eyes looked upslope where the grand Samuel House once stood down and then scanned down to the Rhymney road separating Silver Belle Estate and Sunnyside Farm.

At the base of the slope not far from the road's hedge, Danny's eyes widened to fully take in what he saw.

Chapter 21

THERE WERE FOUR WHITE TOWERS, stood at intervals like sentries, guarding these lowly far reaches of the Silver Belle Estate. They were the image of the ghosts he'd seen in the scrap metal yard.

No wonder they'd coned the traffic off, Danny reckoned. He kept the penknife's blade open and ran to the nearest tent. The opening in the white canvas was flapping on the gusts of wind.

With his back to the tent wall he caught glimpses inside of a masked man in black. Was it Leo?

Back to Danny, the man was sitting at a desk inspecting a laptop screen filled with flickering columns of numbers. Providing the spine of the shelter was a large metal frame. From there Danny couldn't see the top of the structure but it reminded him of the segments of metal scaffolding he'd seen in the Ely Park store barn.

Again the flap in the canvas rode the wind. Inside, Danny caught a glimpse of a large red metal box rumbling away.

Must be the electricity generator they'd need out here, he thought. He saw it as a place to hide.

He circled the billowing walls until he stopped where the rumble was loudest. Back there he discovered several black barrels with orange 'flammable' stickers. He slid under a gap between pegs pinning the canvas down. He then crouched and waited. From this angle he could see the man was wearing a black balaclava. He was certainly big enough to be Leo. His fingers were hovering over a memory stick in the laptop's USB port.

The white screen lit the man's brown eyes as he sat there motionless, seemingly captivated by the data being downloaded. It was like the spreadsheet Danny struggled to use for the yard's accounts but there were even more figures on this screen.

Danny sized the man up and conceded there'd only ever be one winner in a fist fight. He needed backup. Keyes had to see this to believe it and, unlike the spheres in the Ice Room, all this wouldn't make a fool of him by suddenly vanishing.

Covered by the generator and its rumble he punched in the mobile number from the police calling card. As his fingertips felt the impression of the letters SAL left on the cardboard, it suddenly came to him. He realised he wasn't about to call for help. But perhaps making the call would help. He stopped short of pressing dial.

He ripped off the sleeve of his silks. He twisted it like a rope and then pulled it as taught as a tripwire between clenched fists.

With the masked man's partner-in-crime waiting in the car, he suspected his mobile would be left on.

Danny's thumb pressed dial. He then slipped his phone down the top of his riding boots. As soon as he heard the first ring fill the tent Danny charged for the computer desk, silk stretched out before him.

As the masked man fished for the ringing in his jeans pocket, Danny lunged forward and lassoed his thick neck with the silk noose. He then yanked back.

Danny was half his size but momentum sent the masked man toppling back off the steel chair. Before the man had chance to get up, Danny sat on his broad chest, knees pinning the arms down, gravity doing the rest.

'PC Mavers,' Danny said before he'd pulled the balaclava from the man's head. 'Or should that be ex-PC.'

Mavers spat a ball of phlegm up but Danny leant back and let it fall back in his face. 'Get off me!'

'As soon as I felt Sal's name on this card,' Danny said and flashed Mavers the calling card. 'I knew it was you. By shortening her name it told me she was more than just a person on the case or a contact or a suspect.'

Danny looked over at the rumpled black balaclava on the ground nearby and then Mavers' matching sweater. 'See you've been raiding Leo's wardrobe.'

'They're mine.'

'Wouldn't have you down as a Goth.'

Danny then recalled Mavers at the interview on race-day. 'Why were you at Chepstow?'

204

Mavers went quiet.

'It was you I saw out there on the track,' Danny accused. 'In these clothes, not Leo.'

'What did Bert tell you?' Mavers asked.

Danny paused. 'You should know, he was reading off your script. Bert had to toe the line, according to Sal, stick to the same story.'

Mavers looked across at the laptop screen. It's only then Danny saw a download bar gradually being filled blue.

From down there, he reckoned Mavers couldn't see it. Danny said, 'Ages to go yet, you should change your service provider.'

'I've had enough of this,' Mavers said. He fought to free his arms but Danny held firm. 'Let me go and I'll cut you a deal. That screen shows you're worth a fortune. Wales sits on one of the largest shale gas reserves in Europe. With the coal all but gone, in years to come they'll be heralding us as the visionary pioneers in the energy market.'

Danny looked up at the drill structure. 'Why do all this if you already know the gas is there?'

'They know it's there from a 2D satellite image but we don't know the extent. For the 3D picture, we need to drill deep. Early signs suggest there are pockets several hundred feet beneath us.'

'And that's where it's staying,' Danny said. 'Dig up our National Parks and there'd be riots, led by me. You get rejected for the Lancashire licence, so you think it's your right to come down here, cut out the middleman and go ahead with testing in Wales without one.'

'There are drill fields across the States,' Mavers said, 'searching for the new black gold.'

'Soon it'll become like the Wild West over here too,' Danny replied. He recalled all the unsolicited offers for the Silver Belle Estate in recent months. 'I valued the land as priceless long before you lot ever heard of fracking. Why choose us?'

'Don't flatter yourself,' Mavers said. 'There are a host of locations we could've set up test sites.'

Pinned to the Cathedral Road noticeboard, Danny pictured the regional map infested by red dots. 'And one of them was Ely Park racetrack.'

'Much of the area's countryside is protected, look at the Brecon Beacons,' Mavers said. 'This place, Sunnyside Farm and Ely Park are all shale-rich and owned privately by potentially vulnerable targets.'

'Pawns in a game you cannot win,' Danny repeated Sally's words up in Cathedral Road. 'You saw the horses as our weakness. And for Ralph it was the survival of Ely Park.'

'Before you get any ideas, one man cannot get in the way of the insatiable global demand for energy,' Mavers said. 'As populations rise, so does demand. We're merely meeting that demand. It won't be long before the world's natural resources of oil and coal are exhausted. *Then* you would see riots like you have never seen before. The whole of our civilised society would break down. With emergency services dependent on fuel, it would turn into a lawless society, a free-for-all. You see flashes from the future when there's merely a sniff of an oil-tanker strike, the lemmings are queuing for miles at the service stations – imagine the chaos when they really do run out.'

Danny pulled his mobile from his boot. Without a signal, he was suddenly aware he was as good as pinned there too.

Danny checked the Wi-Fi signals picked up on his smartphone. There was only one. It was unnamed. When Danny clicked to join, up came, 'Network password requested.'

'Trouble getting a reception out here?' Mavers replied and then smiled.

'Password, now!'

'Do you think I'm a complete mug?'

Danny looked around him. He saw the thing most precious to Mavers and said, 'I'll drop the memory stick down the drill hole.'

'I'll floor you before you get the chance,' Mavers said.

'Wanna bet,' Danny said. 'I'm a jockey with first run on you.'

'Fuck you, I'll wait for Sal to get suspicious and come looking. You're the only thing keeping me here. You move, I move.'

Danny showed Mavers the shiny blade of his penknife and then made sure he felt its cold steel against his neck. 'Unless you want to end up like Cam, tell me the password?'

Mavers revealed it as Shallow123. Danny breathed out when he saw the Wi-Fi symbol on his smartphone's screen. Using his email account, he thumbed a text: Call police 2 back of S B Estate by Rhymney Rd. Hurry. Lv DR.' He pressed send to Meg's number, hoping she'd have her mobile on. Danny kept the blade pressed against Mavers' stubbly neck.

'Just let me go,' Mavers pleaded. 'We could be business partners.'

'Like the one waiting in the car,' Danny said.

'I'd given up waiting,' came a female voice.

Danny turned his neck enough to see Sally stood at the flap in the tent. The gun he'd seen on the dashboard was now pointing at arms-length his way.

Danny was only too aware he was the only thing keeping Mavers there. If Danny moved, it would be two with a gun against one without.

'Get off him!' she screeched.

He slowly removed himself from straddling the ex-copper and backed away.

'You should join the force, there's a vacancy going there,' Mavers said and brushed himself down as he went to greet her. 'Where's Harry?'

'In the car,' she replied.

She glanced over at Danny, who didn't disguise a look of disgust.

'How could I trust you wouldn't go to the police with his picture and name?' she explained. 'We'd be stopped at airport security, so I went along with you presuming he'd died.'

'He looked ill, white as a ghost.'

'He's the son of a red head,' she replied. 'It's in his genes.'

207

'Why come back for the defaced photo?' Danny asked.

'The same reason why you'd come back for the torch,' she said. 'There were still two identifiable faces in that photo.'

Keeping his distance Danny inched over to the drill hole, wishing he could've swiped the memory stick. As it was he had nothing to bargain with. He checked the thick coil of steel cables of the drill line swallowed up by the hole.

'Where's Gerald?' Danny asked.

'Keep going and you might find out,' Mavers said and then looked down at the black hole.

Danny looked back up at Mavers. 'He fell?'

'With a little help. He was asking for half the profits from mining that data, all for recycling metal to build these frames and avoid the paper trail from buying them,' Mavers said and smiled. 'I heard about five seconds of wailing and it then fell silent. Deeper down, the narrower it gets. There had to be a point when his gut became wedged there, like a cork in a bottle.' Danny swallowed. 'Shame, we could've saved on dropping a frac ball down there.'

Danny pictured the spheres in The Ice Room. 'What are they?'

'They're used to block and divide the drill tunnel to separate and contain the pockets of shale gas released. The farther down we want to block, the smaller the frac ball we used.'

Danny pictured the different sized spheres in the Ice Room. 'Were the frac balls brown?' he asked, playing for time.

Sally said, 'Red.'

Danny recalled the red trail of wet footprints he'd left on the kitchen floor returning from the Ice Room and the matching dust on his fingertips. He then remembered the green light streaming through the grilled ceiling of the Ice Room. Green on red made brown.

'Results were so conclusive at Bert's farm we didn't need to use them all,' Sally said.

'When I returned with Keyes, they were gone, taken,' Danny said.

'Like us all, they're designed to crumble and disintegrate over time,' Mavers explained. 'It saves us trying to remove them from deep underground when we want to bring the gas to the surface.'

'But one of them came for me when I'd touched it,' Danny said but then recalled the uneven flagstones down there. He saw the download bar was near completion. 'What were you going to do with Leo?'

'Bert was the brains behind the operation,' Mavers replied.' Leo wouldn't even provide the brawn. He was nothing to us.'

'Are we done?' Sal asked Mavers and then looked over at the laptop.

'Nearly.'

Danny said, 'And the acid out the back, explains the dead fish and cattle.'

'The hydrochloric acid was used in the preparation stages,' Mavers stated. 'Helps clean up the perforations and widen the fissures in the rock. And the bromate salts and isopropyl alcohol help increase the viscosity of the fracture fluid. Makes the process more efficient and helps us obtain the remarkable results in the data of these four test drills.' Again Mavers anxiously glanced to see the progress of the download.

Danny recalled the flammable sticker on some of the barrels and then the moment he'd turned the tap in Meg's birthday. 'And you're polluting the water, my water.'

'A bit of pollution is a small price to pay,' Mavers said.

'Will you go into hiding, like Bert?' Danny asked.

'I've quit my job and I'll quit the country all in a day,' Mavers said. 'Going to celebrate in someplace hot with no extradition treaty with the UK. I've had it up to here with the rules and regulations in this country, bloody country is drowning in red tape. And our major clients are abroad, so-'

The computer bleeped, like an oven timer.

'It's done,' Mavers said and removed the memory stick. 'And so are we.' He then swiftly turned the gun back on Danny, who glanced back at the steel drill line and then up to the large pulley wheel. He saw there were pads locking it in place.

He heard the click of the gun's safety catch. At that moment it wasn't so much the weapon that scared him but the idea he had planned.

'You told Bert to jump before he was pushed,' Danny said shakily. 'Well, if it worked for him.'

Danny turned on his heels and silently stepped into the black hole. Surface light faded fast as he bear-hugged the thick coil of tiny cables. The surfaces of his torso, thighs and hands all felt the burn as he bid to up the friction and slow his descent. He smelt burning yet still the cable slipped through his stinging hands.

Instinct made his legs kick out to straddle the tunnel, hoping his trusty leather riding boots would act like buffers as they scraped down the walls of jagged earth then rock. He feared his ankles or legs would snap on an outcrop.

Mavers reckoned they'd drilled several hundred feet down. For the first time he prayed to see Gerald in one piece again.

His voice shook as he groaned from the bruising knocks and friction burns. He fought back that pain to get enough purchase on the cable and walls but still he felt a dropping sensation, until his boots impacted something soft.

Danny's hands grabbed the walls as he felt his knees buckle. He didn't want to feel the floor. He stood there in the blackness.

The searing pain of his shredded hands took his mind off the fact he was most probably standing on a rotting corpse. When he sucked in the putrid smell of death down there all doubt was removed. He began to gag. As a child that same stench had filled his family home when a nest of rats had died under the floorboards.

Danny didn't look down at the fat gut that held them both there. He didn't want that bastard's grey face, stringy like melted cheese and hollow raven-black eye sockets, from haunting his dreams.

Instead he kept his eye-line above shoulder height, like a high-wire act. But he lost any focus when he felt Gerald's body slip a few inches lower. Perhaps his decomposing limbs were about to rip off, sending them even deeper. His stomach turned. He started to wish he'd taken a bullet.

He pulled himself up several feet of the steel cable. With his strong thighs acting as pistons, he then pushed his back firmly against the rock wall. The toes of his boots pressed the opposite side of the tunnel. He let friction rather than his biceps take the brunt of his weight.

Danny flicked on his mobile. The screen sent a mural of light up the rough walls.

There were four bars of battery but, as he suspected, there wasn't a single one for signal. The reception was bad enough on the surface of the valleys.

Up above, the dot of light was briefly plugged. Was it them peering down? He quickly flicked the phone off and slipped it back in his boot.

Fearing he'd start gagging, Danny kept his breaths shallow as he hung there, silently. His pulse slowed.

The return of darkness seemed to spark his mind's eye. He began to picture Jack playing and laughing with Mammy Meg on the lawns by the schooling ring. In his imaginings they both stopped and looked up at him smiling in the heavenly summer sunlight.

Suddenly from somewhere energy began to course through his limbs.

He wanted to be buried up here in the valleys but not like this. He had to get out of there.

He shook the tension from his limbs and then began hoisting himself up, a forearm's length at a time. Like a sailor climbing to the crow's nest his crossed legs locked around the thick coil of wires.

Every ten lifts he'd rest up in the back-leg climbing position, letting the toes of his boots and his back take the weight off his tired arms in the long climb.

As he repeated the exercise again and again he worked up quite a sweat and a rhythm. High above the growing circle of light at the end of the tunnel acted like a North Star.

He could feel blood leak from his palms and then trickle down his arms. Yet he kept climbing. He knew it had been important to lose weight and gain strength for the Cardiff Open test, but he didn't know just how important.

After what seemed like twenty minutes, Danny had reached the lip of the mouth.

It wasn't the faces of Mavers and Sal that met him but a wall of heat and blinding light. There was a steady waterfall of clear liquid pouring into the drill hole.

Resting up again, he reached out and wet his fingers. It seemed something like paraffin had lit the furnace.

He imagined Mavers kicking over one of the black barrels and letting the isopropyl alcohol splosh over the tent's ground sheet, before putting a lighter to it. He'd flee with both the evidence and the only witness consumed by flames.

He stared at the waterfall running down the side of the tunnel. Perhaps the hole was acting like a gulley, leaving a protected pathway the opposite side of the mouth. Danny popped his head above ground level and, before being beaten back by the heat, he saw there was a gap in the flames opposite where the liquid had been syphoned down the drill hole.

Danny held himself by his thighs and crossed legs while he pulled what remained of his green and brown silks up over his head.

With his last bit of energy, he hoisted himself up. As his boots reached out, he pushed himself away from the cable towards the narrow path to freedom.

Head down, he ran for his life, bursting through the fiery wall of the tarpaulin. It tore apart like crepe paper. He kept running and then dropped to roll on the ground to extinguish any small flames. He struggled to his feet and saw the four towers ablaze. He stumbled back from the sight.

Had the shale gas been tapped off? If not, would they blow any moment?

He staggered for the cover of the woods, hoping the car with the flat tyre was still there. By now he hoped Meg had seen the text and help was on its way.

Seeing the road he moved silently as a cat burglar. In the dark he could make out the white and red glow of the car's lights through the branches and brambles. He then heard the clunk of a wheel jack.

In the dark Danny lay flat and in a low crawl, dragged his body over the tarmac. He caught glimpses of Sally's face in the mirror again but kept going.

He'd rounded the car. Squinting from the headlights, he could see beneath the driver's door, the boots and knees of Mavers changing the wheel. He crept to the door. When they'd left the tent he remembered it was Mavers holding the gun. He'd leave it somewhere on the driver's side.

Three-two-one! He sidestepped the door and lunged into the car. Deftly his hand reached over the steering wheel and swiped the gun.

Sal also went for it but was pinned back by the seatbelt. Her false finger nails clawed at Danny's bloody arms. She screamed, 'Scott!'

But Danny had already backed out of there in one swift movement. From behind the car he heard the clank of the wheel jack hit the ground.

Mavers appeared but then stopped as if already shot as he saw Danny with the gun trained on him.

Danny glanced into the car. 'Get out!'

'You don't want to do this,' Mavers said, showing his big palms. 'You won't be a vigilante, but a murderer just like us, just as guilty in the eyes of the law. If you put that down, let us go, we can all benefit from this.' He waved the memory stick.

'The police are on their way,' Danny said. 'It's over.'

'You prized fucker,' Sal growled. She clicked herself free from the belt and came for Danny with a feral rage, fiery eyes possessed. Perhaps she was the one that slit Cam's throat.

Danny fired a warning shot over her shoulder. As she came round the bonnet of the Vauxhall, she produced a knife, its blade shimmering in the headlamps.

'Get back!' Danny warned. But she kept coming and was now too close for Danny to fire another shot.

'He hasn't got the balls Sal,' Mavers urged his lover on, stood at a safe distance. 'Butcher him.'

Instead Danny turned the gun on the cowardly Mavers and shot his left leg. A growing black stain spread on his denims. Mavers looked down and then fell to the ground. She changed her course and went to him.

He held the gun firmly in their direction as he took the weight off his aching ankles.

From beyond the bend in the road he heard the distant wail of sirens and then saw blue and red flashes flickering up the wall of the trees. He saw how this would look, so he wiped his prints from the gun's handle and then tossed it away from the scene.

A metallic voice came over the loud speakers. 'Everyone stay where they are!' the officer ordered. Danny saw it was Keyes.

She looked down at the pool of blood growing around Mavers' and then back at Danny. 'It's a game we can never win.'

As the armed officers came over Danny heard the heavy thud of leather boots and clanking AK-45s on shoulder straps.

Danny was helped up by Keyes. 'Took your time didn't you?'

'The four smoke trails led us here.'

'He was after shale gas,' Danny explained to Keyes. 'It was too late to stop him drilling my land, but the results are on the memory stick in his pocket.'

'Who?'

'Over there, a familiar face,' Danny said. 'Like me, you should've looked closer to home for the answers.'

'Mavers?!' Keyes asked as he looked over at the body bathed in blood lit by the headlamps. 'He's behind all this? We'd eliminated all suspects.'

'Including Ralph Samuel?' Danny enquired.

214

'He's on our radar.'

When Danny saw Meg appear from the woodland gloom, it's as if he'd already been given a shot of morphine.

She knelt and blew him a kiss.

He held his bloody palms out in front as if reading a hymn book.

'Looks worse than it is,' Danny said. 'You got the text then.'

'Ambulance is on its way,' she said. 'I got a taxi and ran the rest.'

'Jack!' Danny said and tried to get up.

'He's fine,' Meg replied. 'He's still at the racetrack crèche.'

'What about Salamanca?'

'He's in the stables there,' Meg replied. 'Anything else I can do? I feel so helpless.'

Danny was silenced by a thought. 'There is something.'

'Anything.'

'The cabinet in my office,' he replied and then bit back another surge of pain. 'There's a Jiffy bag that says Prague tapes.'

'When I said anything-'

'Post it to care of DCI Keyes, Rhymney Police Station,' Danny said.

'Is this to do with Ralph?'

'It's my way of flushing out the only bad thing about Ely Park. I was proud to be the architect of the place and allowed Ralph to share that honour,' Danny said. 'I'm not going to let that bastard be the architect of its downfall too. I know you're more forgiving but he did threaten to kill you on that tape recording.' He then groaned again. Where the bloody hell were the medics?

'I'll do it first thing,' she said and ran a gentle hand through his hair. 'Oh Danny, what am I gonna do with you?'

He looked down at his own bloodied colours. 'Perhaps I should qualify as a plumber,' he replied and then smiled. 'Reckon it's safer.'

'But a bit of you will die inside,' she said. 'Live to live, that's my motto.'

215

For once he smiled because she was right and he was wrong. 'One more thing.'

'Yes.'

'Would you be up for playing a bigger role in team Rawlings,' he said and swallowed.

She looked confused. 'Assistant trainer?'

'I already see you as that,' he said. 'No, much more.'

'Are you asking-' she said, shaking almost as much as him.

Danny managed a nod. He then saw the yellow of an ambulance as it pulled up behind the squad cars.

'Can't really do this properly,' he looked at his hands.

'I'll get down on one knee for you,' she said and wobbled there. 'See how you're making me feel,' she said. He smiled. Keyes was directing the medics over.

'Megan Jones, will you be my wife?' Danny asked.

'Of course I bloody will,' she said. Her watery eyes sparkled in the car lights.

A man in green also knelt beside. Danny didn't feel the needle go in his arm. An oxygen mask was then snapped round Danny's face. He pulled it away and told Meg, 'In the top of my breeches, you'll find a ring.'

Her finger wormed its way along the top of his bloodied whites. She pulled out a diamond ring.

'It's lush Danny,' she said, eyes flitting between the cut stone and her fiancé.

The medic smiled briefly and said, 'The morphine should be kicking in. Can you move your limbs?'

Danny nodded but eyes remained firmly fixed on Meg. 'Put it on quick, see if it fits.'

She slipped the ring on her wedding finger and then showed it off.

In the ambulance, she said looked at the drip attached to his arm and then the ring on her finger, 'The drugs aren't making all this happen?'

'I got the ring last week,' he replied. 'It was all premeditated, Your Honour.'

The medic was preparing a booster jab of morphine. Danny opened his mouth but stopped himself from asking whether he'd be fit by March. He didn't want the answer, deep down he already knew.

Instead he stopped fighting the drugs and allowed his eyelids to fall. He began to dream of jumping the final fence with a clear lead in the Cheltenham Gold Cup and then being led into the winners' enclosure by wife Meg, who looked up and mouthed, 'Live to live, Danny.'

Printed in Great Britain
by Amazon

64529266R00124